FRACTURED

BOBBY AKART

The Nuclear Winter Series
First Strike
Armageddon
Whiteout
Devil Storm
Desolation

New Madrid (a standalone, disaster thriller)

Odessa (a Gunner Fox trilogy)
Odessa Reborn
Odessa Rising
Odessa Strikes

The Virus Hunters
Virus Hunters I
Virus Hunters II
Virus Hunters III

The Geostorm Series
The Shift
The Pulse

Martial Law

False Flag

The Mechanics

Choose Freedom

Patriot's Farewell (standalone novel)

Black Friday (standalone novel)

Seeds of Liberty (Companion Guide)

The Prepping for Tomorrow Series (non-fiction)

Cyber Warfare

EMP: Electromagnetic Pulse

Economic Collapse

PRAISE FOR BOBBY AKART AND THE CALIFORNIA DREAMIN' NOVELS

"If Bobby Akart ever decided to write screenplays for the movies, he'd be happy and rich as Croesus. His novels read like a Roland Emmerich disaster movie, which is to say, of the highest quality!" ~ Amazon review for ARkStorm

"I love the way you are drawn into the lives of the characters in Bobby's books. It's like you're there with them and cheering them on to not give up." ~ Amazon review for ARkStorm

"Bobby Akart is one of the most REAL writers I've ever read. Bobby's writing is so visceral. It contains the perfect balance of fact, fiction and fun! I always read anything with his name on it!!" ~ Amazon review of ARkStorm

"Bobby Akart's writing weaves current happenings into believable stories. One can put themselves in the story and literally sense the disaster." ~ Amazon review for ARkStorm

"I cry for the injured and defenseless, rage at the bad guys, and scream with impotent rage when one of my favorite characters are hurt or killed! Such is the artistry of the author. Such is the realm of Bobby Akart." ~ Amazon review of Yellowstone

"Love the intensity of his stories, his through research, his creativity, the characterizations and the abundant action and realistic locations." ~ Amazon review of New Madrid Earthquake

FRACTURED

by
Bobby Akart

Copyright Information

DEDICATIONS

To the love of my life, Dani, and our little princesses in training, Bullie & Boom. Every day, you unselfishly smother me with your love, support, and merriment. I may be the machine that produces these words. You are the glue that holds me together and the fuel that winds me up each day so I can tell these stories. I will love you forever.

EPIGRAPH

As seismologists gained more experience from earthquake records, it became obvious that the problem could not be reduced to a single peak acceleration.
In fact, a full frequency of vibrations occurs.
~ Charles Francis Richter, developer of the Richter Scale

Battle not with monsters, lest ye become a monster, and if you gaze into the abyss, the abyss gazes also into you.
~ Friedrich Nietzsche, German Philosopher

We imagine *the end* as a world-devastating event, but every time there's a terrible earthquake, a tsunami, or an outbreak of disease—that's apocalyptic on a micro-scale.
~ Marjorie Liu, American Author

I said shake rattle and roll!
~ Big Joe Turner, 1955

People shouldn't be living in certain places—on earthquake faults or on flood plains.
But they do, and there are consequences.
~ Vaclav Smil, Czech-Canadian Scientist

You can no more win a war than you can win an earthquake.
~ Jeannette Rankin, American Politician

I used to sleep nude—until the earthquake.
~ Alyssa Milano, American Actress

PROLOGUE

California, USA

Don't panic!

Mac Atwood repeated the words under his breath until his mind took over. He debated with himself. *Isn't that what they always say in the movies? Easy for them to say.* That was fiction, and this was very real.

He fought the urge to sleep. Drift away until the god awful ordeal ended. Until the spinning stopped. When he'd awaken to the sun shining brightly on his skin.

However, his mind had other ideas.

His brain was flooded with memories of that

mid-December day when he'd just completed the first semester of his senior year at Dyersburg High School. The town where the Atwood family had put down roots in West Tennessee in the early 1900s was about eighty miles north of Memphis and a dozen miles from the Mississippi River.

He and his buddies had piled into their pickups and raced one another to Reelfoot Lake, where a keg party was raging. They couldn't contain their excitement. Everyone with a boat would be there. Every cute girl in school would be there. Every red Solo cup would be full of beer or Jack and Coke. Country music would echo through the woods. The Christmas break party, known to all the parents in Dyersburg, was a rite of passage for the teens as they navigated the transition from high school to college.

On that particular day, it became a nightmare the survivors would never forget. It was the day the New Madrid Seismic Zone awakened after two hundred years. It was the day that Reelfoot Lake opened up and began to swirl like water draining out of a massive toilet bowl. It ruined the party for hundreds of teens, who were sucked into a turbulent black hole until they drowned or were crushed by boats circling wildly in the current.

It was Mac's exceptional swimming skills and quick thinking that saved him that day. Exhausted, he made his way to the banks of the lake. His fingers were tingling, and his toes were numb. He shivered uncontrollably. His limbs ached. His mind raced as he tried to make sense of it all. To be sure, the Atwood family had experienced tremors around the New Madrid Seismic Zone before. However, this was different.

There was a monster beneath the earth. Hungrily gobbling up the dirt, shaking the surface in search of sustenance. When the beast needed to quench its thirst, it sucked the Mississippi River through an enormous, supernatural straw, causing it to flow in reverse for the first time since, well, the last time it had reared its ugly head in 1812.

When it was over, bridges had collapsed into the river. St. Louis, Memphis, and Baton Rouge had been decimated. Hundreds of thousands had perished. However, Mac had survived.

Now, here he was, deep in the darkness under more than a hundred feet of water. Swirling around and around in a powerless submersible. Begging for it to stop. Praying for the beast below to release its grip on him.

He wanted to heed those words, *don't panic.* So he didn't. He simply asked himself, *Are they even looking for me? Am I gonna die?*

Maybe I'm already dead.

And so it begins ...

CHAPTER ONE

Late June
Lake California, USA

Mac Atwood had found his rhythm. His body glided through the water as his freestyle strokes propelled him along. His form was perfect, thanks to an excellent swim coach during his high school years. He maintained a strong body position, with elbows kept high to ensure long strokes. His powerful legs kept a consistent two-beat kick.

Mind and body were in perfect sync. His long-distance swimming routine had become as natural as walking down a sidewalk. As his right hand speared into the water, his left arm circled, completing the stroke. His left leg kicked, alternating with the right as he swam. Some people went for a walk to clear their heads of the clutter that invaded their brains from everyday life. Mac swam.

Now in his early thirties, he was at the peak of his athleticism. Growing up in West Tennessee, where he was surrounded by parks, forests, lakes and *Old Man River*, Mac had spent every available moment outdoors. You name it. Hiking, running, swimming, and fishing. He never owned an Xbox or PlayStation. He owned fishing rods and hunting rifles while enjoying the freedom the outdoors afforded him.

By his calculation, and with the aid of his Garmin Triathlon watch, he'd reached the center of Vacaville, or where it once stood. The center of town was now ninety feet below the surface of Lake California. The town of a hundred thousand was not the only one submerged under the lake formed years ago. Others that had joined a fate similar to the mythical Atlantis under the surface of Lake California included Sacramento, Stockton, Modesto, and parts of Bakersfield.

The massive body of water had been created from an atmospheric anomaly known as an ARkStorm. *ARkStorm*, a term that immediately connotes the story of Noah's Ark in the Bible, was certainly biblical in impact. From a scientific perspective, *ARk* represents atmospheric river, a thousand-year flood event. *Storm*, while easily envisioned, was certainly understated for those who lived through it. Apocalyptic was more appropriate.

Years prior, California had been besieged by a series of atmospheric rivers that formed near Hawaii and brought Pacific Ocean moisture to the state's shores. When it was over, in just a matter of weeks, water equivalent to the volume of the Mississippi River times twenty-two had been dumped on California's Central Valley.

The landscape of the state had changed drastically. The deluge caused mountain ridges to collapse. The resulting mudslides dragged earth and debris, including structures, into the valleys below. Wildlife and human life perished. Most of the debris found its way into Southern California, where concrete dams around Los Angeles failed in dramatic fashion.

During the multiweek catastrophic event, the floodwaters joined the Pacific Ocean along the beaches of Los Angeles County. Ships and barges were broken from their moorings and forced into the city. Earthen debris and demolished structures eventually began to congregate in the La Crescenta Valley, creating a nature-made choke point. The accumulated earthen debris and man's shattered improvements effectively held the floodwaters in the Sacramento, San Joaquin, and Crescenta Valleys.

After the spring thaw brought millions more gallons of water from melted snow out of the mountains, the newly formed lake began to rise to its present-day levels. Los Angeles eventually dried out, so to speak, after the United States Army Corps of Engineers took immediate action to ensure the new lake didn't burst through the nature-made barrier holding the water in the Central Valley.

The rest of California's breadbasket paid the price for rescuing LA. The fertile farmland and cattle ranches were flooded. The homes and businesses were lost. The cities were buried under silt and covered by the lake. Millions were displaced.

Mac was one of the lucky ones.

After living through the massive earthquake at the New Madrid Seismic Zone, Mac felt compelled to volunteer in the cleanup and rebuilding effort. It helped that the federal government was offering a full scholarship to Oregon State's College of Earth, Ocean and Atmospheric Sciences for a select few who participated full-time in the effort. The New

Madrid Earthquake had a profound effect on Mac, and he vowed to join those who needed to not only understand what was going on under the Earth's surface, but how to warn people of a major quake event.

With a deep breath, he turned and began to propel himself toward his home. The peaks of the Vaca Mountains separated Lake California from the populated regions around Santa Rosa to the west. Beyond Napa Valley was the Pacific Ocean, quietly minding its own business, for now.

California had suffered a terrible fate that winter when the ARkStorm events occurred. After the rains subsided, the recovery efforts began. When the snowmelt made its way into the lake, the rebuilding of what remained of the land mass of California began. And with that, the land grab by government and opportunists alike began.

CHAPTER TWO

Mount Vaca, California

After Mac graduated from Oregon State, he received a job offer from the United States Geological Survey, commonly referred to as the USGS, the agency whose primary focus was the detection and study of earthquakes. It was an entry-level position at the Earthquake Science Center at Moffett Field in Sacramento. The facility had just relocated from nearby Menlo Park due to its need to expand.

The Earthquake Science Center was the flagship research center of the USGS in the western U.S. for nearly sixty years. Mac was intrigued by the extensive laboratories, research facilities, and scientific monitoring infrastructure at the USGS complex.

He'd barely gotten his feet wet in his new position when the ARkStorm descended upon California.

After receiving the job offer, Mac had purchased a small cabin at the base of Mount Vaca overlooking the town of Vacaville. His property included ten acres along the ridgeline that he planned to clear for nature trails and a larger home when his finances allowed.

He was single and wasn't in a hurry to undertake the improvements. He'd dated a classmate for a time during their last months at Oregon State. She'd taken a different track in her studies, which led her to become a volcanologist. Mac stayed true to his goals of studying earthquakes.

Since the move to Mount Vaca, he'd dated a few women but never truly connected with any of them to enter into a longer-term relationship. His cabin had been the epitome of a bachelor pad with spartan furnishings and generally unkept.

Mac wasn't home the day it floated away during the ARkStorm. He'd packed for a two-week temporary duty assignment in Denver to liaise with the geophysicists on a new project the USGS was preparing to launch. While he was away, the worst of the storm hit on New Year's Day. Still, despite the catastrophic nature of the ARkStorm, Mac never imagined his humble cabin in the mountains would be affected.

The devastation was beyond belief. The world was hungry for information. NASA made its satellite imagery available to displaced California residents to determine the status of their properties. Mac studied them daily. He'd reached a conclusion as to the fate of his cabin, but he needed to see for himself.

It was two months before the state of California allowed people to return to their homes. Mac had to drive toward Mount Shasta, located north of the partially submerged town of Redding, and then wind his way through the Vaca Mountains until he reached the ridges overlooking Lake California.

He hiked the familiar trails and made his way to where his home once stood. Only a storage shed holding his kayak, fishing gear, and some tools remained. With a look of bewilderment on his face, he studied the shoreline of the enormous freshwater lake. His acreage stretched several hundred feet along the water from one protruding rock outcropping to another. He was familiar with them all. Without the benefit of survey markers or signage, the result of the ARkStorm was unmistakable.

One man's loss is another man's gain, as the saying went. Mac had lost the old cabin and his belongings, such as they were. He'd gained pristine frontage on the new Lake California. He'd smiled that day as he turned his face toward the sun. The loss of the cabin was devastating, but he'd find a way to start over. He was beginning to visualize his new home.

Unfortunately, the state of California had other ideas.

The recovery effort was unparalleled in modern history. It required all of the resources of the state and federal governments to stabilize the land around the lake and to construct dams to keep the water in place to prevent additional damage.

The costs were astronomical. Trillions of dollars were spent to rebuild government facilities and infrastructure. The state of California was forced to relocate its capital from Sacramento to Santa Rosa, located in Sonoma County twenty miles from the Pacific coastline. The USGS, among many other displaced federal agencies, followed the state's lead. To accomplish the monumental task of relocating the government facilities, properties were seized by eminent domain to house the federal government agencies and the state capitol.

Relocating the state and federal government was only the beginning of the land grab. The governor of

California had the same euphoric feeling that Mac had when he first viewed his newly attained lake frontage. Under the auspices of protecting the public, the governor ordered the attorney general's office to systematically condemn and declare a hazard of all the lakefront properties from Redding in the north to south of Bakersfield. Millions of acres of privately owned land were subjected to seizure lawsuits filed by the state.

Eventually, the scandal and corruption came to light. At the southern end of Lake California, the state's condemnation proceedings yielded a valuable haul of real estate. The wealthy residents of LA were interested in rebuilding on higher ground, and the allure of lake frontage was too strong to resist. Bluffs overlooking the lake near the Los Padres National Forest were in especially high demand.

The governor's office orchestrated a series of executive orders exempting parts of the ridges overlooking Lake California from the condemnation order. After the property was seized from the original owner, it was then sold to wealthy insiders and political cronies for a large profit. Along the way, everybody got a small bite of the apple.

The governor justified the taking and the subsequent sales as being necessary to pay for the recovery and rebuilding of the state. Others screamed nepotism and tried to fight the state in court. They lost, so the state of California continued the land grab.

Mac couldn't afford a lawyer. He received pennies on the dollar from the insurance settlement, as every major insurer in the state filed for bankruptcy weeks after the ARkStorm. The Federal Emergency Management Agency, or FEMA, had a loan program available, but the backlog of applications stretched for years into the future. As a result, he was certain he'd lose his property to the state.

Then the Corps of Engineers issued a change in its regulations to help them deal with the enormous costs associated with stabilizing the land from further erosion. If landowners along Lake California would undertake certain remedial measures to shore up their water frontage in accordance with the Corps of Engineers' guidelines, they would be given a federal exemption from the state's onerous condemnation proceedings.

This set up a battle between California and Washington that quickly landed in the lap of the United States Supreme Court. A spotlight was shined on the governor's nefarious actions in the national media. He was facing threats of impeachment and federal racketeering charges. Just as the Supreme Court case was approaching oral arguments, he ordered his attorney general to back off. Nonetheless, realizing political winds can shift with the next election, out of an abundance of caution, Mac complied with the Corps of Engineers' guidelines.

While he stabilized his land along the shoreline, he also applied for a permit to build a floating dock. The federal government had jurisdiction over the permit and granted it. Mac built a dock, bought a floating house, and couldn't be happier with the way things turned out.

CHAPTER THREE

Mount Vaca, California

Mac finished his swim and pulled himself up the ladder affixed to the end of the dock. Water dripped off his body as the sun warmed him. He paused and took a long look around, reminded of the natural beauty of the Vaca Mountains. If he hadn't lived through the ARkStorm and witnessed the destruction firsthand, he would never have known how devastating its impact had been on California.

A merganser swooped down and dove for a fish just beyond the bow of his houseboat. The state had struggled for years of punishing drought until the ARkStorm. Despite the toll the series of atmospheric rivers had wrought, it was a reminder to Mac that nature had a way of fixing things. California's waterfowl and flocks of migrating birds were now enjoying a rare bounty of water along the vast swaths of the Central Valley's landscape.

For the first several years, the waterfowl experienced a die-off during the warm summer months due to botulism. Botulism occurred naturally in the soils of the Central Valley and especially in the Tulare basin. When the water temperatures rose, the waters became stagnant. Botulism boomed, and thousands of waterfowl died. To combat the stagnant waters, the state encouraged people to use the vast lake for water activities. Tax breaks were given to new boat owners and to those who built floating, rather than stationary, docks on the lake. By the third summer following the ARkStorm, the botulism threat was lessened.

The merganser's dive reminded Mac to check the droplines he routinely tied off before his swims. He gently tugged on each to check its weight. The lines were equipped with small lead balls to keep the baited hooks near the bottom. Daily, Mac caught a variety of fish ranging from crappie and bluegill to the occasional small bass.

He pulled up two of the lines and dropped a

couple of crappies into a bucket. After work, he planned on filleting the small fish, which he'd smother in Cajun seasoning and butter. It was Monday, and his team would meet in the lunchroom to discuss the week's activities. The catered food was usually too heavy for Mac's liking, especially since it seemed to make his fellow geophysicists sleepy.

With a towel wrapped around his waist to cover the Speedo bathing suit that he wore only for swimming because he despised the skintight nature of the garment, he prepared to board his floating house to get ready for work. That was when a woman emerged from the woods and waved at him.

She wore khaki cargo pants and a vintage logoed tee shirt promoting a rock concert to benefit victims of the 1989 Loma Prieta earthquake in the Bay Area. Her bucket hat was pulled low over her eyes to block the rising sun. Her disheveled look stood in far contrast to Mac's beach-boy appearance. His sun-kissed skin, chiseled body, and shoulder-length blond hair apparently grabbed her attention because she was speechless after Mac addressed her with a nonchalant *good morning*. So he tried again with a little more forcefulness.

"Hey! Is there something I can help you with? Are you lost?"

Mac walked up the dock onto the grass to intercept her. He didn't want her to come any closer. She looked like a groupie of some sort.

"Um, no. I'm not lost. I don't think. I'm looking for the home of Mac Atwood."

"Whadya need?" he asked.

"Rita Charles," she responded as she extended her hand. She'd forgotten that she was holding a cell phone. "With VHP."

Initially, Mac was confused because she'd caught him off guard. After a moment, he found his bearings. VHP was an acronym for the USGS Volcano Hazards Program, which monitored active and potentially active volcanoes. Mac was perturbed that the interloper would bother him at his home.

"I have an office, you know? And a phone just like yours." He pointed at her cell phone, which she immediately shoved into her cargo pants' pocket.

"Yeah. Um, I'm sorry to arrive unannounced. There must be problems with cell communications because I couldn't get through to you. I've been calling for an hour."

"I've been swimming for an hour. Phone's in there." He nodded toward the houseboat.

"Right. Um, there's a situation we need your

help with. My boss has already cleared it with your boss."

"Cleared what?"

"I can explain it in the chopper," she began in response. She turned around and looked at the forest she'd just found her way through. "Um, it's back over that way. I think."

Mac sighed. He hated being thrown curveballs on a Monday, or any other day for that matter. Mac shook the excess water out of his hair and lowered his eyes to focus on the woman. He studied her for a moment and then asked, "You look familiar to me. What do you do at VHP?"

"Well, this is my last month there. I'm being assigned to another project."

"Where did you go to school?"

"Cal Berkeley at first. Then Oregon State to enter the VIPER program. That's an acronym for—"

Mac finished her sentence. "Volcanology, igneous, petrology, and economic geology research. I know of it."

"Cool. Well, anyway. Would you mind getting ready? They're waiting."

Mac studied the young woman. "I went to Oregon State as well, and I know somebody associated with the VIPER program. Do you know Ashby Donovan?"

Rita smiled. "Of course, Dr. Donovan will be my boss. We've been assigned to study volcanoes along the Ring of Fire as well as Yellowstone."

"Is this about Yellowstone?" he asked, his voice clearly excited, as his interest had been piqued. "And will Ashby be, um, wherever it is you're taking me?"

"No and no. She's at Kilauea at the moment, and it's not about Yellowstone. We're unsure, but it's possible Cascadia is involved, we think. That's why we need your help." She was referring to the Cascadia Subduction Zone, a six-hundred-mile fault that runs from Northern California to British Columbia in Canada.

Mac's shoulders slumped, as he'd hoped to make contact with his old flame. Their romance had been typical of college trysts. Mainly physical with the occasional conversation about their studies. He resisted the urge to pry into Ashby's personal life further. VHP thought highly enough of him to send this young woman to fetch him from his swim, which puzzled him.

Lastly, he asked, "Why me?"

Rita smiled. "They call you the earth whisperer.

They say you're some kind of seismic detective who can sense trouble when others can't."

Mac looked to the sky and smiled. He'd heard this before around the USGS Santa Rosa campus; however, he ignored it. He had no idea his reputation stretched to Vancouver and who knows where else.

Without another word, he hustled inside to dress.

CHAPTER FOUR

Mount Vaca, California

As Mac led Rita up the trails to where the helicopter had found a clearing, she revealed to him that they were headed to the USGS Cascades Volcano Observatory in Vancouver, Washington. Vancouver was six hundred miles away. He grumbled that he should return to the houseboat to pack clothes for an overnight stay. She assured him it wouldn't be necessary.

"It's just a three-hour flight," she said, slightly out of breath as they approached the top of the ridge.

Mac wasn't intimately familiar with helicopters, but he was skeptical of her claim. This chopper would have to be fast with a long range to make it to

Vancouver in three hours. When they entered the clearing, he nodded and smiled.

A dark gray United States Air Force AW139 helicopter stood quietly atop a ledge. The massive chopper awaited its passengers. Mac laughed.

"That's a lot of chopper for just the two of us. This must be pretty important."

"It is. And if you can shed some light on the seismic aspects of the unusual readings we've received, you might be taken elsewhere."

Mac looked at the young woman again. She had a way of disarming him with her casual appearance and unassuming manner. She was holding back information, and he didn't like being dragged along with the promise of a treat at the end. He stopped in his tracks and thrust his hands on his hips as he surveyed the aircraft.

"Okay, Rita. It's time to spill. This thing probably cost the government millions, and lord knows how much it costs to operate per hour. I'm not getting on until you tell me what's going on."

Rita's eyes darted between the pilot, who was peering through the large windows at the front of the Leonardo AW139, and Mac. "Mr. Atwood, um, Mac, we've discovered what I can describe as a firehose of water spewing nonstop from the ocean floor fifty miles off the Northern California coast."

"That's not unusual," interrupted Mac. "Leaks similar to this have been discovered along the ocean bottom years ago. Hell, it's likely been there for fifteen hundred years."

"Yes." She nodded as she continued, "Naturally, CVO is familiar with all of these, and they continue to monitor their emissions. However, the prior seeps were off the coast of Oregon. This is closer to Eureka. You know, Northern California." CVO was the USGS acronym for the Cascades Volcano Observatory.

"I know where Eureka is," said Mac in a stern tone. "Are you saying it is a newly discovered seep?"

She nodded and then glanced at the pilot, who was tapping on the window and pointing at his wristwatch. She took a deep breath and stepped closer to the chopper.

"Mac, please. We can cover this in detail on the three-hour ride to Vancouver." She gestured toward the open door to the passenger seating.

Mac furrowed his brow and looked in the direction of the Pacific Ocean. "You have the details in there?"

"All of it, including some underwater imagery obtained from our sailing drone. Can we please go?"

"I might be able to shorten our trip," he replied as he walked past Rita toward his ride. "If that's true, I don't need to waste my time in Vancouver. I wanna see it for myself."

"Excuse me?" she asked, now hustling to catch up with Mac as he boarded the chopper.

"If you can get one of these things to pick me up, you can probably get a submersible. Am I right?"

"Um, yeah. I think so."

"Good." He slid into a seat with a view of the pilots. He leaned between their backrests. "Take us to Eureka. There's a heliport at Arcata. Let's go!" He waved his arm to the young woman, who scrambled aboard. She would have to explain to her boss that Mac Atwood had his own way of doing things.

CHAPTER FIVE

Aboard the USAF AW139
Mendocino National Forest, California

Mac immersed himself in the research and data accumulated by the Vancouver CVO team. Ordinarily, this information would've been discerned by the California equivalent known as CalVO. However, when Sacramento had been submerged under Lake California, the satellite offices throughout the state took on their own duties and were assigned specific volcanos to monitor.

The five volcanic observatories under the purview of the USGS performed a number of important tasks, including the one Mac's team spearheaded as the project chief of the National Strong Motion Project.

At the NSMP, Mac's team studied the recordings produced by hundreds of strong-motion instruments throughout the West Coast where seismic activity was greatest. These seismic data loggers recorded underground motion accelerograms to understand the characteristics of any earthquake rupture. It fit Mac's career goal of helping create a warning system that actually gave people time to find safety or even evacuate a high-risk location.

Unfortunately, since the ARkStorm, Mac and others in the NSMP had been pulled away from their normal duties to help rebuild the system of monitoring arrays destroyed by the landslides and flooding. Nearly one thousand ground and subsurface seismic recording instruments had been rendered inoperable under the lake. This made Californians vulnerable to quake sequences because they had no warning until the ground shook.

At first, he was puzzled as to why the Vancouver CVO office would pick him out to review this data. Certainly, there were others in the Santa Rosa office of the USGS capable of giving their opinion.

However, he'd gained extensive experience using submersibles to identify the locations of the damaged seismograph equipment along the bottom of the lake. Depending on the location of this newly discovered seep, he'd potentially be deep diving in the Pacific. He wasn't sure how he felt about that.

As if she were reading his mind, Rita proudly announced, "I've secured your submersible. The best I could do on short notice was a Blue Wolf variant of the equipment you're familiar with."

"Am I going down alone?" asked Mac, trying to conceal his trepidation by avoiding eye contact.

"Um, yes. The Navy couldn't free up a pilot to accompany you. Your boss said you'd be familiar with the sub."

Mac probably would be. He was an accomplished scuba diver, although his deepest dive had been just over one hundred feet. This was much different. Rita noticed his concern.

"I'd be glad to ride along though I wouldn't be much help. I've never been in a submersible except the 20,000 *Leagues Under the Sea* ride at Disneyland."

Mac laughed. Ashby Donovan got lucky with this one. If Rita weren't a volcanologist, he might have stolen her away for his team.

"I'll be fine," he muttered. "Thanks anyway." Mac continued to study their findings.

Cracks or fissures in the ocean floor are common along the Cascadia Subduction Zone. These seeps, as they're called, gush liquid or gasses from the sandy bottom and form a column of water until they dissipate. Sometimes cold seeps can spew methane, petroleum, carbon dioxide or hydrogen sulfide.

Then there are the hydrothermal vents, or hot springs as they were commonly called, associated with underwater volcanoes. Hot mineral-laden fluids leak up from below the ocean's surface, indicating volcanic activity below.

Mac furrowed his brow as he thumbed through the pages of the report. He frequently turned the pages back to compare the findings to determine a pattern. This seep didn't fit the standard geologic definitions. His first inclination, in accord with the CVO scientists, was this was a cold methane seep not unlike thousands of others in the region.

However, this seep was much warmer. It had an uncharacteristically low salinity reading. Most notably, the water sample taken by the sailboat drone registered components such as boron and lithium that aren't found in other seeps or elsewhere on the ocean floor.

Here's the kicker, Mac thought to himself. The seep wasn't found within the Juan de Fuca Plate or even the Gorda Plate that bordered the Cascadia Subduction Zone. It was farther south. At the leading edge of the Pacific Plate.

Near the San Andreas Fault.

CHAPTER SIX

**United States Coast Guard Station
Humboldt Bay
Eureka, California**

The helicopter pilots took Mac directly to the U.S. Coast Guard Sector/Air Station at Humboldt Bay near Eureka. Known as the Guardians of the Lost Coast, Sector Humboldt Bay covered two hundred fifty miles of rugged coastline from Sonoma County to the Oregon Border. If Mac was going to navigate the submersible to the bottom of the Pacific, he'd be more comfortable knowing this outfit had his back if something went awry.

The San Andreas Fault was perhaps the most famous in the world. It stretched along a major fracture in the Earth's crust for eight hundred miles from the northern end of the Gulf of California near Eureka through Western California, where it meandered into the Pacific Ocean near San Francisco and then ultimately into Los Angeles County along the San Gabriel Mountains.

The tectonic movement along the fault has been responsible for some of the largest earthquakes in modern American history, including the San Francisco quakes in 1906 and 1989 as well as the destructive Northridge earthquake in suburban LA in 1994.

Incredible forces were at work beneath the fault that posed great risk to buildings and inhabitants above. Two major tectonic plates, the Pacific and the

North American, slip and slide against one another, creating one of the most seismically active regions on the planet. Each year, the plates' movement relative to one another was around two inches. In 1906, during the San Francisco quake, which was estimated to be around a magnitude of 7.9, it was determined that parts of the tectonic plates moved as much as twenty-one feet.

Because of its potential for disaster, a massive earthquake along the San Andreas Fault of magnitude eight or greater has been dubbed the *Big One*. While a magnitude 8.0 quake would be devastating to California, the potential for a larger quake of 9.0 or greater is possible. In the last hundred years, megaquakes have occurred in Alaska, Chile, Indonesia, Japan, and Russia. Because the magnitude of an earthquake is related to the length of the fault on which it occurs, a magnitude 10 or larger is not possible on Earth. The 1960 Chilean quake recorded a magnitude 9.5 because its fault stretches a thousand miles. It was deemed to be a megaquake.

The San Andreas Fault is one of the most studied in the world and had once been extensively monitored until the ARkStorm. The seismic monitors were either missing or offline due to the debris and the weight of the silt filling Lake California.

Government's resources were limited to coping with the massive rescue and recovery efforts, followed by the reconstruction of the state's homes and businesses. The USGS worked diligently within the bounds of their budgetary and personnel constraints to restore the monitoring system of San Andreas. However, it was far from complete and therefore deemed unreliable by many.

As a Navy team prepared the submersible and loaded it onto a Coast Guard ship equipped with a small crane, Mac wandered across the grounds toward a rocky point where the Pacific's waves covered him in sea spray. Without a doubt, California's coastlines, mountain ranges, and now lakes were the most beautiful in the world.

He could've taken any assignment within the USGS he wanted. There were even private employers who would've loved someone with his skills. He chose California despite what he knew about what was under the state that should've scared him away after his childhood experience. He remembered the day he'd picked out the cabin on Mount Vaca. He knew of its proximity to the San Andreas Fault. But then, he surmised, how do you find a safe place to live when you can't drive ten miles in any direction without crossing a fault line? To him, it was like standing in the middle of a frozen lake that suddenly decided to thaw and crack just before you sank below the water's surface.

That was California. His new home. And his gut told him something was wrong underneath his feet.

CHAPTER SEVEN

Pacific Ocean
Southwest of Eureka, California

Mac had been given a heads-up from the Coast Guard that the SS *Princess Clementine* and a tow vessel had capsized in the late nineties near the location of the seep. He was told the offshore gambling cruise ship and the accompanying Sea Tow vessel stretched one hundred twenty feet, although they'd settled on the ocean floor in a jackknifed configuration.

As he approached the coordinates for the seep fifty miles off the coast, southwest of Eureka, the wrecked ships appeared out of the dark, gloomy waters like a man-made reef made of steel. Sand, moved by the force of the Pacific Ocean, hugged the wreck. The paint on the hulls had long since worn off, leaving a grayish skin, dark and discolored from decades of exposure to the salt water.

As he reached the bottom, Mac powered on all the external lighting of the five-man submersible. The wreck came into view, revealing streaks of algae, rust, and layers of barnacles, confirming the vessels would most likely remain there for eternity.

Mac guided the submersible around the wreckage, taking in every detail the underwater lighting afforded him. The *Clementine* had wedged in a steep, narrow subsea canyon that required him to be mindful of striking the sheer walls. The rear-facing cameras reminded him of the close proximity by sending clouds of silt billowing through the water.

Once he cleared the wreckage, he patiently waited for the sand and silt to settle before easing deeper into the narrow canyon. His video recorder continued running, although he was certain the wreckage had been explored and surveyed more than once. Many universities on the West Coast studied the effects of deep-water currents on ocean acidification and carbon storage levels. The sunken cruise ship had first appeared during a sonar survey of the San Andreas Fault twenty years ago.

Although Mac was alone in the submersible, he was not completely alone. Three thousand feet above him, a very capable Coast Guard crew stood at the ready to send single-man rescue submersibles to retrieve his vessel in the event of a malfunction. This particular Orca model came equipped with full-time underwater breathing devices, which Mac wore at all times. In addition, the submersible's cockpit was encapsulated and would always maintain an atmospheric pressure commensurate with its depth in the event of an unforeseen breach.

Mac checked his coordinates and continued toward the location of the seep. Racks of computer monitors, electronics and a baffling amount of encased wiring filled the concave instrument panel. Mac took in his surroundings once again, puzzled as to how a five-man crew could fit in the watertight coffin.

He was more experienced at navigating the depths of Lake California than he was the Pacific Ocean. Although, his first experience in a submersible had been at a similar depth off the coast of Oregon while he was in college studying Cascadia. At three thousand feet below the surface, he was in the mid-ocean twilight zone, the depth just beyond the reach of sunlight. At this depth, the water was cold, and its light was dim but teeming with flashes of bioluminescent radiance produced by living organisms. The marine creatures in the twilight zone ranged in size from microscopic to among the largest on the planet.

It was the refrigeration effect within the twilight zone that helped discover the new seep. An unmanned sail drone had discovered the temperature anomaly created by the seep, and its data had been reported to NOAA. The safety-orange sailing ship had been commissioned to survey forty-five thousand square miles of the Pacific from Northern California to the coast of Vancouver, Canada.

Its data had revealed the temperature anomaly emanating from a portion of the canyon near the wreck of the *Clementine*. At first, analysts thought the anomaly might have been related to the wreck. Perhaps a leak from a fuel or water tank on board the boat had finally ruptured. They programmed the sail drone to return to the area to perform a grid-pattern search of the ocean floor. That led the team at USGS Vancouver to declare the discovery of the new seep.

The sail drone was not capable of identifying the geologic transformation responsible for the seep. In a way, it was a very flat-Earth type of surveying vessel. Hence, the reason for a submersible to be sent to the ocean floor.

Mac continued forward at a slow, steady pace, expecting to find a fissure of gurgling bubbles rising out of the canyon. He studied a previous map of the ocean floor and compared it to the actual appearance of the dark landscape before him.

He lowered his eyes as he compared the visual through the glass enclosure to the computerized survey. He brought the submersible to a full stop and pressed his body back in his seat. He took manual control of the submersible's lighting to view the canyon walls from left to right. He checked his depth.

Forty-two hundred feet below sea level. *Did I wander that far down without noticing, mesmerized by my surroundings?* He was piloting the vessel, and it was possible he'd lost track of his depth.

Regardless, he thought to himself before speaking aloud, "Where the hell did this mountain come from?"

CHAPTER EIGHT

Pacific Ocean
Southwest of Eureka, California

Mac's heart was beating out of his chest. He continued to shine the spotlight on the previously uncharted seamount rising twelve hundred feet out of the canyon. It was as if a giant set of hands had scooped the sand out of the canyon, shoved it into a plastic beach bucket, and emptied it on the ocean floor, much like a child would do at the beach.

Seamounts were essentially remnants of volcanos, ranging in size from Hawaii's Mauna Kea, the dormant volcano, which is actually the tallest mountain on Earth at thirty thousand feet from its base to the crater, to what he'd just discovered. More than half of Mauna Kea is beneath the surface, which hides its massive size. The vast majority of seamounts, especially near the Southern California coast, are closer to two thousand feet.

There were three seamounts well off the coast of San Francisco that were irregular-shaped knolls, mounds, and ridges worn down by ocean currents and time. Seamounts typically follow a geologic pattern of initial growth, subsequent volcanic activity, sinking, and eventually extinction when volcanic activity has ceased.

It was this knowledge of geology that struck Mac as odd about this particular formation. As he slowly encircled the seamount with the submersible, he thought of famous seamounts like Mount Fuji, which was characterized by sloped sides topped by a crater. As he navigated around this seamount, he marveled at the steep, vertical sides. It rose out of the canyon's seafloor like a tower. It was a textbook example of a seamount undisturbed by the forces of the Pacific.

Mac found a moment of hilarity as he spoke to himself. "Kinda like a Bundt cake. An enormous Bundt cake."

He continued to study its shape as he rose higher

toward the top rim. One side was higher than the other, forming a gradual summit. The round, bulging top was irregular due to the variability of the slope. *The shape is not unusual per se*, Mac thought to himself. But the size of it was. He was unaware of a conical-shaped seamount rising to this size.

"And so quickly. How new is this thing?" Mac alternated between speaking to himself aloud and internally. He glanced at his oxygen levels to make sure everything was in range. He wished he had more time but cautioned himself against pushing the envelope, a characteristic he wished he could shed.

He rose above the seamount to observe the seep. Looking downward in the limited light, he understood how the tall, narrow seamount could be missed by other research vessels. The narrow opening spewing material was barely noticeable. However, the readings he was receiving from the outside water temperature were definitive. This seamount had not been created slowly by the piling on of marine snow, that shower of organic sea material from the upper waters of the Pacific. *Millennia of fish poop*, as Mac's professor at Oregon State liked to say. Definitely recent, as evidenced by rocks and debris rolling down the sides periodically.

Mac mumbled as he observed the entire rim.

The submersible was equipped with sonar videography, enabling it to capture an image of the crater. Warm, chemically distinct fluids gushed out in the form of bubbles. Some darted higher than others, alternating turns as if dancing to underwater music.

He spoke aloud. "Not necessarily unusual considering our proximity to the plate boundaries. It's the fault's way of relieving stress between the plates. But the levels of boron and lithium are astounding. Like no other we've seen before. And the water flow rate? Incredible!"

Mac circled the crater, taking video from multiple angles while observing the seamount's characteristics. He continued to narrate his observations although they weren't recorded.

"No doubt it's volcanic. And it had to be super hot and super quick. It may still be growing." Subconsciously, he looked upward toward the surface, wondering if its growth might form a new volcanic island. There were more than ten thousand seamounts around the world, but fewer than three hundred had been surveyed. A very small percentage reach the surface. Even fewer become active volcanoes.

Mac sighed as he considered the consequences of this discovery. To him, it was not about the prospect of a volcanic eruption creating a new island. It was what had shifted below it that had created the seamount in the first place.

"The plates could be locking. Too much stress. The water outflow is probably fresh, chemically dehydrated by the heat."

Mac considered the ramifications of this hypothesis. The water between the Pacific and North American plates was necessary to regulate the pressure and alleviate the stresses, allowing the two massive tectonic features to slip-slide against one another. Losing this fluid, the lubricant required to relieve the stress, meant only one thing.

The question was how large and when.

CHAPTER NINE

**United States Coast Guard Station
Humboldt Bay
Eureka, California**

Mac didn't want to return topside. If he had his way, and the ability, he would've put on his scuba gear and touched the damn thing just to see if it was real. Unfortunately, at that depth, he'd be dead within seconds from nitrogen narcosis or hypothermia.

As the submersible breached the surface, the crew of the Coast Guard ship were anxiously waiting to hoist the vessel on board. Mac had pushed the limit of his time on the ocean floor, and the captain of the forty-seven-foot rescue vessel had been on the verge of sending a team down to bring him back.

Mac sat on the bow of the boat, taking in the sun while he nourished his body with fluids and a snack box designed to avoid dehydration. After he steadied his nerves and allowed his adrenaline levels to come back to earth, he tried to separate fact from hyperbole.

Undoubtedly, he'd still have to go to Vancouver to meet with the folks who summoned him. They'd need to download the data on board the submersible. However, that wouldn't be enough. He was certain they'd want his take on what he'd observed. Anybody could've driven the submersible around the seamount. Mac was the guy they needed to make sense of it all.

As soon as the boat was in view of the Coast Guard facility, Mac saw a contingent of a dozen or more people gathering at the point, shading their eyes from the sun. The captain navigated the fast-response rescue vessel through the channel toward the dock. He took a deep breath and exhaled. It wasn't that he was uncomfortable speaking to a group of any size, regardless of their relative status on the government's totem pole.

Rather, he needed to force himself to curb his

enthusiasm as well as his concerns. This seamount was anything but ordinary. The seep reflected its unique nature. He was genuinely concerned they'd discovered a tectonic time bomb along the San Andreas Fault.

After the captain gave him a nod, indicating he could disembark, Mac made his way onto the dock with the wetsuit he'd been provided pulled down to his waist. He wasn't much for trying to impress anyone with the way he was dressed. Plus, it would've taken a heckuv an effort to pull the suit back onto his sweaty upper body.

His eyes darted from one member of the contingent to the other as he attempted to identify who was present. There were several unfamiliar faces. Noticeably absent was Rita Charles. She'd given him the impression she hadn't been interested in the outcome after fetching him from Mount Vaca. He imagined she'd found a military transport or some other means to make her way to Kilauea to meet Ashby.

A young man hustled to Mac's side and handed him a Coast Guard logo duffel bag with his clothing inside. He whispered to Mac that he could have use of the officers' showers if he wanted to clean up. Mac thanked him and then turned his attention to a large man with a toothy grin.

"Dr. Atwood, I'm Evan Papp, scientist-in-charge of the Cascades Volcano Observatory. Miss Charles sends her regrets, but she was anxious to go to her new assignment."

"Nice to meet you," Mac greeted as he wiped the sweat off his neck and shoulders. "Please call me Mac."

"Well, Mac, we're grateful that you were able to assist us in this endeavor. Your reputation for providing a straightforward assessment of what's happening within a seismic system warranted our efforts to bring you here. Now, if you don't mind, please tell us what you've learned."

Mac stepped forward and quickly repositioned himself to the side of the group, as most of them had been shielding their eyes from the setting sun. Only one woman standing in the rear of the group was wearing sunglasses. He gave her a lingering look, as she was completely out of place to the rest of the group.

Scientists had a certain way of dressing. Well, like Rita. Casual. Clothes that were loose fitting with lots of pockets. They looked more like they were ready to dig for prehistoric bones in the badlands of the Dakotas than study computer screens and seismic monitoring devices.

This woman was different. She was dressed head to toe in Vineyard Vines apparel. Her Ray-Ban Clubmaster sunglasses were a classic throwback to the preppy look she sported. At first glance, he thought she was a wife or girlfriend of one of the Vancouver contingent. Or maybe she'd decided to follow them around for grins and giggles. A reporter? Definitely a possibility.

In any event, she knocked him off his game for a moment, forcing him to pause and rethink his approach to the CVO's lead scientist's request.

"I'll try not to get into conjecture. However, what we have down there is certainly extraordinary. Once you pore over the data from the submersible, I think you'll find a tremendous outflow of low-salinity, high-temperature, mineral-rich water. By tremendous, I mean the flow rate is astonishing. The date readings on the submersible noted a significant rise in temperature around the rim of the seamount."

"Seamount?" asked one of the attendees. "The sail drone didn't indicate anything other than a seep in the ocean floor."

Mac presumed this man was late to the party or

unfamiliar with the technology of the sail drone. "The sail drone isn't capable of providing any point of view except straight down. This is the interesting aspect of this seep. A seamount formed in the middle of the canyon a couple of miles south of the shipwrecked cruise ship and the Sea Tow vessel. The canyon widened, and the seamount has risen to approximately fifteen hundred to two thousand feet above the canyon floor."

"Are you sure?" asked another man. "We've surveyed this part of the coastal region for years."

Mac was perturbed but bit his tongue. He had no idea who these people were. He didn't need to get fired.

"The videotape will provide you the imagery. It is conical in shape and very steep. I've never seen anything like it."

Papp asked, "What about the temperature of the water? You mentioned it was warmer."

"Yes, at least twenty degrees warmer. And the volume being released is significant, which could have an impact on the tectonic plates."

"What do you mean?" asked a woman standing next to Papp.

"Loss of fluid from the offshore megathrust interface through these strike-slip faults increases the friction between the oceanic and continental plates."

He'd given a very scientific answer, resulting in puzzled looks across several faces in the contingent. *They must be the politicians,* he thought to himself. He was about to clarify in layman's terms when the preppy woman in the back spoke up.

"Think of an air hockey table. In a strike-slip scenario like Cascadia and San Andreas, a high-pressure fluid lessens the friction. It's similar to the air being turned on during an air hockey game. There's less friction, allowing the puck to slide smoothly on the table. On the other hand, if the fluid pressure is low, as Dr. Atwood indicates, the two plates will lock, and stress can build up."

"And result in a seismic event," added Mac. He studied the woman, then provided her an imperceptible nod and smile. He was impressed and intrigued. He continued, "It will be important for you to analyze the water samples I took. If the chemistry suggests this fluid is coming from the plate boundary, then we might be looking at something significant."

Mac answered a few more questions, all of which would be answered by the data on board the submersible. At the end of the briefing, he got the impression most of the people quizzing him seemed relieved that the newly formed seamount was not within the Cascadia Subduction Zone. They spoke amongst themselves as they wandered off toward their vehicles.

All but one.

CHAPTER TEN

**United States Coast Guard Station
Humboldt Bay
Eureka, California**

The preppy woman waited behind. Mac was
beginning to think she was a tourist who decided to
hang around to see what all the hubbub was about.
They awkwardly stared at one another for a moment.
Mac turned around to see if anyone was lingering
nearby he hadn't noticed. No, it was just the two of
them. She had to be a reporter. A very knowledgeable one.

When he made eye contact with her again, she
began laughing. Mac started laughing, too. He held

his hands to his sides and shrugged as if to ask, what's next?

She stepped closer to him. "How'd you like the air hockey analogy?"

Mac jutted out his lower lip and managed a slight smile. "Not bad. I kinda figured some of those people weren't geologists, so it helped."

"Most were from the governor's office from Washington and Oregon," she added. "They'll go back and pop the cork on some nice champagne to celebrate the seep being along San Andreas. Those two states benefitted the most from the ARkStorms. Their tax bases grew exponentially."

"Good point. Which governor's office are you from?" Mac continued to assess the woman, who had an uncanny ability to disarm his normally guarded nature.

"None of them. We're teammates, sort of," she replied with a laugh. "I work for Papp."

Mac was genuinely confused and scowled at her response. "Oh, more like a double agent."

She'd continued to move closer to him. "I'm Taylor Reed with CalVO. Nice to meet you." She extended her fist to bump, rather than shake, Mac's hand. He gently bumped her fist.

"I haven't seen you around campus in Santa

Rosa," he said. Mac studied her attire again. And then her face. And then her body. It was the opposite of most assessments by the male of any species. "You must be in one of those fancy corner offices with a view of the Russian River."

"Nope. Ya wanna guess again?"

She was toying with him. Flirting, in fact. He tried to nonchalantly glance at her left hand in search of a wedding ring. Apparently, he wasn't nonchalant enough. She wiggled her fingers to let him know she'd busted him.

Mac was mad at himself for getting caught. He scowled and looked over his shoulder as the sun began to sink into the Pacific. "No, I don't wanna guess. I need to catch a chopper home." He started to walk away, although he didn't want to.

"Wait." She reached out to touch his arm. "I'm sorry. Um, I just got off a PJ at the airport and had a couple of drinks before I came to greet you."

"PJ?" asked Mac.

"Private jet. I was on an Alaskan cruise with my parents. When we returned to Vancouver, I was instructed to come here. The agency arranged for the plane. It wasn't really a PJ per se. It had propellers. It was small. It stank a little. Not to mention the pilot rudely asked how much I weighed before he assigned me a seat. After it was over, I needed the drinks."

Mac chuckled. "How much?"

Perplexed, Taylor tilted her head and asked, "How much what?"

"How much did you weigh?"

Mac burst out laughing at his bold question, and the look on Taylor's face was priceless. Up until that moment, her confidence had given her the impression she had the upper hand in her exchange with him. Just like that, he'd turned the tables on her.

"Noneya!" She subtly flipped him a bird.

This set Mac off into a laughing fit. "All right. You're clearly important enough to warrant a chartered plane of any kind; how are we part of the same team?"

"Formally, I'm the CalVO scientist-in-charge at Mammoth Mountain and the Long Valley Caldera. In reality, my team consists of me, myself, and I, plus a couple of part-timers. *You guys* stole my help to rebuild the seismic sensor array beneath the lake."

Mac raised his eyebrows and glanced at the setting sun again. There was a lot to unpack with this volcanologist, Taylor Reed. He started with the obvious.

"You're a long way from home." *Probably five hundred miles*, he thought to himself.

"I am, although my next stop is Santa Rosa. I have to brief my boss about your findings to determine if it will impact California. I'm supposed to rent a car, but ..." Her voice trailed off.

"Lost the PJ, did you?"

"I almost threw up, twice. I told them I'd rather walk to Santa Rosa than fly in that puddle jumper again."

Mac pointed toward the awaiting helicopter. "I've got room on my ride. I'm sure the pilots would be glad to drop you off. That is, if you are willing to ride with one of the *guys* who stole your staff."

"Whadya mean?" she asked.

"In addition to heading up the National Strong Motion Project, I'm also overseeing the rebuilding of the San Andreas sensor array."

"You're the one!" she shouted, pointing her finger at him playfully.

"Not true. I made a request for warm bodies. I had no idea where my boss would pluck them from."

"Whatever. I'll rent a car." She began to walk away.

It was Mac's turn to reach out for her. "Come on, Taylor. It's two hundred miles down the one-oh-one in the dark. It'll take you three hours at least. And you've had a couple of drinks."

Taylor stopped and looked at the ground. "Fine, you win. But along the way, you can expect an earful about why the seismographs aren't in place, and I want answers on when you'll be sending back my people."

Mac grinned. Taylor Reed was Ashby Donovan on steroids. If they knew each other, he'd probably ask the chopper pilot to drop him off first. Anywhere. He'd walk back to his quiet house on the lake alone.

CHAPTER ELEVEN

**Aboard the USAF AW139
Northern California Coastline**

After they reached the heliport, Mac and Taylor boarded the chopper. They settled into their seats, and the pilots quickly lifted the four-ton twin-engine helicopter skyward. Mac asked them to skirt the coastline as the sun dropped into the Pacific. It was an incredible sight to see, and had he and Taylor been intimately involved, the memory of the romantic moment would last forever.

Nonetheless, it served to calm Taylor down about her aggravation over the earthquake monitoring system that was in disrepair. Mac didn't need to hear it from her. He was frustrated as well. He'd worked for the USGS long enough to know that his need for human resources was not always aligned with his superiors'. The restoration of the seismic monitoring array required many steps, including the demolition of submerged structures located where underwater seismographs had to be installed.

He battled with the USGS. They battled with the state of California. They battled with environmental interests. They all did battle in the courts from time to time. None of them seemed to care that the most dangerous fault in the world, San Andreas, was still there. Lurking. Waiting for the opportunity to shake the earth and everything on the surface.

Mac opted to make small talk with the attractive volcanologist. She was charming in a bossy sort of way. He looked at her as a challenge. On the surface, she looked like some of the Chi-O sorority girls at Oregon State. Chi Omega was very selective in their membership, and many of them came from well-to-do families. In reality, her cruise-wear apparel from Vineyard Vines was simply her way of playing a part for her family. After half an hour of flight time, he found her to be very laid-back and unassuming.

"I was born and raised outside of Denver in Aurora. I was given a golf scholarship to the University of Colorado in Boulder; however, I only played my first year before I got serious about school. My freed-up schedule gave me time to intern within the geological sciences department to pursue a career path. That's when I fell in love with rocks."

Mac laughed. She didn't appear to be an entitled princess under the surface. Her preppy attire had nothing to do with who she was. It was simply the obligatory cruise outfit everyone picked out because it was expected.

"They have one of the top volcanology programs," added Mac. Along with Oregon State, Hawaii and Alaska-Fairbanks, the University of Colorado was highly respected.

"Yeah, and I was lucky to get in. Their acceptance rate was down near ten percent, but I had an inside track because I made friends in the geological sciences department during my internship."

Mac paused the conversation to direct her attention to the Point Arena Lighthouse sitting atop a rocky part of the coast. The one-hundred-fifty-year-old lighthouse had survived the devastating 1906 earthquake sequence that had nearly leveled San Francisco.

"San Andreas runs practically underneath Point Arena. The lighthouse was rattled but withstood the tremor. Still, they were concerned about its structural integrity and the safety of the wickies, so they rebuilt it."

"Wickies?" she asked.

"Yeah, sorry. That's a nickname for the lighthouse keepers, who had to crank a huge weight up the center of the structure to keep the lens turning. A hydraulic oil lamp kept the light on, and the lens sent out the signal."

"Who knew?" she said jokingly.

The copilot announced they were entering Santa Rosa airspace, and they would be touching down at the Charles M. Schulz–Sonoma Airport, named for the famous creator of the *Peanuts* characters—Charlie Brown, Snoopy, and friends.

Mac continued, "Listen, um, we didn't have time to talk about the seismograph project."

"That's okay. I realize your hands were tied, anyway."

"Yeah, but there's more. Um, I was wondering. Um, tomorrow afternoon, if you get freed up, would you like to go fishing?"

Taylor leaned back and tried to get a better look at Mac's face in the darkness. "Well, that's random. I mean, we just met, and now you wanna take me fishing? Is that some kind of code word for your true, nefarious intent?"

Mac was caught off guard once again. It took a lot of courage for him to ask her out on a sort-of date. He thought of a way to throw it back at her.

"Nefarious? No, not at all. Fishing is fishing. But if you're afraid of fish, I understand. Just say so."

Taylor laughed and playfully punched him. "No, I'm not afraid of fish. I'm afraid of you."

CHAPTER TWELVE

Mac's Floating Home
Mount Vaca, California

Mac was soaked with sweat when he awoke at five o'clock that morning. Anxiety had never been an issue for him. One of his favorite axioms was that nature had a way of fixing itself. Another one was don't fret about the things you can't control.

Two things had kept him tossing and turning that night. One was the seamount and its relationship to San Andreas. That, he couldn't control, although he'd reached a conclusion about its importance. Throughout the night, the numbers had scrolled through his brain, keeping him awake. His recollection of the seamount, its unusual formation, and sudden appearance caused him to be on edge. He needed to get a handle on all of the data and video observations.

He needed a working theory on the impact the seep might have on San Andreas. But first, he needed to clear his head of the other matter that was giving him the night sweats.

Her name was Taylor Reed, and she could become a real problem for him.

He replayed their interaction over and over as he tried to find sleep. There was something about her that grabbed him. She was the first woman who'd had the combination of dry wit and intellect to keep him interested in more than a casual date or roll in the hay, as they used to say back in Dyersburg. The concept of dating someone on a regular basis, even on a long-distance basis, was unsettling. Mac was married to his career, and he didn't think there was room for another love interest in his life.

He knew he was in trouble when he skipped his morning swim in favor of cleaning up his bachelor pad. It was certainly outside the norm. While he had been completing his dock and shoreline improvements, Mac had researched houseboat options. He'd applied his own form of logic to his selection.

He'd separated his options into two groups. There were houseboats that were more boat than house. Then there were floating homes. Mac had no desire to cruise up and down the lake in a forty-foot-plus behemoth in search of a quiet cove to do cannonballs off the roof. He needed a place to live. So he chose a floating home.

The floating home was seaworthy to the extent a tow vessel could drag it to a dock and secure it. It was a barge with a home built on top, together with external amenities suitable for lake living. Mac had chosen the Zion, a fourteen-foot-by forty-seven-foot home totaling six hundred and fifty square feet. It suited his lifestyle perfectly.

Mac slid out of bed to get his day started, one that was filled with meetings and capped by an evening fishing outing with Taylor.

As he straightened the living area and kitchen, he recalled viewing the Zion for the first time.

The salesman had chattered in his ear about the fact it could sleep eight and that the state-of-the-art chef's kitchen could host a party of forty. Mac didn't need all that. Yet he was amazed such a large living space could encompass only six hundred and fifty square feet.

What he liked most about the floating house was the third of the structure that would face the lake. A covered deck included a hot tub, grill and full bar on the roof and plenty of room for seating below. Mac stored his fishing and dive gear on the bottom deck and used the top deck to relax alone, as he never entertained.

The unkept state of his home added to his cluttered mind. Mac was taking her fishing. He'd never said anything about dinner, although the late afternoon fishing trip might imply dinner. Besides, he couldn't keep her out of his home, either. He silently cursed himself for being such a slob and vowed to treat his modest digs with a little more respect.

As he cleaned the kitchen, the sun began to rise, casting an incredible orange glow on Lake California. The water was like glass with only the occasional ripple being created by a fish breaching the surface or a bird trying to snatch the fish in its beak. The peacefulness had a calming effect on Mac, allowing him to focus on his meeting with the executive team at the Santa Rosa USGS campus.

He thought back on the events of yesterday. The Vancouver contingent had been too giddy when they learned their new discovery wouldn't impact the Cascadia Subduction Zone. He frowned and shook his head. San Andreas could trigger quakes across the entire North American stretch of the Pacific Rim. Quakes, in turn, could trigger volcanic activity.

These were the issues that weighed on him as he dressed and started his days.

CHAPTER THIRTEEN

USGS Santa Rosa Campus
Santa Rosa, California

Mac enjoyed his occasional hour-long drive across Mount Vaca into Santa Rosa. If his job required him to be in the office every day, he might've considered giving up his floating house. However, the majority of the time was spent in the field, reconstructing the array of seismographs up and down Lake California or studying earthquake swarms. Sometimes he used his fishing boat to commute to work on the lake, and the USGS covered the maintenance and cost of his fuel. He was very pleased with the arrangement.

His Jeep Rubicon was the perfect vehicle for his

overland commute. Mac had discovered Forest
Service utility roads that allowed him to take a more
direct route over the mountain. The weather in
Northern California is often wet, so the Rubicon
enabled him to traverse the muddy trails without
much difficulty. The winch on the front bumper had
pulled him out of a ditch more than once.

The USGS campus shared a beautiful stretch of
property with several U.S. government agencies
displaced from Sacramento. Once farmland amidst a
string of a dozen lakes, the property had been seized
by the government, and the structures were built
well above grade to avoid damage from future flood
events. This afforded every structure a magnificent
view of the Russian River, which separated the
valley from the lower end of the Northern Coast
Ranges.

Upon arrival, he was surprised to learn that his
meeting with a handful of superiors had become a
full-blown presentation in the campus auditorium.
He'd hardly prepared to provide the detailed explanations and analysis the entire executive team at
USGS Santa Rosa would expect. However, it was a
reminder to him of how significant this discovery was
and what it could mean for the West Coast.

Before he summoned his team leaders, he

stopped by the monitoring center. He gently pushed open the door and squinted his eyes to adjust from the bright illumination in the corridors to the near darkness in the carpeted room filled with cubicles. Computer screens provided the bulk of the lighting, and the steady hum of the computers created a pleasant form of white noise. However, it was the muted chatter between the scientists and analysts that caught his attention.

Many workstations revealed a screen filled with alternating lines of blue and red, with numbers darting upward and downward, as the seismometer readings were unusually active. The frenzied activity meant that there was an earthquake swarm along the West Coast.

Mac made his way to the desk of an analyst from his department. He gently placed his hand on the young man's shoulder so as not to startle him. Nonetheless, the intensity of the swarm had drawn his complete attention, so he jumped slightly at Mac's touch.

"Shit!" he exclaimed under his breath as he turned to see who had interrupted his train of thought. "Oh, sorry, Mac. I didn't know ..."

"No worries. I should've waited. What's goin' on?"

He responded with a single word. *Hayward*. The Hayward Fault ran parallel to the San Andreas on the east side of San Francisco Bay. It was very short compared to San Andreas, only stretching forty-five miles from Berkeley to the north and just past San Jose to the south.

The USGS had placed a significant emphasis on the monitoring of Hayward, even declaring a major earthquake was increasingly likely. The last major quake there had been in 1868, six years after the ARkStorm of 1862. In addition to the usual threats of damage and loss of life, the Hayward Fault bisects significant communication and internet lines between Silicon Valley and the rest of the U.S. The cost of a disruption of these services was incalculable.

"How many have been registered in the swarm so far?" Mac asked as he leaned over the analyst's shoulder.

"It started just after four this morning. We're at one-ten between M3.5 and M4.0."

"Any particular trigger event?" asked Mac, whose mind immediately sought a connection between the seamount and the earthquake swarm at Hayward despite it being a different fault from San Andreas. Understanding the interconnection between fault lines beneath the Earth's surface was an inexact science based mostly on studying recorded history and the consensus of geologists.

"Most of the team wants to point to the bayside soil conditions. Since the ARkStorm, the lower elevations near San Francisco Bay are water saturated combined with mud and sand. It's a function of the marshland development a hundred years ago and the impact of the atmospheric rivers."

Mac glanced at his watch. His presence would be expected shortly in the auditorium. He wondered if the Hayward Fault activity might postpone the meeting. He could've used the extra time to prepare. He got his answer a moment later via a text message from his assistant. She'd seen his Jeep in the parking lot, but he was nowhere to be found. She reminded him of the meeting and then admonished him to wash the mud off the Rubicon. Mac chuckled. She obviously didn't understand that allowing mud to cake on was a Jeep thing.

He instructed the analyst to text him if anything new developed, and then he headed toward his office. He checked in with his assistant, told his team to expect to work through lunch, and tossed his computer bag in his cubicle. Mac hadn't requested an office although he would've been entitled to one.

He didn't want to be tied to a desk. If he needed to meet one-on-one with a subordinate for disciplinary reasons or to review work performance, he'd take them outside to the picnic tables by the river. In fact, he'd set up shop out there if they'd let him.

He took a deep breath, gathered his thoughts, and made his way to the auditorium. When he pushed open the swinging double doors, he was astonished to find a packed house.

CHAPTER FOURTEEN

USGS Santa Rosa Campus
Santa Rosa, California

Mac thought he was unprepared for the hastily arranged briefing. However, it was not unusual for him to underestimate himself. He was too humble to repeat the words from music artist Bob Dylan, who once famously said *I've forgotten more than you've ever known*. In Mac's case, it might've been true, although he would never give himself credit for it.

He hated standing on a stage looking down at the people in attendance. The auditorium was designed to provide video presentations to visiting students of all ages. The theater-like seating was comfortable for viewing, but, like a theater, it was well below the stage level.

They'd set up a folding table for Mac, and a microphone was placed in the middle. As he settled into the chair, he looked around and took inventory of who was in attendance. It was a who's who of the USGS on the West Coast. There were even a few suits in the front row, flanked by both the volcanic and earthquake regional directors of the Santa Rosa offices. He suspected several had flown in from Washington, DC.

Within a minute of speaking, Mac abandoned the table, pulled the cordless microphone free of its stand, and sat on the end of the stage, with his legs dangling beneath him. He felt like some poor sap who'd just been called before Congress to get interrogated.

Through a combination of recounting his observations and answering questions, he was able to set the table for the ultimate question on everyone's mind—what does it all mean?

Mac explained the worst-case scenario.

"What struck me as odd when I was navigating the submersible through the canyon is how it suddenly widened at the base of the seamount. I'd need to study available mapping of the ocean floor in that area to determine if this canyon has remained static or it has grown apart recently. Typically, a chasm of this type opening up, whether it be on land or below a body of water would generate noticeable seismic activity.

"However, that's not always the case. Let me give you a point of reference. In 2005 a significant split formed in the Ethiopian desert. The USGS was invited into Africa by the governments of Ethiopia, Kenya, and Uganda to study the seismic activity. When we were done there, it was determined this was the only place on Earth where a continental rift could become an oceanic rift.

"The East African Rift, as it was named, only stretched thirty-five miles. However, over time, the Red Sea and nearby bodies of water could flood the void, forcing the rift to widen. A million years from now, a new ocean could form.

"What I observed at the bottom of the Pacific was possibly a new rift in the making." Mac paused as his audience began to mumble to one another. He sensed their skepticism.

"Here's why it is important. If the strike-slip dynamic of the San Andreas Fault has changed by, for example, becoming locked, then instead of the two massive plates sliding smoothly against one another, they'll be punching each other for supremacy.

"It's the same scenario experienced at New Madrid. The two plates can bounce back, creating a rift along San Andreas."

"All of it?" asked a man's voice from the middle of the auditorium.

Mac thought for a moment and then replied, "It's hard to tell because we're in uncharted territory here. That said, in theory, the answer is yes."

He took a deep breath and continued, "Here's the thing. The development of a rift, regardless of location, takes time. While it is true that the possible change in width and the resulting seamount is an indication that we might be in the early stages of rifting, I can't say with certainty that we are facing an immediate threat of a seismic event along San Andreas."

"Mac," began Sierra Kemp, the director of the USGS Santa Rosa region and Mac's boss, "what I'm about to bring up may or may not have a bearing on your discovery off the coast. We have discussed the concept of earthquake weather and the theory that heavy rains could trigger earthquakes. You know, as a result of the ARkStorm, for example."

Mac hoped Kemp wouldn't go there. In fact,

Mac's theory would be considered fringe by many geologists, who would view the concept with skepticism. Nonetheless, it was on the table, so he responded.

"As we all know, water pressure in any strike-slip transform fault is important to the competing plates' lubrication. All fault zones contain groundwater, and when the pressure of the water increases, the fault can become unclamped."

"Is that a new scientific term of art?" a voice shouted to a cacophony of jeers and laughter.

Fine. Skeptics. Naysayers. Mac bristled but continued by throwing it back at them. "No, not yet, anyway. However, studies have shown that injecting water into any seismic system, whether fault lines or the plumbing of a volcano, can disrupt the way a geological fault slips. Look at fracking, for example. Tremors are triggered in areas with miniscule fault lines compared to what we have in California.

"Further, an Oxford study found that rain-triggered seismicity occurred in Germany, France, and Switzerland in the summer of 2002. There were several variables distinct to the region, but the scientific study was peer-reviewed." He then went on to cite the magnitude 7.0 earthquake that had devastated Haiti in 2010 after eighteen months of unusually heavy rainfall. The magnitude 6.4 quake in Taiwan followed a major typhoon in 2009.

"How does this relate to the ARkStorm?" a woman in attendance asked.

"By all estimates," began Mac in response, "the atmospheric rivers that came ashore dumped a volume of water on the state's Central Valley equivalent to twenty-two times the volume of the Mississippi River from its headwaters to its mouth. All of this water is now settled in over the state, including many hundreds of miles of the San Andreas Fault.

"It's my opinion that the weight of the water may have a profound effect on the San Andreas Fault and the thousands of smaller faults that are nearby."

"Sir, isn't it true that since the ARkStorm, activity along the San Andreas has subsided? If anything, the exact opposite has occurred."

Mac couldn't argue with that. The state was extremely tectonically active due to San Andreas, although the so-called *Big One* had held off since 1906. Over the past one thousand years, the average interval of large earthquakes had been one hundred eighty years. Sometimes, the media would get caught up in the concept of a quake being *overdue*, Mac thought to himself. What they didn't consider was the significant intervening events like an ARkStorm.

Mac gathered his thoughts before responding, "As we all know, the friction of the tectonic plates is the primary driving force behind earthquakes. Another factor to consider should be the weight of the water created by Lake California. Let me give you a couple of examples.

"A hundred fifty years ago, when a series of atmospheric rivers filled the reservoirs of the state, Lake Cahuilla was full of water as well as other lakes in the Coachella and Imperial valleys. Over the years, the lake drained and left us the Salton Sea. Seismic activity practically ceased.

"Then came the series of atmospheric rivers that predated the recent ARkStorm. The lakes in that region refilled. Within two years, earthquake swarms were being noticed. The swarms only intensified following the ARkStorm. Many of the faults across the state have increased tension, like a taut rubber band ready to snap." Mac caught his breath.

"The number of smaller quakes recorded may be because the excess lubricant available to the fault has decreased the pressure between the two tectonic plates. I recognize that many of my peers have debunked the concept of earthquake weather because of the conventional belief that arid days are prime for tremors. All I'm saying is the ARkStorm is entirely different from anything we've studied in the past. I firmly believe the weight of the water is having a profound effect on what's beneath it."

His words hung in the air as a few nodded their heads in agreement while others had a good chuckle at Mac's expense. Shortly thereafter, the meeting came to an end. Mac hung around to answer a few more questions. He was exhausted and was anxious to retreat to the solitude of the lake. He glanced at his watch and realized it was just after ten o'clock. Then a voice from behind him made it seem all better.

"I believe you," said Taylor in a quiet voice.

Mac smiled as he turned around. He changed his voice to imitate a hostess at a restaurant. "True believers, party of two. Your table is ready next to the fire exit. Your server today will be Chicken Little."

Taylor laughed and playfully shoved him. "It's not that bad. Your boss didn't do you any favors. So, can you forget about it?"

"Probably. Maybe. Who cares, right?"

"Actually, I do," she replied. "So when do you think you can blow out of here?"

"Three hours. Max." He'd have to cancel everything his assistant had set up for him. He didn't care.

"Are you still up for fishing, or do you wanna sulk alone?"

Mac laughed. "Fishing is the best antidote for sulking."

Taylor checked her watch. "I'll meet you at your car in three hours."

"How do you know what I drive?" he asked.

"I saw you pull in when others in my wing laughed at the mud all over your Jeep. I get it. It's a Jeep thing, right?"

Mac grinned and looked shyly at his feet. *She gets it.*

CHAPTER FIFTEEN

San Andreas Fault
Beneath Lake California

After an earthquake occurs, geophysicists can explain where it started and what type of fault led up to the event. Scientists would uniformly admit they were unsure of what happens under the Earth's surface during the moments leading up to the quake event.

Most seismic events were gentle, occurring as tectonic plates meet and glide against one another. From time to time, the friction created by this movement exceeds the strength of the rock of the plates, leading to a failure at a fault line. This frictional stress can happen at any time or for no reason what-soever. Or it can be caused by a change in the dynamics of the seismic system.

In the early years of the modern scientific study of quakes, earth scientists wanted to believe that something exotic, even supernatural was occurring underground to create the massive upheavals of rock. It wasn't until recent history that the concept of fric-tional sliding between tectonic plates became under-stood. Still, it was impossible for the human eye to see and confirm.

When the sliding is inhibited or altered by external pressures, a violent displacement of the Earth's crust follows, leading to a release of elastic, strained energy. This energy takes the form of shock waves radiating across the Earth's surface.

Certainly, most tremors and earthquakes are gentle compared to the massive upheavals that took place billions of years ago when the planet was formed. As history has proven, the earthquake along the San Andreas Fault of 1906 would look quite different from one in the present day although the strength measured by magnitude might be the same. The erection of buildings, infrastructure, and roads could not survive the energy released by a massive quake of a similar nature as the 1906 seismic event.

Scientists use the ferocity of a hurricane as their example. The category five hurricane that hit Galveston, Texas, in 1900 was devastating, but its economic costs paled in comparison to Hurricane Rita, an equally powerful hurricane, that struck the same coastline in 2005. The storms were similar in strength and wind velocity. The only difference was the size of the population and the number of structures in Rita's path.

Geophysicists frequently lamented their inability to recreate the moments leading up to a major earthquake. They wanted to create a warning system to give people an opportunity to protect themselves. Buildings can be rebuilt; lives cannot be restored, they'd say.

That day, as Californians went about their business, two massive, hard, weight-pressurized rocks slabs passed against each other. Ordinarily, the Pacific and North American plates do this every day without a noticeable seismic event. However, on this day, the friction began to generate heat as one stubborn force opposed the motion of the other stubborn force.

The fault had changed over the past several years as, inexplicably, it had begun to lose water, the fluid lubricant necessary to maintain a proper temperature as the plates slid against each other. With increasing frequency, the friction grew in intensity. With insufficient lubricant, the rock began to melt under the immense heat. *Flash heating,* as geophysicists called it, occurs when the faults become stuck in place.

For some period of time unknown to any human being, the San Andreas Fault had become stuck.

CHAPTER SIXTEEN

USGS
Santa Rosa, California

The snickering in the auditorium still chafed Mac's ass. Because his theory was still unproven except for isolated examples that might or might not have been evidence of his hypothesis, he would've preferred to keep the concept out of today's conversation. It was the seamount and its unusual activity that should've been the focus of attention. Not the ARkStorm, earthquake weather, and the weight of the lake putting pressure on San Andreas.

He'd hastily finished up his work for the day and

had twenty minutes to kill before he met Taylor at his Jeep. Their first meeting and the quick interaction in the auditorium had taken the edge off any nervousness he had about their first, semiofficial date. He wasn't sure if a fishing outing constituted a date. Most people would consider dining over a bottle of wine and candlelight an official date. Mac laughed to himself. If that was the definition of an official date, it was no wonder he'd never kept a girlfriend. He'd never technically dated.

He moseyed into the monitoring room and surreptitiously wandered through the workstations, peeking over the shoulders of the entire team. They were still abuzz over the activity at the Hayward Fault, which did not surprise him. Seismic activity near a major population center, like the Bay Area, garnered more attention than a tremor in the middle of the Central Valley that only a bunch of cows, or now fish, felt.

If anything, the filling of Lake California by the ARkStorm had drawn attention away from a third of the state. The USGS was constantly under pressure to predict the next big quake in order to save lives and minimize property damage. The submerged towns and rural farms under Lake California couldn't be saved at this point. Therefore, the San Francisco area and the newly constructed Los Angeles properties took away the bulk of the monitoring team's resources.

When this had been mentioned to Mac in a senior staff meeting after he was hired to oversee the recreation of the seismic monitoring array, he'd rightfully pointed out that just because a third of the state was now submerged under Lake California, it didn't mean the nearly sixteen thousand known faults had gone away. Before the ARkStorm, most Californians lived within thirty miles of an active fault in the state. That number had grown a hundred times as displaced residents found new places to live in the Sierra Nevadas, Northern California and along the coastal regions.

He made his way to the analyst he'd spoken with earlier. He eased up to his workstation to avoid startling the young man like he'd done before.

"How's it goin'? Anything new?"

"Still rumbling," replied the analyst as he deftly switched screens to show Mac the data thus far. "It doesn't appear that it's letting up. *Did you feel its* are coming in from San Jose to the homes along San Pablo Bay in the north."

The USGS had established a system for citizens to phone in or text their experiences during an earthquake event. The DYFI, an acronym for *did you feel it*, assisted the USGS in creating a map indicating the location of the tremors and the level of damage sustained. It had proved to be an effective tool to provide a rapid assessment of the extent of damage for emergency responders. It also helped the USGS fine-tune their research.

Mac nodded and was about to comment when the analyst continued, "How's it going with you? I was just in the break room ..." His voice trailed off as he gulped. Clearly, he wished he hadn't broached the subject with Mac.

"News travels fast, huh?" he said rhetorically.

"People suck," the young man added dryly as he continued to switch between screens and make notes.

Mac couldn't disagree. He changed the subject. "Have you seen any activity at the north end of San Andreas? Southwest of Eureka?"

"In the ocean?"

"Yeah, in the ocean," Mac replied, perturbed. A major earthquake in the Pacific could generate a tsunami that would swamp the rest of the state along the coast.

The analyst banged away on the backlit keyboard; the changing brightness of the LED lights under the keys twinkled like stars on a clear night.

"Nada," he said, leaning back in his chair and pointing at the screen.

"Okay, thanks. I'll be outside of cell coverage this afternoon, but text me anyway if something develops. If I catch a tower, or when I return to the house, I'll get in touch."

"Fishing?" he asked.

"Yeah. I need to clear my head."

Mac exited the monitoring center and hustled out of the building before anyone else could engage him in conversation. He wanted to put the morning briefing behind him and focus his attention on something that made him smile.

As he wandered through the parked cars to his Jeep, his scowl disappeared, and a toothy grin replaced it. Taylor was waiting for him, casually leaning against a shiny, red Kia parked in the adjacent space.

Mac began to laugh. "Whadya have against leaning against my Rubicon?"

Taylor ran her hand slowly along the boxy fender her butt rested on. "This one is cleaner."

"Yeah, but it's a Kia."

Taylor closed one eye and grimaced. "Good point. Ready to roll?"

He was, and they headed toward the lake, with a stopover at the Safeway on Sonoma Highway to pick up provisions.

CHAPTER SEVENTEEN

San Andreas Fault
Beneath Lake California

Before the San Andreas Fault became stuck, the friction plummeted to near zero, causing the faults to slide faster than normal. It became slippery at multiple contact points like two skaters gliding across a frozen pond. Heat was generated, resulting in a high-temperature cushiony flash of light. The super-heated gas and plasma yielded no detectable melted material. Yet.

Then the plate movement suddenly slowed down to stick tight to one another. The precipitating event of this sudden anomaly was the ARkStorm.

The weight of the water, calculated in the millions of tons, fundamentally changed the surface of California. Crevices and caves filled with water. Soils once starving of moisture were now saturated and being crushed by the enormous pressure of the lake above.

The San Andreas Fault was feeling the pressure as well. At first, it enjoyed the extra lubricant. The ease of the two plates gliding against each other resulted in an extraordinary calm on the planet's surface. However, over time, the unfathomable power of the Earth to fight back began to reveal itself.

First, it was an imperceptible seep here and there in the Pacific Ocean, considered normal by those who studied the ocean floor. Then seamounts began to form, like the one off the coast of Eureka. As more and more of the additional water was converted to superheated gas and expelled, the result was a lack of lubrication along the fault line.

Now the plates were stuck as the planet seemingly overcorrected. Rather than slipping and sliding along the fault, they butted heads like two rams on the side of a rocky mountain. Subtle at first and then with more frequency until a chasm began to develop. This chasm, stretching along portions of the lakebed near the San Andreas, quickly filled with silt and debris, both man-made and as a result of the massive mudslides. This enabled the fault's unusual activity to avoid detection.

That, and the lack of monitoring devices.

The frequency of the pressure between the two plates increased. The severity of the ramming effect was unprecedented in modern times. The resulting change to the Earth's surface, deep beneath the waters of Lake California, was hidden from view. However, the push and shove of the two powerful tectonic plates became increasingly violent. The battle would rage until relief came.

Until then, the ground above would suffer.

CHAPTER EIGHTEEN

Mac's Floating Home
Lake California

Mac and Taylor put the workday behind them after leaving Safeway. He picked up burger fixin's in case their big fishing haul didn't materialize. After playfully quizzing him about whether he had any pots and pans, Taylor agreed to make the sides, including her grandmother's recipe for hush puppies. They picked up a case of Corona and a dozen limes to complement their day in the sun.

As Mac traversed the backroads and trails of Mount Vaca, they made small talk about the change in the landscape of California since the ARkStorm.

Mac relayed the political machinations behind adopting the name Lake California for the new body of water.

"Naturally, those politicians from SoCal who thought the world revolved around LA and Hollywood insisted upon referring to the lake as the Lake of Angels, a nod to the damages incurred by the City of Angels. Others around the state objected because of the biblical connotation by using the word angels in relation to the lake created by the ARkStorm. They clearly didn't understand there was no relation to Noah's Ark. But that didn't matter."

"You know how people are," interjected Taylor. "They'll find any reason to bicker. Heck, they'll make one up if it doesn't exist in reality."

"It's that way all over," said Mac. "Anyway, historic-minded politicians wanted to call it Tulare Lake, which used to be the largest freshwater lake west of the Mississippi. It was intentionally drained over a hundred years ago to create more farmland in the fertile Central Valley. The decision to drain Tulare was devastating to three Indian tribes who fished the shores and relied upon the fresh drinking water. Its disappearance resulted in the Indians referring to it as Ghost Lake."

"I see," said Taylor. "Then Ghost Lake returned."

"That's right. Ghost Lake, or Tulare Lake, was proposed. However, the state's politicians were split, and an infrastructure for voting on it as a referendum wasn't in place, so a compromise was reached."

Taylor finished his thought. "Lake California. Seems simple enough."

Mac nodded as he focused on steering his Jeep down the narrow, tree-covered trail. Taylor grabbed the handle affixed to the dashboard and braced herself in her seat.

"I know. Not much of a driveway. I like it that way. I don't want anyone else coming down here by car. The occasional four-wheeler full of hunters makes their way until they see that sign." He pointed at a pair of signs nailed to redwood trees that read:

PRIVATE PROPERTY
TRESPASSERS WILL BE SHOT

"Would you?" she asked.

Mac frowned. "Would I what?"

"Shoot them. You know, if they trespassed."

Mac chuckled. "If they come onto my land and then leave when I asked, the answer is no. If they mess around on my dock, they're gonna get a rifle pointed at them. If they enter my house, then it's game over."

"Really?"

Mac set his jaw and nodded. "Without hesitation."

"Okay."

He sensed she was bothered by this. "Let me explain. I grew up in a rural area of West Tennessee around Reelfoot Lake. We fished and hunted. We were willing to protect ourselves from anyone who might try to harm our families. After the New Madrid Earthquake, looting was a problem. Law enforcement was overwhelmed. The National Guard had to focus its efforts on what was left of Memphis. We were on our own in the country, so we defended ourselves.

"The situation in California wasn't much different after the ARkStorm. I didn't personally experience any looting because my cabin was gone. However, the same can't be said of other properties that managed to survive the catastrophe. Desperate people do desperate things. I have no intention of being someone's victim."

Taylor thought for a moment and then nodded. She asked, "Your cabin is gone? Where?"

Mac pulled into a clearing overlooking his dock, the houseboat and his fishing boat. "Thataway." He pointed toward the south. "The rising waters picked it up off its foundation and carried it south. I've never been able to find any remnants of it."

"Wow. I'm sorry, Mac."

"Hey. Look, I'm better off for it."

"I can't wait for the grand tour," said Taylor as she eagerly exited the Jeep.

CHAPTER NINETEEN

Lake California

Mac and Taylor hustled to unload the Rubicon of the refrigerated foods first. Then she returned to grab her USGS logo duffel bag. The black canvas duffel featured the USGS, *Science for a Changing World* logo embroidered on the side.

Mac noticed it immediately. "I'm impressed. Where'd you get it?"

"Etsy."

"Who?"

"Etsy. It's an online shopping website that can do personalized stuff, too."

Mac laughed. He playfully lowered his eyebrows and locked eyes with her.

"Taylor Reed, are you a geek?"

"Sometimes. So, are you gonna show me around?"

Mac smiled and held his arms wide as he spun around twice. "Well, what you see is what you get. Welcome to my humble abode."

Taylor walked around the combined living-kitchen space. It was small but very functional. She glanced up at the bunk area accessed by a wooden ladder. She pointed toward it.

"Guest room?"

"Yup. It had two side-by-side queen beds, but I took one out to create an office space. The far end opens up to the deck and a nice view of the lake."

She wandered toward his bedroom cabin. He was glad he'd straightened up early and made the bed for the first time in more than a week when he washed his sheets.

"I love it!" she exclaimed suddenly. "I really do. I mean, it's cozy but has everything you need. No wasted space."

Mac was relieved. He'd only brought a few women back to his houseboat, and they'd uniformly turned their noses up at his living arrangements.

He pointed out a few other things. "The lake is normally very smooth unless some idiot roars past on a large boat, creating a wake. Or during a rare storm. Even then, it gently rocks and is actually soothing."

She glanced through the windows as she returned from his bedroom. "Are you worried about the lake levels receding? California is known for overusing its water resources."

She was right. The state was largely to blame for the drop in water levels along the Colorado River and Lake Mead in Nevada. Many in Nevada, in particular, lamented California taking more than its fair share of the valuable water resource. After the ARkStorm had replenished state lakes and reservoirs, the Colorado River not unexpectedly began to rise on its exposed banks.

"I was approved for a forty-foot floating dock and took full advantage of that. The water could drop nearly thirty feet without it affecting my floating house."

Taylor was still dressed in her khakis and USGS polo shirt. She looked around for the bathroom. "Where can I change?"

"Use my bedroom. I've got some shorts on the boat and the rest of my gear. While you get ready, I'll stock the coolers and check my drop lines from this morning. Today, we'll be fishing for largemouth bass.

I'll pull those rods, reels, and tackle out of the hold. Take your time."

Earlier, Mac had checked the weather forecast. It was supposed to be a warm day, in the mid-eighties, with no chance of rain or wind. He boarded his twenty-eight-foot Boston Whaler center-console boat. The Dauntless model was designed for both open-water fishing on the Pacific as well as the enormous lake that now covered a third of California.

After securing the Coronas with the ice in the forward coolers, he rummaged through the bow storage lockers for the necessary fishing gear to pluck a few largemouth bass out of the water. Mac had had great success of late fishing several favorite fishing spots along the mountainous shoreline. He didn't want Taylor to be disappointed in their outing.

"Anything I can do to help?" she asked, startling Mac out of his thoughts. He turned to respond and found himself without words.

When Mac was younger, he had been shallow like many men in their twenties. You know, good looks were tantamount, and whether she could put together a complete sentence came a distant second. It was the typical choosing process of many men who tended to think with, well, you know the saying.

Naturally, he'd noticed Taylor was attractive the

first time they met at the Coast Guard station. She had been well dressed and obviously took pride in her appearance. Even in her work attire, she impressed him. Now his mind raced as he tried to stifle his reaction to the short jean shorts she was wearing and the bikini top. He wanted to shout out to her, you are beautiful. Instead, he kinda blurted out a stupid question.

"Um, your top is the official USGS green, right?"

I'm an idiot, he thought to himself.

What was worse for Mac was the fact that Taylor picked up on his uncomfortable reaction to her choice of fishing outfit. She was a little less enamored with the thought of fishing and more interested in getting some sun with this intriguing guy. She decided to tease him.

She reached behind her and grabbed the strings holding her top in place. "Too work-related? Would you rather I take it off?"

Mac's Ray-Bans hid his eyes growing wide. "No. No. No," he stammered. "You're good. Um, I think we're ready."

"Okay, Cap'n," she said laughingly. "I can handle the dock lines for you."

Mac studied her. "Really?"

"Sure. My uncle lived on the Horsetooth Reservoir just outside Fort Collins. He and my aunt work as epidemiologists at a CDC facility there. We'd visit them a couple of times every summer to go horseback riding and take their boat out."

Mac made his way around to the bow, forcing himself not to stare at her. "So you do like the outdoors?"

"There's nothing better," she said as she untied the aft dock line and made her way up to the cleats on the bow. She quickly unwrapped the line from the eight-inch dock line and held it in place for a moment until Mac gave her the thumbs-up. She tied off the line to the Boston Whaler's cleats like a pro.

"Do you wanna stretch out up front or ride behind the console until we get there?"

She answered his question with a smile as she settled on the narrow bench seat just in front of him with her back against the center console. Mac slowly pulled away from the dock and kept his idle speed for several hundred feet until his wake would be clear of his floating house. Then he gently nudged the throttle, and the bow rose in response.

Taylor's long, brunette hair flew around in the breeze, crossing over the top of the fiberglass center console until it tickled Mac's hands on the wheel. He closed his eyes to regain his composure as a shudder came over his body. The oddly intimate sensation gave him a momentary shiver of unease.

When he spontaneously invited her to go fishing, he'd realized he wanted more than a working relationship with Taylor. Now he couldn't imagine a moment without her, and they'd just met. He could never recall feeling this way about any woman.

After they reached the center of Lake California, more boats and jet skis appeared. The Fourth of July weekend was only a few days away, and it was obvious many people took the entire week to enjoy the water. In fact, due to the lack of wind and natural turbulence of late, the state's Division of Boating and Waterways had encouraged the governor to suggest people use the lake, to aerate the lake water, which had become stagnant in places. Propellers helped exchange surface water for that on the bottom, a form of oxygenation. Lake California had been experiencing a lack of that constant exchange of living water following the early spring snowmelt. The turbulence of watercraft was expected to help alleviate the problem.

A couple of chiseled young guys approached the Boston Whaler from the rear. They increased their speed and jumped the wake of the boat's powerful twin Mercury engines. As they raced by on both sides, Taylor never glanced in their direction. She was relaxed and enjoying the ride. In turn, Mac was enjoying the view.

After twenty minutes, Mac cut his speed and idled towards the Mount Diablo cut where Interstate 580 once connected Modesto with the Bay Area. A large sound had been created on the other side of the cut, surrounded by the mountains. The water was deep, clean and teeming with largemouth bass.

"Here we go," he announced as he pulled back on the throttle. The engine continued to run as he moved around to the front of the boat to pull out the anchor. Taylor pulled her long legs in to give him room to work. Once again, Mac found himself ill at ease as he tried not to gawk at her beauty.

"What was it like living through the New Madrid quake?" she asked suddenly. "You were there, right?"

Mac nodded. "Less than thirty miles from the epicenter. Most of the homes had a little damage from the quake. It was when the Mississippi River flowed backwards that the levees were breached, and the farms were flooded. Our family avoided that fate. It was sad for the others."

Taylor looked around to study the mountainous terrain. Then she looked down to the water's surface.

"These people suffered, too. At least they had some warning. Quakes don't give us much advance notice."

"You're right. I knew the history of New Madrid and how the river was impacted in the 1811–12 quake sequence. When the ARkStorm hit us years ago, very few people understood how severe the atmospheric rivers could be. They could've had more warning, but they were either kept in the dark or ignored them."

Taylor stood and joined Mac as he made his way to the stern to prepare their fishing gear. She sat on the railing as she spoke. "You know, people go through their day. Working, playing, living their lives. They have no idea the greatest threats they may face come without warning."

"New Madrid was practically right under our feet," added Mac. "We all knew it but assumed it would never happen to us."

"That's exactly my point," she continued her thought. "It's happened before, so it can happen again. However, most people don't recognize that. They think that we're too modernized. Electronically sophisticated. Smart. Whatever. New Madrid was a great example."

"Same with the ARkStorm. Some scientists tried

to warn the public that it had happened in the 1860s and could happen again. Everyone waited 'til the last minute to evacuate. They never made it out."

"Natural disasters are what people like you and me focus on," said Taylor. "Everyone else watches the news or takes to Twitter to see if China has fired nukes at us."

Mac shook his head in disgust. The news hyped nuclear war every other day lately. He never doubted it was possible. He just wished the media would provide equal coverage to the threats from nature.

They made small talk about the various threats the world faced, both man-made and naturally occurring. They agreed that the man-made threats, namely nuclear attacks, paled in comparison to the potential planet killers such as a series of volcanic eruptions along the Ring of Fire, massive asteroid strikes, or even a rare gamma-ray burst from space. It was certainly not light, casual conversation except for two people who studied the threats of earth-quakes and volcanos to mankind.

They caught a couple of bass, and then Mac suggested they try another spot. Taylor made sure the captain of the vessel always had a cold Corona in hand, earning her first-mate-of-the-year honors in Mac's mind. He was easing through the cut when

Taylor, who had retaken her seat on the bow, suddenly stood and pointed to their right.

"What the hell is that?" she asked.

Mac pulled the throttle back and allowed the boat to drift on its own wake. At first, he thought there was a boulder floating in the water. Then the massive snapping turtle raised its head just above the surface.

"That can't be," he exclaimed.

"It's a dinosaur!" exclaimed Taylor as she eased toward the boat's railing to get a better look.

"No, it's definitely an alligator snapping turtle. We used to have them around some of the lakes when I was growing up. It's weird because they're not native to California."

"It's enormous. Maybe the lake has brought the dinosaurs back to life. Where's *T. rex*?"

Taylor was having fun with the sighting of the strange creature. She finished off another beer and made her way to the cooler to get a replacement. She handed Mac another one, and he swigged the remains of his second beer first. He tipped his Corona toward the turtle.

"He may be the reason why the fish aren't biting here. They'll eat everything. Dip your foot in the water and you'll lose it."

"I guess skinny-dipping is out of the question, huh?"

Mac laughed. Taylor was getting tipsy. "All the dipping is out of the question. At least here. Let's find another spot."

"Carry on, Cap'n!" she said with a grin. She settled back into the seat in front of the console and tilted her head back to soak in the sun. Taylor knew how to unwind. Mac could learn some lessons from her in that regard.

He eased the throttle down, and the boat picked up speed as it sailed over the top of where Interstate 5 was once located. The West Side Freeway, as it was called, had stretched along the mountains in a north-south direction. Almost due west of Merced was the former San Luis Reservoir nestled in between the ridges.

The reservoir, which once had a depth of two hundred fifty feet, was now nearly six hundred feet at its deepest level. The once rocky banks were now tree lined as the waters of Lake California consumed it.

It was another quiet, out-of-the-way spot, perfect for fishing and relaxing with a new friend. It was also directly adjacent to the San Andreas Fault undergoing stresses no one ever envisioned.

CHAPTER TWENTY

Lake California

Taylor slid off the bench seat and took up a spot next to Mac as he turned into the cove created by the lake merging with the reservoir. There was one other boat nearby, a couple of older men working the bank in a bass boat.

"Okay, Cap'n Mac, I need to say something before we talk shop."

Mac's back stiffened, and he prepared for impact. This was how things often went when he found a woman he was interested in. *You're a nice guy, but ...* He'd be disappointed because he really liked Taylor. Smitten, actually.

"Okay." He dragged the word out as he waited

for her to continue.

He steered the Boston Whaler to a bank that was full of fallen trees and brush in the water. Bass aren't normally found in open water, as they prefer the cover of vegetation near the shoreline. It was getting later in the day, and he expected they'd have better luck fishing, although it was possible his luck with love was about to get doused.

"So here's what," she began. "I'm a little drunk, so I need to say this now before I throw back a few more beers with you. I am not going to sleep with you."

Mac swallowed hard and stifled a laugh. Her statement was so candid she had to be joking with him. He wasn't sure what to say, so he didn't.

"I really, really like you. A lot, I mean. I don't know why. Well, I do, but, um, it's a lot of things. But I don't sleep around, and I'm not gonna sleep with you. Tonight, anyway. Okay?"

"Okay, I promise," said Mac, who'd always been a gentleman when it came to relationships. "How about this, though. We have more fishing to do. Then there's cooking our catch. And talking about stuff, because I really, really like you, too."

She hugged him and smiled before whispering, "Thank you." Mac wasn't sure why she was thanking him at this point other than he'd made her feel safe. Suddenly, he felt this need to protect this woman who'd unexpectedly appeared in his life. He wanted to make her laugh. He wanted to dry her tears if she was sad. He wanted to help her in her career. He wanted her closer to him. So many thoughts flooded him as he considered what to do next.

"Promise?" she whispered in his ear.

"Pinky swear." Mac held up his right hand with his pinky finger extended. This brought out a hearty laugh from Taylor. They shook pinky fingers and hugged again. He racked his brain in search of another reason to pinky swear with a follow-up hug, but he didn't want to push his luck.

She slowly pulled away from him. "Beer?"

"Absolutely," he replied. Their intimate moment had subsided. "Let's catch a few more and then call it a day before it gets dark. Since we've made this pact, are you okay staying over? We can ride into the office together tomorrow."

Taylor covered her mouth and opened her eyes wide. "Scandalous! What will the people in the cubicles think?"

Mac laughed. "I have an idea. We'll stop by the car wash and clean up the Jeep. They'll never know it's us."

"Brilliant!" she exclaimed as she pumped her fist in the air. His wit earned him another hug. A longer one this time.

Then Mac had an idea for a second date of sorts. "Say, you seem to like the water."

"I do."

"Are you claustrophobic?"

"No. I used to go caving all the time as a kid. You can't get any more surrounded and closed in than that."

"I have to inspect some of our recently installed seismic sensor stations underwater the day after tomorrow. I know it's not enough, but it will bring the ShakeAlert system up to forty percent completion. Whadya think?"

Taylor did a slow pirouette with her arms raised above her head. She grabbed the rail to steady herself as she realized that wasn't the best of ideas.

"I'd love it. It'll help me to see what you're up against in restoring the system."

"Sounds like a plan," said Mac as he prepared to drop anchor.

"You know, Mac, I've had first dates and second dates, and sometimes I ventured into the whole dating process. I can't recall ever taking sunset helicopter rides, fishing trips, and as a cherry on top, a trip in a submarine. You really know how to impress a girl."

"Stick with me, Taylor Reed. You'll never be bored."

Truer words had never been spoken.

Mac prepared the rubber-coated cast-iron anchor by attaching a digital thermometer to it to gauge the water temperatures. The new technology enabled the gauge to record depth and temperature while transmitting the data to a device attached to the boat's console.

"Okay, let's get ready because I'm sure they'll jump in the boat as soon as we cast our lures."

"Where's the net? I'll get ready."

Mac and Taylor continued fishing and exchanged stories about their experiences at the USGS. Mac learned more about Taylor's duties at Mammoth Mountain and the Long Valley Caldera. Inevitably, comparisons were made to the Yellowstone supervolcano during the conversation. Both agreed that the Long Valley Caldera, like the New Madrid Fault Line, was often overlooked in discussions of natural disaster threats.

Mac wandered past the console and glanced at the temperature gauge connected to the underwater digital thermometer. He swiped over to the depth gauge. The depth gauge recorded fifty-seven feet. Puzzled, he rummaged through a storage box under the console. He found his old digital thermometer that he'd used before the new one was introduced.

Without saying a word to Taylor, he leaned over the bow and dropped the gauge just below the water's surface to record the temperature. When he pulled it out, it read seventy-four degrees, which was normal.

"Mac, what's wrong?"

"I don't know. Maybe nothing. I have this new digital thermometer that transmits underwater temperatures to a gauge on the console. It's reading in the low nineties. Nearly twenty degrees higher than the surface temps."

He began to pull up the anchor line at a some-what frenzied pace. Something was wrong, he could sense it. He removed the digital thermometer from the line and replaced it with the older model. He then handed the digital version to Taylor.

"Would you mind holding this just below the water at the back of the boat. You can sit on the transom to be more comfortable. I need to know if this thing is defective."

"No problemo," she said as she hustled to the stern and opened the latched door.

Mac lowered the anchor with the older device firmly affixed to the line. He wanted to allow it several minutes to get an appropriate reading before he'd quickly pull the anchor back to the surface.

He waited patiently for nearly two minutes before Taylor interrupted his thoughts. "Mac, it's pretty consistent at seventy-four or five. Do you want me to keep checking?"

"Nah, come on back."

He turned his attention to the anchor line and vigorously tugged on the hundred-pound anchor to hoist it to the surface. He cursed himself for not getting the working anchor option that included a winch when he bought the boat. Still, it took him less than twenty seconds to pull the anchor to the surface. With a final heave, he dropped the anchor back into its box and hurriedly removed the older thermometer.

"Ninety-three degrees," he muttered.

Suddenly, the other boat appeared within thirty yards of Mac's boat. One of the older fishermen shouted across the water, "You folks having any luck?"

Mac was slightly aggravated by the intrusion but responded, nonetheless, "No, not really. You?"

"Same here. Except for the dead ones. Never

seen anything like it since the lake formed."

"Yeah," added his friend. "At least a dozen large-mouth floating along the shore plus quite a few bluegill."

Mac gave them a thumbs-up and turned his attention to Taylor, signaling that the conversation was over.

"I don't like this, Taylor."

She held her hands up to calm Mac down. He was obviously hyped up. "Look, there are a lot of possible explanations for the dead fish. And you know lakes turn over with the change of seasons although these numbers are not at all normal."

"I've thought about that. Also, this lake, even the reservoir that was here before the ARkStorm, has been subjected to a lot of shore erosion. There is a substantial amount of silt caught in gullies at the bottom. Silt tends to hold more heat, which could cause a temperature anomaly."

"See, that's all a possibility," Taylor interjected. Then after thinking for a brief moment, she looked across the water toward the other side of the reservoir. She shook her head and frowned. "Ninety-plus in deep-water cover is way too high."

Mac began stowing the fishing gear. Taylor gathered up the empty beer bottles and stuck them in the empty hold at the stern bench seating. Their fishing day was over.

Before he started the boat, Mac checked his watch. He sighed. "I've got to get a team out here to do some analysis. They also need to take water samples throughout the reservoir."

"Liquefaction?" she said inquisitively.

"Liquefaction would make sense, except it doesn't," replied Mac. Liquefaction took place when loosely packed, waterlogged sediments at the Earth's surface lost their strength due to a tremor or significant quake. "During the '89 Loma Prieta quake, liquefaction of the soils and debris used to fill in a lagoon caused horizontal sliding of the ground surface throughout the Marina District of San Francisco. As bad as that quake was, it could've been much worse. We haven't had any tremors in this area for many months."

"Are you thinking a seep?" asked Taylor.

Mac slowly nodded as he rubbed his temple. His mind raced as he considered the ramifications of a seep in this area. It meant something was occurring along San Andreas that wasn't caused by the movement of the seismic plates. In fact, there was no movement.

"Calm before the storm," he muttered.

CHAPTER TWENTY-ONE

USGS
Santa Rosa, California

The next day, Mac and Taylor, who'd lived up to their promise of not sleeping together, woke up early to head into the office. Both wanted to have a day to spend together without the concerns of the unusual activity occurring along San Andreas. They reminded one another the three-day July 4 weekend was coming up, and there'd be plenty of time for fun in the sun. For now, they wanted to ease their minds as to what was going on along the fault.

They'd stayed up late into the night considering the possibilities and agreed that research teams needed to be dispatched to the reservoir as well as other parts of Lake California. Mac also wanted to conduct his own underwater investigation, and Taylor begged him to let her come along. After all, she'd said, earthquakes often trigger volcanic activity, which was her way of justifying spending the day away from her own duties. Although she questioned whether the Long Valley Caldera would be affected by the seismic activity in Northern California.

Mac dispatched three of his senior-most personnel to join with the NOAA personnel at the American Canyon marina on the north end of San Pablo Bay. NOAA maintained several of their vessels there for oceangoing research and allowed the USGS to team up with their crews if an issue arose on Lake California.

A dam with locks had been constructed at Sears Point at the Carquinez Strait where Lake California met San Francisco Bay. The research ships were able to travel through a series of locks to navigate into Lake California where the Sacramento River once emptied out into the Pacific.

With the three research boats allocated to his teams, Mac would need to travel to one of their floating submersible stations, which were anchored in several parts of Lake California. As the monitoring

devices were installed and declared to be fully opera-
ble, the moorings holding the floating docks were
removed, and the twelve-thousand-foot platforms
were towed to the next locations where underwater
work was to be performed. Each of the stations was
assigned a submersible not that different from the
one Mac had navigated to the bottom of the Pacific
to view the seamount.

After doling out responsibilities to everyone on
his team, he returned to the monitoring room to get
an update on the Hayward Fault and to determine if
any activity had been reported near the former San
Luis Reservoir where he and Taylor had discovered
the heated lake water.

He approached the same analyst from the day
before. He was no longer studying the Hayward Fault.

"Is it over?" asked Mac, who tried to identify the
locale attracting the young man's attention.

"Oh, hey, Mac," the young man greeted. Mac
had insisted that everyone address each other on a
first-name basis. "Hayward fizzled out. The swarm
was intense for most of the afternoon, and then after
midnight, it suddenly stopped."

"Have you been able to establish any kind of
connection to San Andreas?"

The young man grimaced and shook his head. "Not at all. You may not have heard because we just got word of it. Another seep has been identified just off the coast near Point Delgada."

"How far from the other one?"

"Fifty miles to the southeast. I mean, we were shocked at the proximity to the shoreline. Some early morning paddleboarders scalded their legs from the knee down."

Mac stood up and looked around the room. He ran his fingers through his hair, as he often did when his stress levels increased. He closed his eyes briefly to visualize the location of the San Andreas Fault. It ran along the coastline and jutted out into the Pacific near Point Delgada. Subconsciously, he'd been holding his breath. He forced himself to exhale before turning back to the analyst.

"Anything else?"

"No, all quiet. Well, except for, um, I guess a mini swarm near Hollister. Eighteen tremors of $M1.5$ or greater in the last twenty-four hours."

Mac's eyebrows rose as he digested this information. *Another coincidence? Doubt it.*

Hollister was just southwest of the reservoir where he and Taylor had been fishing. The small city was located on the edge of the San Andreas Fault along the Diablo Mountain Range.

He pulled his cell phone out and navigated to his Notes app. There was a floating submersible station above where the town of Hanford was once located, two hours away from the reservoir. It was the northernmost of the three stations that had been focused on restoring the early warning alert systems to the residents around LA and Santa Barbara.

He'd planned on taking the submersible out the next day to monitor the seismic activity and to receive reports back from his three teams. Instead, he pushed his plans forward. He was about to walk out of the monitoring station to see if Taylor could leave early, when several of the analysts began speaking to one another excitedly. And just as quickly as the cacophony of chatter began, an eerie hush came over the room within seconds.

He turned back to his two analysts, who were typing frantically on their keyboards. "Talk to me!"

The analyst stared in silence before speaking. "We have a tremor along the San Jacinto Fault," one of them replied without making eye contact.

The other analyst was equally calm as he spoke. "Fifteen seconds," he said before pausing. "Twenty seconds."

"We're approaching M7 range," the other said in between.

"Twenty-five," he said as he lowered his voice. A hush fell over the room as if the entire monitoring team of the USGS Santa Rosa facility held their collective breath. The young man whispered, "Wait. Wait. That's it. Twenty-eight seconds."

"Estimate is M7.2. A big number for San Jacinto. There'll be damage."

The San Jacinto Fault Zone was a major strike-slip fault that stretched one hundred thirty miles from Santa Barbara to the Mexican border. San Jacinto created tremors more often than San Andreas but of a lesser magnitude. An M7 was sizable for that region.

What bothered Mac was the proximity of the quake's epicenter, identified as Cajon Pass near San Bernadino, north of LA. Typically, geophysicists believed that earthquakes would remain confined to a single, well-established fault zone. However, at Cajon Pass, the two major fault lines almost intersect. Mac, and a handful of others at the USGS, maintained the close proximity of the two faults could result in shared earthquakes during which one tremor would trigger another on the adjacent fault.

He remained in place as he took in the chatter

that exploded throughout the room. He needed to gather as much information as possible, forcing himself to curb his desire to run out of the building and find his way into a submersible.

He texted his assistant and asked her to arrange for an amphibious helicopter from the nearby Coast Guard facility to pick him up as soon as possible. She was to get his boss involved, if need be, to gain the necessary approvals.

Mac paced the floor as he listened to the initial reports of damage around San Bernadino. He was not one to look at isolated incidents as being connected. However, his gut told him otherwise. Something had changed along San Andreas, and the signs were starting to reveal themselves.

His next text was to Taylor. Undoubtedly, the news of the Cajon Pass quake reverberated through the USGS campus, so he dispensed with the preliminaries. He wrote he'd be leaving as soon as the chopper arrived, and if she'd like to go with him, she'd need to come to the monitoring room now. The instant he sent the message, the recognizable notification ding of an Apple iPhone was heard near the door. Mac swung around.

Taylor was already there.

CHAPTER TWENTY-TWO

Lake California
Above Hanford, CA

The Coast Guard amphibious helicopter rested on its skids at the heliport located adjacent to the Russian River. Mac carried a backpack filled with his laptop, a satellite telephone, and an underwater global positioning device that had been used by his crews to locate the coordinates for the replacement seismograph stations. While he had no intentions of scuba diving that day, the device provided a secondary navigation tool in the event the submersible malfunctioned. His experience fishing that day reminded him of his rule of redundancy. Always have a backup.

The modified R44 Raven with its pop-out floats had been commissioned by the Coast Guard for the USGS project. They were a far cry from their other seaworthy aircraft like the massive Grumman Albatross. However, with a cruising speed of one hundred thirty miles per hour, the chopper was able to deliver Mac and Taylor to the floating dock in the center of Lake California in less than two hours.

While en route to the platform, Mac recalled the crew using the submersible to the floating docking station. It was already early afternoon, and they'd be ready to return to Santa Rosa in a couple of hours anyway. This allowed the platform crew to refuel the submersible and have it ready to launch upon their arrival.

Just as they arrived, more details on the Cajon Pass earthquake had been delivered to Mac. It was a confirmed M7.1 quake with its epicenter directly beneath the pass separating the San Bernadino and San Gabriel Mountains. It was only miles away from where the San Andreas Fault ran through San Bernadino. A landslide had partially filled the pass, blocking a major highway. Many older buildings had succumbed to the tremor. Search and rescue operations were underway throughout the area.

"Good afternoon, sir," greeted Johnson Pollock, one of the supervisors aboard the floating platform, as Mac and Taylor walked across the floating rails and stepped onto the deck. The amphibious chopper pilot had made an expert landing and had pulled the aircraft parallel to the decking. Pollock took Taylor's hand to assist her onto the platform and nodded. "Ma'am."

Seconds later, the chopper had pushed away and was airborne, racing back toward Santa Rosa as the sun began to drop below the horizon. Mac had lost track of time that day as he bounced between his offices and the USGS monitoring room. During the ride to the platform, he and Taylor didn't speak much, as both were deep in thought. The interior confines of the chopper were loud even with the headsets on.

"Hi, Johnson, are we ready?" asked Mac anxiously.

"Yes, sir," Pollock replied. Mac recalled aspects of the man's résumé. He was former military, either Navy or Coast Guard. He was clean cut, sharply dressed and polite. He'd been on his team since the beginning. "Sir, normally at this hour, this facility will be on lockdown with only a single security guard on board. As you know, we stopped night installs and demolition following complaints received by the state."

Mac understood. He'd laid out a plan that would've completed the seismograph array a year ago if he'd been given trained personnel and been allowed to run twenty-hour shifts. Soon after the project began, residents in the San Bernadino area who'd built hillside homes overlooking the lake complained of the underwater demolition required to install the seismographs. The governor ordered the after-hours work to halt, and eventually, Mac's crews were limited to an eight-to-five schedule. The decision tripled the time necessary to complete the monitoring array.

"I know, and I appreciate you for reminding me. I can handle the submersible, and Miss Reed is more than capable of assisting with the docking procedures. Is your guard knowledgeable on the procedures as well?"

"Yes, sir. He's been trained, although he's never had to do it in practice. Sir, I'd be glad to stay and assist. I just need to call ..." His voice trailed off as Mac raised his hand.

"Johnson, thank you. That won't be necessary,

though I appreciate the offer. We'll be fine. I'll be starting just north of Hollister and working my way southward through the Carrizo Plain along the ridgeline."

"Sir, um, if I may?" the supervisor asked. "I'm not sure what your mission is this evening, but I might remind you of the significant amount of rock and debris at the base of the ridges. None of that area has been cleared or excavated yet."

"Understood," said Mac with a smile. He'd always liked Pollock. "We'll stay well offshore. I have certain coordinates already preprogrammed into my handheld GPS unit. Once we hit the area east of San Luis Obispo, we'll return here."

"That's a long return, sir. Keep in mind you have the Parkfield Junction platform as well, if necessary."

Mac smiled and nodded. Pollock persisted. This facility was his baby, and he wanted his boss to be safe.

"Don't forget, our team will be continuously monitoring the sub at Santa Rosa."

"Yes, I know. Thank you, Johnson."

Mac and Taylor spent the next several minutes going over the docking procedures with the crew before they left for the day. He met the evening security guard, who was one of three off-duty Tulare

County deputies who made extra money tending to the floating facility.

He turned to Taylor, took a deep breath, and asked, "Ready?"

"You bet."

"Well, then. Welcome to Orca."

CHAPTER TWENTY-THREE

Lake California
Near Hanford, CA

The Orca five-man submersible was designed to take its crew to depths of thirteen thousand feet, certainly more than the darkest depths of Lake California. However, it was its surveying and research capabilities that had won Mac over when he was putting the project together.

"Okay, I'm not sure what I imagined this thing to look like from the outside. I visualized the torpedo-style submarines with a periscope sticking out of that, um, hat-looking thing on top."

Mac laughed. He loved it when Taylor was being cute. "That's the sail."

"Okay, the sail. Looks more like a fin."

"That's what the Brits call it."

"Whatevs," said Taylor. She settled onto the bench seat opposite Mac. "Tell me about the Orca."

"Well, the first thing you gotta know is that it's safe. It was designed by a team of entrepreneurs who wanted to be astronauts but then realized there were vast parts of our oceans that remained unexplored. One of their first projects was to dive to the wreck of the *Andrea Doria* off the coast of Massachusetts. Once they achieved that feat, they set their sights on deeper wrecks."

Taylor rapped her knuckles on the hull. "Sounds solid."

"It is. Five-inch-thick carbon fiber with three-inch titanium, hatched on both ends for crew access. With the advanced pressurization, we're able to have all of our electronic components for every aspect of the project. In the Orca, it doesn't matter if you're on the surface or at ten thousand feet below it, the functionality isn't altered."

Mac took a deep breath and looked around the interior. It seated five, which resulted in cramped surroundings. He and Taylor would have the ability to move around to study the video monitors, the data screens and even look through the thick glass inserted into the two hatches.

He tapped on the keyboard to notify the submersible team in Santa Rosa that he was preparing to launch. They gave him a thumbs-up, which caused him to laugh. Keep it simple, as they say. He made eye contact with Taylor.

"Last chance. If you wanna bail out, I'll totally understand. You can hang out here, or I'll send for the chopper."

"Not on your life!" she exclaimed. "This is better than Disneyland. Let's go."

Mac made several entries on the keyboard, and the sound of four large winches springing to life could be heard through the thick hull.

"What's that?" asked Taylor as she gripped the edge of her bench seat.

"There are several ways to launch the Orca. In the ocean, they use a specially made Zodiac boat to carry it to its initial destination. A research ship then uses a powerful crane to drop the Orca on a platform tethered to a Zodiac. The sound you heard was a similar platform being lowered into the lake."

WHOOOSH!

"Geez, now what?" she asked. Mac sensed a tinge of nervousness in her voice.

"Those are the ballasts on the platform releasing their buoyancy. We'll drop about thirty feet into the lake at this point. If you look through the hatch windows, you'll see the water getting darker the deeper we drop. Light doesn't benefit us when we're at depth. It's pitch black at the bottom, which is why we could've operated crews twenty-four seven to complete the project without anybody noticing." He was still aggravated that his team was restricted to what amounted to a forty-hour workweek. He argued lives were at stake and used the analogy of an interstate highway bridge collapsing. Motorists would lose their minds if the crews only worked eight to five to make repairs.

The platform abruptly came to a stop at thirty feet, and the ballasts stopped releasing air. Mac powered the thrusters and pulled away from the platform. He immediately switched on the fore and aft external lamps, which emitted fifty thousand lumens of light. Taylor was mesmerized by what she saw.

"Look at all the stuff floating around. Big fish, little fish. Twigs, leaves, trash."

"That's right," added Mac. "Lake California is still in its infancy, geologically speaking. Freshwater lakes are usually deemed to be clean when there is a lack of silt and debris. Visibility is limited but still better than this. Of course, we don't help matters with our demolition on the lakebed. Over time, the lake will be beautiful and afford divers a lot of opportunities to visit the ruins of the submerged towns."

Taylor thought for a moment and then shuddered. "Underwater graveyards. Kinda morbid. No thanks."

"Well, I agree. So does the state, which is why scuba diving is against the law on Lake California. First, it's unsafe, as the structures below are unstable. Second, there may be curiosity seekers; however there are probably more looters. Both are disturbing the dead and their belongings."

Mac pulled away from the docking station and turned the submersible in the direction of the San Luis Reservoir where they'd detected the temperature anomaly. He knew entry into the reservoir would be treacherous, as the rising lake water had simply covered massive rock outcroppings and tall trees, which still stood beneath the surface. If he was unable to navigate into the cove created by the flooding, he'd at least be able to check water temperatures along the ridgeline in the vicinity.

After confirming the multiple 4K cameras and

laser scanners were providing data to the console, he set the navigations system to guide the Orca to the coordinates of the San Luis Reservoir. Once they were alerted of their destination, he'd take over navigation using the manual steering system. He leaned back on his side of the sub and smiled at Taylor.

"Having fun yet?" he asked teasingly. She seemed unsure of what she'd gotten herself into.

She pointed at the navigation station and the steering system, which resembled a PlayStation controller. "Um, aren't you gonna steer this thing?"

"Onboard nav will take it from here. Once we get to our fishing hole, I'll take the manual controls."

"That thing? It looks like a toy."

Mac laughed and took her by the hand. "Come on, first mate. You did pretty good on the fishing boat; let me show you. Sit next to me."

"No," she replied stubbornly, pulling her hand away from Mac's.

"Whadya mean no?"

"I mean I don't think I need to touch anything on this tube thing. I can just imagine crashing into a building or a floating semitruck or something."

Mac grinned and shook his head. "Okay, here's the thing. We're above miles of farmland. There are no buildings, but if any suddenly appear, the

Orca will warn us. Its navigation system is kinda like an airplane that issues warnings to a pilot that they're flying too low. The Orca has the same capability."

"That's swell," she said with her arms crossed in front of her. "The answer is still no. I'd rather enjoy the ride."

"Okay, but if you change your mind, it's not that difficult."

She gave him a thumbs-up and turned her attention to the thick glass insert at the front of the sub. As they dropped in depth, the water became cleaner. Taylor began to feel more at ease, so she expressed her concerns to Mac about the earthquake early warning systems being inoperable.

"I get it, even with the ShakeAlert system, we only get a few seconds' advance notice after the first P waves are detected," she began. "Now, a large area of our state has no warning system in place. It's archaic."

Earthquakes begin with the first waves of motion, P waves, followed by the next set of waves, which cause the most shaking. These are the slower-moving S waves. The period of time, usually measured in seconds, will determine the magnitude. The ShakeAlert earthquake warning system provided precious seconds for people to take cover and avoid injury.

"I will say this," began Mac. "We have made great strides by incorporating artificial intelligence into the new early warning system to predict how the ground will move during these temblors. We call it DeepShake."

"I've heard rumors about it. I didn't know it was being deployed yet."

"Santa Rosa is trying to keep it under the radar of the media. It's one of those situations where Deep-Shake's capabilities could be overhyped, and even successes can be declared to be failures."

"Why would it be unsuccessful?" she asked.

"DeepShake uses a vast neural network, of sorts. Basically, through the use of AI, the DeepShake brain identifies patterns of past earthquakes in order to predict how the shaking of a new quake will travel along the fault. In theory, this will lead to faster processing and easier predictability across the quake-prone regions near San Andreas."

Taylor was puzzled. "It sounds phenomenal. I still don't see the problem."

"The USGS made the decision not to input past data on earthquakes because it wasn't as accurate as what DeepShake can adsorb and analyze in real time. It goes back to that old saying *garbage in, garbage out*. The developers believe the future accuracy of DeepShake will be based largely on what it has been able to experience rather than what geologists believed to have happened prior to bringing the system online."

Taylor nodded as she gained some clarity. "It makes sense. The AI of DeepShake can beat the ground-motion prediction equations in use by ShakeAlert."

"Yes, but there is a learning curve. Just consider this. After a quake event, our people need numerical data solvers, running on supercomputers, to provide a semi-accurate assessment of what happened along the fault lines. It can take hours to process. With DeepShake's AI, you can run twenty different scenarios based on the data received, and within six milliseconds, you'll have a complete analysis of the quake event. Blazing fast."

"But it's not working yet?" she asked.

"Only in part, near the low end of San Andreas. As you know, due to politics, LA and surrounding communities were given the most attention following the ARkStorm. DeepShake is limited to that geographic area so far."

Taylor thought for a moment as she watched the

video monitors. The display registered every moment of the Orca's travels. She asked a question about the displays before she continued the conversation.

She pointed toward the console. "Does that transmit back to Santa Rosa in real time?"

"I wish. I'd love to have another set of eyes studying the data and providing the Orca's onshore operations team instant feedback. However, once we're at depth, we'll be on our own. Later, the moment we're docked at the floating facility, the data is transmitted via satellite link. It's still kinda old school considering the Orca's other technological capabilities."

Taylor returned to the discussion of DeepShake. "Alright, we had the M7.1 north of San Bernadino. What kind of warning did we receive?"

"Well, I didn't stick around for an analysis. But, as you know, I was there. I think it was somewhere between three and ten seconds. At Santa Rosa, we monitor and study. We don't warn. California takes care of that part themselves."

A subtle warning signal began to accompany a series of flashing lights on the control panel. The Orca was approaching their destination, indicating that Mac should take over manual controls. He quickly slid down the bench seat and sat on a small, swivel seat. It was a stainless disc sitting atop a tripod on wheels.

After tapping on the touchscreen monitor, he gently began to use the center toggle to steer the submersible through the opening to the San Luis Reservoir. Mac's eyes stayed focused on the sonar readings, occasionally glancing at the video feeds, which were less reliable at depth.

As he expected, the entrance was narrow. The skeletal remains of the massive trees lining the ridges on both sides of the opening provided little margin for error. Yet Mac was determined to inspect the reservoir's floor for the cause of the near one-hundred-degree water.

He set his jaw, lowered his eyebrows, and studied the video feeds as he entered the dark waters of the circular-shaped reservoir in search of answers.

CHAPTER TWENTY-FOUR

San Luis Reservoir
Lake California

The San Luis Reservoir was a man-made lake surrounded on all sides by the eastern slopes of the Diablo Range, which ran parallel to the Pacific Ocean coastline. At the eastern end of the reservoir where it opened up into the Central Valley, an embankment dam had been constructed to hold back the thirteen-thousand-acre body of water. When the ARkStorm hit, the dam, made of compacted soil and rock, never had a chance. The weight of the water burst through the dam and began to flood the small town of Santa Nella and Interstate 5 that ran through it.

That was the beginning of the deluge. Within days, the water that filled the entire Central Valley had merged with the reservoir. The depth of the reservoir had doubled, and the rocky surrounds had disappeared below the surface, allowing vegetation to appear sporadically along the banks.

Mac breathed a sigh of relief as he cleared the entrance to the reservoir. The earthen dam had left odd formations below the surface that couldn't be accurately portrayed on his video screens. The last thing he needed to do was to wreck the Orca. He could only imagine what the submersible's price tag was.

Mac methodically searched the lakebed in search of the temperature anomalies. Because he was below the surface, it was difficult to get his bearings in relation to where they had been fishing previously. He didn't dare hug the slopes of the reservoir and intermingle with any submerged vegetation for fear of getting entangled. He was certain that the odd temperature readings would appear near the lakebed if they were related to a seep, as he suspected.

"What can I do to help?" Taylor's face was

pressed against the aft window. She was fascinated by the creatures found in the deep water of the reservoir.

"You wanna help monitor the gauges? If we find the heated water, we're gonna want to make a note of the GPS coordinates."

"Doesn't the onboard computer do that for you?"

"Yeah, but extraction of the information requires leaving one program and opening another. There just wasn't enough room within the submersible for multiple workstations."

Taylor slid down the bench seat until they were touching. "Is this a good spot for me to sit?" she asked in a sultry voice.

Mac liked it. "Closer would be better," he joked.

She wasn't joking as she pressed against him. "This is, like, our sixth or seventh date, you know."

Mac remained focused on the navigation panel. "How do you figure?"

"Well, the first one was on the helicopter and the sunset."

"Okay. One."

"Then we had a shopping date."

Mac leaned back to study Taylor's face. "Shopping date? Did I miss something?"

"At Safeway. Didn't we have fun strolling through the aisles, picking out things for our fishing date?"

Mac laughed and shrugged. "Good point. That's two."

"Then later that day, there was fishing and cooking and eating."

"Three, four, and five."

Taylor continued, "Another chopper ride, this time one that landed on water. That's six."

Mac was enjoying playing along. "And I suppose the ride in the Orca is number seven?"

"Yup," she replied as she stretched her arms and nefariously wrapped them around his waist when she was done. She whispered in his ear, "You know what that means?"

"I have an idea, but I wanna hear it from my date."

She lowered her voice as if the Orca were full of scientists. "You get to kiss me proper, Cap'n Mac."

A wide grin came across his face. His heart raced as he contemplated christening the Orca with Taylor. He began to sweat as his body warmed. He reached to the keyboard to place the Orca in an idle status.

Mac tried to focus. His body shuddered. Or was it the Orca?

Then he realized why he was sweating, and it wasn't because this beautiful woman was nibbling on his neck.

CHAPTER TWENTY-FIVE

Near Hollister, California

At 8:28 p.m. as the sun set over Diablo Range near Hollister, a tiny crack in the northern wall of the San Andreas Fault suddenly splintered. The Pacific and North American tectonic plates had been locked together in a battle for underground supremacy. Their normal dance of striking and slipping that continued throughout the millennia had halted. They continued to dance, but it was cold-blooded. Harsh. A ferocious cage fight to the death.

Then as if a seismic referee shouted *break it up, boys,* they did. Both sides suffered damage, and in an instant, a gap between the two plates emerged along the eastern base of the Diablo Range.

Above the surface of the planet, tourists and locals alike enjoyed the setting sun, marveling at its beauty as the colors of the Pacific and the skies above it changed from blue to orange to violet. The serenity was destroyed as the ground began to shake.

The first to detect trouble was the animals. They always seemed to know when trouble lurked from below. Birds took flight. Wildlife scampered to a place of perceived safety. Cats dashed under beds. Dogs stood and howled.

And the water in normally calm, glass-like Lake California began to rock and roll.

Approximately twenty miles below the planet surface, the two massive slaps of rock strained to move against one another before abruptly bouncing back. The jagged and deadly San Andreas fault line stretching the length of the state became agitated.

For centuries, the walls of the seismic plates remained relatively quiet and in harmony with one another, with many thousands of tons of pressure preventing one plate from overtaking the other.

Until now. Inexplicably, the plates moved apart ever so slightly, opening a chasm underneath the shores of Lake California. Although the ground shook, it didn't open up this time. Except where the soils were the most vulnerable.

At the bottom of the lake.

CHAPTER TWENTY-SIX

Aboard the Orca
Lake California

"Are you okay?" Taylor asked as she noticed Mac's change in demeanor. The words were barely out of her mouth when the San Andreas answered her question.

Underwater, the concussive effect of the earthquake shoved the Orca onto its side and then into an uncontrolled roll toward the rocky slope. As the quake continued, the submersible began to turn end over end. Its inhabitants were tossed like bingo balls in a revolving cage.

"Arrrgh!" Mac groaned as his body was battered

against the monitoring console. With every violent roll of the Orca, another part of his body found steel or the carbon-fiber hull.

"Mac, help me." Taylor was barely able to speak above the roar of the earthquake reverberating under the water and the thumping the Orca was taking as it was pounded against debris dislodged by the turbulence.

The lights had dimmed inside the cockpit, and Mac tried to get his bearings as the submersible seemed to stabilize. His mind raced as he debated whether to regain control of the vessel or to help Taylor. With the Orca adrift and floating upside down, he opted to crawl to Taylor.

Her body had been tossed around like a rag doll. She was wedged in the aft hatch area, curled up in a ball. Her face and upper body were covered in blood. Her breathing was frantic and shallow. Her pulse was too fast to count.

Mac tried to calm her down. "Hey. Hey. You're gonna be okay. Can I take a look?"

She tried to nod her response as she continued to approach a state of hyperventilation. Mac gently patted the blood off her face before examining her scalp. Head wounds were known to bleed profusely, and he suspected she had a gash of some kind.

He was right. On the side of her head near her temple, a deep gash was allowing blood to pour out. It trickled into her ear, but the most volume hit her face because of her positioning in the hatch area.

Mac had to act quickly, as Taylor was on the verge of hyperventilating. He remained calm and tried to use a soothing tone of voice. "Come on out of there. Let's get more comfortable."

She released the tension on her muscles and allowed Mac to ease her away from the hatch. The Orca was slowly turning onto its side. Mac glanced through the aft hatch window. The powerful light beam revealed a torrent of activity. There was near zero visibility as the silt began to swirl around them. He begged the Orca to stabilize as the turbulent water continued despite the noise subsiding.

His instincts had taken over the moment the submersible had been struck by the shock wave. He tried to count the seconds in his head. As a kid, when they'd played pickup football in somebody's back-yard, the standard measure of a second was *one Mississippi*. He adopted a more accurate measure, honed by years of practice measuring the duration of a tremor.

One potato, two potato. He'd tried to focus as he, too, was being thrown about the Orca's hard interior.

He eventually settled on eighteen potatoes. Eighteen seconds. Another earthquake but lower in magnitude than the previous one at Cajon Pass. Foreshocks, his trained mind concluded.

The best is yet to come, as they say.

Mac focused on helping Taylor; he cursed himself for not knowing more about the Orca's emergency procedures. He recalled the briefing that had explained the significant innovation known as real-time hull-health monitoring. It was equipped with acoustic sensors and strain gauges throughout the hull. The system made it possible to analyze the effects on changing pressure and to warn the occupants if the hull's integrity had been compromised. Thus far, there hadn't been any bells, whistles, sirens or electronic voice warnings issued.

At least we're not gonna drown in this coffin, he thought to himself. He took a moment to wipe the blood off his own face and then cleaned Taylor's. While he held his blood-soaked shirt firmly against her scalp, he spoke to her in a soothing tone of voice.

"Honey," he called her, using a term of endearment usually reserved for the one you love, "I need you to calm down. Can you hold your breath for a moment?"

Taylor never heard a word after he called her

honey. She held her breath, but not because he asked her to. Her mind struggled to confirm what her hearing delivered to it. *Honey. He called me* honey.

She blurted out her response. "I love you!"

The threat of hyperventilation was erased with a simple word of care and tenderness. She began to laugh as tears rolled down her cheeks. Mac tried to pat them dry as they mixed with the blood coming out of her scalp. Then he gently kissed her on the lips.

Mac wanted to talk about so many things with her. He wanted to explain why she had him from the moment they met. What he hoped for their future. How nothing on earth mattered except them being together.

But first, he had business to attend to.

"I love you, too. More than you can imagine. Can you sit up straight and press this against your head?"

She nodded and winced. The lights inside the submersible had inexplicably dimmed, making it difficult to evaluate the extent of her injury. Perhaps it was an automatic function when the vessel was imperiled. Regardless, the Orca was listing on its side. He needed to right the ship and get them to the surface. He'd figure out how to get out of the partially submerged hatches at that point.

With the Orca turned on its side, the navigational control panel was on the ceiling, requiring Mac to twirl the console chair to face upward with his back against the hull. He visualized astronauts sitting at the end of a powerful rocket, their control panel in front of them, and space out there somewhere. Once he regained operational control, he'd have to brace himself to fall out of the chair. His body was beaten enough.

"That was a powerful quake," said Taylor, who was beginning to recover from the ordeal.

"Seventeen or eighteen potatoes," mumbled Mac as he ran a systems check on the Orca.

"Huh?" she asked.

"Oh, sorry. I tried to count the length of the tremor. I think it was seventeen or eighteen seconds. Potentially an M6.3 or 6.4."

Suddenly, the Orca was struck with a loud thud. Then another. And another.

It was getting pummeled with rocks rolling down the steep slope of the ridges surrounding the reservoir. The earthquake had shaken them loose, causing an avalanche. Because of the Orca's close proximity to shore, it was taking a beating.

He shouted at himself, "Come on, Mac! Fix the damn thing!"

He worked furiously, banging on the keyboard, searching for the reason the submersible was powerless. He tried to use the toggle controller to roll the submersible into an upright position.

Then the lights inside the cockpit returned to their normal levels. He was able to look around and see the carnage wrought by the quake. Taylor was soaked in blood, as she was now discovering. Her breathing became rapid again. Anxiety was about to overtake her. Mac needed to right the ship.

He worked with the steering controller, easing the toggle while gently pressing the buttons, sending signals to the many jets designed to propel the Orca. Mac was still puzzled as to how the submersible was able to be rolled so easily by the forces of the quake. Most submarines were designed to maintain a certain weight in relation to their buoyancy. Perhaps it was because the Orca was so small, it didn't have the means to adjust the buoyancy. So he used the Innerspace electric thrusters to achieve the propulsion necessary to maneuver the Orca.

And it was working. Slowly, despite the Orca being smacked with softball-sized rocks, it responded and began to turn upright.

"Okay, Taylor. We're almost there. Give me just a second."

Mac continued to take corrective action until the Orca was back into its proper orientation. He clapped his hands once, pleased with his effort. With a huge grin on his face, Mac turned to share his excitement with Taylor.

She was slumped over in a heap under the bench seat. Unconscious.

CHAPTER TWENTY-SEVEN

Aboard the Orca
Lake California

"Taylor!" Mac exclaimed as he dropped to his knees, hitting the floor hard enough to send a jolt of pain into his lower back. He pulled her lifeless body from under the bench seat and leaned it upright against a cargo hold.

He tried to wipe her bloodied face with the palms of his hands, only for her scalp to cover it once again. He didn't want to check her pulse, but he had to. *She can't die!* he screamed in his head.

Mac needed to wake her, but he also needed to get the bleeding under control. His shirt was lying across the floor, soaked in blood. Her shirt had turned from white to crimson. He made sure she was securely propped against the cargo door before he made his way to the Orca's head. The small bathroom was barely big enough to sit in but was there for the occasional need for the passengers to use it for bodily functions, including vomiting.

He located two rolls of toilet paper and began unrolling them. He pressed the somewhat rough, office-grade paper against the gash in Taylor's scalp. He was glad it wasn't some kind of *squeezably soft* brand that tended to disintegrate when used. She was already susceptible to taking in bacteria. She certainly didn't need bits of toilet paper in her wound.

He searched the Orca's storage compartments for anything that might help him. A case of bottled water was a great start. He used the first bottle to cleanse Taylor's wound. He poured the entire pint over her head to flush it out, using his bloodstained shirt to soak up the moisture before it hit the floor. After applying pressure once again, he used the second bottle to slowly wash off her face.

The cool water worked its magic to revive Taylor from her unconsciousness. At first, she winced and reached for her head. Mac had continued pressure on the wound, which stemmed the loss of blood.

"Geez, my head is pounding," she said breathlessly. "It's so hard to breathe in here."

For the first time, Mac noticed that it was more difficult to breathe. He attributed it to that brief period when the Orca had been either powerless or underpowered. He felt like that situation would improve, so he tried to calm Taylor's concerns.

"I think I've fixed that. Look, we're upright again."

She nodded. She was still breathing rapidly but not as bad as before. Yet it appeared that she was gasping for breath.

Mac lovingly pushed her blood-soaked hair behind her ears. Near her temple, her soft, brunette hair became matted and dark. "Can you sit up straight?" She'd been slumped ever since he'd discovered her unconscious.

Taylor tried to arch her back and then groaned. She immediately slumped back into an almost fetal position.

"Let me help you move away from the door so I can take a look." She relaxed, and Mac easily slid her to the side on the blood-covered floor. "I'm gonna pull your shirt up."

"Please take it off. I'm hot, and it's yucky."

Mac scowled. Her voice was almost childlike. The trauma she'd suffered went well beyond the gash on her head. He slowly pulled her shirt over her head and used it to wipe the blood off her upper body.

"Okay. Tell me if this hurts. I'll be gentle."

He tenderly pressed his fingers against her back, paying particular attention to the area behind the lungs. Her responses told the story.

"You've taken a hard enough hit on your back to possibly bruise your lungs. Try to take a deep breath."

It didn't go well. She broke out into a coughing fit.

"Okay. Okay. I'm sorry, honey. Do the best you can without going too fast. Slow, short breaths are good."

Taylor managed a smile. "That's twice."

Mac studied her face. "Twice?"

"Yep. You've called me *honey* twice."

Mac chuckled. He propped her up against the cargo door again and helped her cross her legs in front of her for stability. He positioned himself in front of her so he could make direct eye contact.

"Now, you listen to me, Taylor Reed. I love you.

I'm gonna fix this. And when it's over, we're gonna talk about how many times I wanna call you honey for the rest of our lives."

Her smile broadened until the stretching of her face seemed to impact her wound. She pressed harder on the toilet paper compress as she spoke.

"Are you seriously proposing to me right now? When bloodied and battered and probably brain damaged?"

"You're not brain damaged, and I'm not proposing to you."

Taylor feigned a serious look. Despite her injuries, she was enjoying the playful back-and-forth with Mac, whom she adored. "Why not? Why aren't you proposing?"

Mac leaned back so he could get a better look at her face. "Because I need to do it on one knee, with a ring, in a fancy restaurant. You know, the whole nine yards."

"We don't need that. Just pop the question."

Mac took a deep breath and smiled. He maneuvered until he was on one knee. He stared into her eyes.

"Taylor Reed, will you marry me?"

She appeared thoughtful as her eyes moved side to side as if she were contemplating her answer.

"I don't know. I need to think about it."

Mac sat back on his heels and glared at her. "You gotta think about it? You just said ..." His voice trailed off.

"This isn't very romantic, Cap'n Mac. And you've got us in a helluva pickle. So, yes. I need to think about it. Now, take me home, please. I have a headache." She placed the back of her free hand against her forehead and did her best Scarlett O'Hara swoon.

Mac laughed and turned his attention to the control console. It was time to get his dramatic, maybe soon-to-be-betrothed sweetheart safely above the water. He felt good. After all, she didn't say no.

However, the Earth wasn't done with them yet.

CHAPTER TWENTY-EIGHT

Aboard the Orca
Lake California

After locating his handheld GPS unit, he confirmed their coordinates in relation to the Orca's readings. Both were accurate. Then he thought for a moment. It would be impossible for them to exit the Orca without having at least one of the hatches free of water. The pressure inside the cockpit would prevent them from opening it. Likewise, any attempt to intentionally run the Orca aground might cause it to be damaged. If he was unsuccessful in beaching the submersible, they might be stranded with no ability to navigate back to the floating docking facility.

"Now or never," he muttered as he prepared to pull the Orca away from the rocky slope leading up to the shoreline. He wanted to get away from any potential entanglements like fallen trees. Plus, they'd already been peppered by falling rocks. Although he couldn't see them due to the churned-up silt, they felt softball size to him. Closer to shore, the rocks could be the size of a small car.

He backed away from the shore and smiled when the Orca's thrusters functioned properly, allowing him to turn the vehicle toward the center of the lake, away from danger. He constantly glanced toward Taylor to confirm she was still conscious and not in need of his help. The first couple of times, she gave him a thumbs-up. Once, she flipped him a bird. That was when he knew she'd be all right.

Nonetheless, she'd lost a lot of blood, and he needed to get her to safety. First order of business was exiting the reservoir. Then they'd decide between the floating dock or some other location along Diablo Range where they could get help.

Once he was clear of the rocky underwater embankment, he began to turn the Orca toward the gap between the ridges leading into the main body of

Lake California. At first, he kept his speed below what was generally considered a safe cruise level. The Orca had been battered, and he didn't want to test the integrity of its propulsion system or the hull.

He also used the toggle steering controller to rise upward. He no longer had an interest in personally observing the water temperatures. He'd allow the Orca's onboard video recording devices, coupled with the many external sensors, to gather the data for later study. His priority was getting Taylor to safety.

As he made the adjustments on the controller to turn the Orca to the surface, he sat upright on the stool and furrowed his brow. He used the buttons on the controller to increase the propulsion speed. It made no difference. They weren't rising toward the surface.

Mac rubbed his temples and then rolled his head around his neck to relieve some tension. He blinked rapidly and opened his eyes wide, thinking he'd lost focus.

He studied the control panel. The jets appeared to be functioning properly. He had to think. Was he traveling in reverse and therefore underpowered? Supposedly, the Orca was capable of moving through the water toward the aft or stern hatch equally.

Stymied, he decreased the propulsion until the Orca was floating. It remained upright. A good sign. Using the thrusters, Mac turned the Orca to reorient it. He knew this was not necessary, but he had to determine if he could travel faster by mentally exchanging the fore and aft positions.

As he turned, he felt a jolt. It wasn't from a boulder. There was no thud.

He studied the video camera feeds. He cursed the silt around them. He looked for any obstruction that might have caused the submersible to shudder like that.

Then it happened again. It was as if the side of the Orca had been punched with a fist.

Taylor screamed and scrambled on top of the bench seat despite the pain she was enduring. In her hurried state, she slammed her back hard against the Orca's hull, causing her to groan and cough again.

"I can't seem to get it to ascend to the surface. It's like it's underpowered or being held back somehow. Surely, there isn't any seaweed or vegetation attach—"

Mac stopped mid-sentence as the Orca turned rapidly, rotating as if it had been set on a hard surface and twirled. Mac was knocked out of his chair and hit the bench seat. He hit his ribs so hard that it knocked the wind out of him momentarily. Once again, Taylor was thrown to the floor but managed to hold onto the toilet paper wad against her head.

"Mac! We're moving!"

"I placed us in an idle position!" His response reflected his confusion. He scrambled to get back in front of the console.

He never made it. The Orca lurched upward and then was immediately pulled downward. Mac lost his balance. He tried to crawl on his hands and knees to pull himself up to the controller, only to be knocked backwards as the Orca was turned on its end.

"What the hell?" he shouted, not expecting an answer from the devil or anyone else.

Mac gathered himself and got back into his chair. He grabbed the controller and tried to gain control of the Orca. It was a fruitless exercise. Any attempt to use the thrusters failed. The Orca's propulsion system was no match for the open-water phenomenon that had the state-of-the-art submersible in its grasp.

CHAPTER TWENTY-NINE

Aboard the Orca
Lake California

When the quake struck along the San Andreas Fault at the Diablo Range, it caused cracks to appear at the lowest elevations on both sides of the mountains. The Diablo Range was formed over millions of years by the collision of the Pacific and North American continental plates. The rugged and jagged rock masses were made of a rocky combination that was easily chiseled or broken apart. The Hollister quake acted like a jackhammer on the region, easily breaking apart the planet's surface.

When the earth separated below the San Luis

Reservoir, the weight of the water sought a way through the crevass that formed. As the reservoir drained, the water began to circulate through the opening in a clockwise direction, forming a massive eddy, a whirlpool-like phenomenon ordinarily found in the ocean.

However, what was unfolding along the San Andreas Fault was anything but ordinary.

"What's happening, Mac? I can feel us getting pulled downward!"

Mac focused on the controls. His eyes darted from monitor to monitor as he watched their steady descent. He battled to pull free of the grip of the turbulent water. However, the Orca's propulsion system was not designed to fight the powerful, unseen beast.

The submersible was broadsided by a jolt of water, causing it to spin repeatedly. Mac was thrown out of his chair again, while Taylor was sprawled out on the blood-covered floor, trying to hold on to the bench seat supports.

The spinning stopped, but the whirlwind ride did not. The Orca was caught in the swirl of the eddy. Steadily at first, the submerged cylinder rolled over and over, tossing its passengers from side to bottom to side to top. The forty-foot-wide eddy was merciless in its attack. It gobbled up anything floating nearby. Fallen trees. A night fisherman and his bass boat. Black-tailed deer who'd found themselves too close to the lake when the quake hit.

Mac left the controls and dropped to the continuously changing bottom of the submersible as it rotated. He wrapped Taylor in his arms and assisted her in holding the bloodied mass of toilet paper against her wound.

"No, let go," she said with a groan.

"Why?" He tried to grab her arms as she pulled loose and turned away from him.

That was when she vomited. A harsh, ugly projectile retch brought on by the continuous tossing and turning of her body. Her spew caused Mac's stomach to heave as well. The air flow in the submersible was minimal. The stench of blood and vomit was overwhelming. He fought it. He tried to find the head, but the never-ending rotation of the Orca caused by the eddy made it impossible.

Seconds later, he hurled the contents of his stomach. He had the presence of mind to point his projectile vomit away from Taylor, but as the submersible rotated, all of the nauseating fluids smeared together and covered their bodies.

"Mac, I can't do this!"

He felt helpless. He tried to regain his composure. He wanted to help Taylor. He wanted to help himself. He wanted this hellish ride to end. He had to regain control of the Orca.

The turning subsided momentarily, allowing Mac to try to regain his seat at the navigation console. The steering controller had been dangling from its cord and repeatedly smacked against the counter, the monitors and the hull throughout the ordeal. He wasn't sure if it was still functional. He was not trained on a keyboard bypass of the device. Not that it mattered. The keyboard had sailed off the counter during the ordeal and out of sight.

Mac sat in the seat, drew his knees up to his chest, and forced the bottom of his feet against the countertop. He pushed hard against it to wedge himself in place in the event of the submersible beginning a chaotic rotation again.

"We're stuck in a whirlpool. Like an eddy."

"How the hell?" asked Taylor, who was taking advantage of the Orca's current stability. She'd grown accustomed to the traveling in a circle. It was the initial turbulence that had caused the angst in her stomach.

"The quake must've caused a crack in the rock

formations along the bottom of the lake. The water is literally draining out."

"Like a toilet or a bathtub?"

"Yes, actually," replied Mac as he glanced at the water temperature readings. They were over a hundred degrees and steadily rising. They were slowly descending as well. The Orca was being sucked into the earth.

He took a deep breath. He couldn't relay any of this to Taylor. She had enough trouble. He came up with a game plan.

"I can't fight the swirling motion. The best I can do is navigate the Orca with the current and try to slingshot out of it."

Taylor began opening cargo drawers in search of a first aid kit or anything that might help control the seepage of blood out of her scalp besides the soaked roll of toilet paper. She located the bottled water and two blankets. There was also a roll of paper towels and a bottle of glass cleaner.

As the submersible continued to spin in the eddy, both Mac and Taylor displayed a remarkable level of calm. Battered and injured, they dug deep as they mustered the courage to endure the unfolding disaster. There was never any doubt in their minds they'd survive it.

"Okay, I think we have something!" Mac exclaimed as the Orca suddenly began moving at a rate of speed triple its capabilities using the propulsion jets. The centrifugal force created by the submersible following the rapidly swirling current within the eddy forced Taylor to abandon her search for the first aid kit and take a seat on the bench near Mac. She gripped the seat and pressed her legs against the opposite bench, similar to Mac's positioning.

Mac studied the 4K video monitors, which revealed the turbulence of the water and the amount of silt swirling around them. He had zero visibility.

With a deep sigh, he turned to Taylor.

"We're blind."

"We have to try. I can see the monitors, Mac. You should've told me. I'm a big girl." She pointed toward the digital readouts indicating the water temperature and their continued descent toward the bottom of the lake.

"I'm sorry, I should've ..." His voice trailed off as he glanced at the video screens one more time.

"Go for it, Mac. If it doesn't work, keep trying. We've got nothing to lose. I know which way we're headed."

Mac took a deep breath, firmly grasped the

controller, and prepared to execute a slingshot-like escape from the water draining into the planet. *Don't panic; you've got this.* He repeated the words in his mind as if he was cheering himself on.

Don't panic.

CHAPTER THIRTY

Aboard the Orca
Lake California

"Almost! I can feel us pulling out of it!" Mac's exuberance was contagious.

"I feel it, too. C'mon, Orca, get us the hell out of here!" Taylor was pumping her left fist in the air, urging the submersible on.

Then the Orca crashed into an immovable object and was flipped upside down. Another object bashed into the side of the hull, forcing it into another spin. As a result of the two massive blows, the submersible lost power, and the interior went dark.

Mac was thrown upward out of his chair, taking a direct blow on the crown of his head against the ceiling. He landed hard on top of the command console before being thrown toward the back of the sub, where he crashed into Taylor's body, which once again lay motionless against the aft hatch.

In his semiconscious state, Mac tried to make sense of what had happened. He tried to speak but couldn't. His vision was blurry although he couldn't see in the darkness anyway. He fought the urge to sleep, somehow knowing he might never wake up.

He felt around the interior to get his bearings. His hand found Taylor's khaki pants. Using his feet, he slid his body along the floor without regard for the blood and vomit that would soak his own pants. None of that mattered. The stench that filled his nostrils didn't matter. If anything, it helped to keep him conscious, much like smelling salts would do for a trauma patient.

"Taylor!" His voice was strained, breathy. He was having trouble breathing. He crawled closer to her until he could find an arm. "Taylor, please answer me."

Nothing.

He closed his eyes and reopened them. He

begged God to end the torture. He asked Him to save Taylor. He promised to do anything to make the nightmare stop.

It didn't.

Suddenly, the Orca lurched downward and began tumbling out of control. Their bodies slid in unison down the floor of the sub just as it rolled onto its side. They crashed into the bench seating. Mac groaned in pain. Taylor did not.

He wrapped his arms around her, trying to protect her battered body from further abuse.

The Orca rolled again, turning end over end at the same time. Mac held her tight, struggling to shield her from harm.

And then he felt it. The submersible was back in the swirling current of the eddy. Round and round like in a massive centrifuge attempting to separate their souls from their bodies.

In the pitch darkness, Mac had no way of orienting himself. The eddy, much like a black hole in space, was devoid of light. Like a cosmic black hole, it refused to let anything escape its powerful clutches.

The Orca was now turned sideways as it spiraled with the eddy. Mac wiped the blood-matted hair out of Taylor's face. He felt her pulse. It was weak. He wiped the blood off his ear and pressed it to Taylor's chest. Her breathing was shallow. She was alive. She had a chance.

Mac tried to stay positive. He searched for hope in the throes of despair. He knew the submersible had an oxygen supply of ninety-six hours. However, was that the case when all power was lost? He didn't know and cursed himself for not being more knowledgeable about emergency protocols.

He considered the hatch. Was there an emergency pull that would allow them to escape the swirling coffin? But then, why bother? Their bodies could never swim out of the powerful eddy.

Helplessness began to overtake him. As he held Taylor tighter, tears streamed down his face. She was a beautiful, intelligent woman with her whole life ahead of her. He should've never brought her along. He'd been selfish. He wanted her by his side. She had won his heart from the moment they'd met. Now he was responsible for her dying.

The Orca tumbled again, causing them to slide to the other end. Mac's ribs crashed into the navigation desk. It stopped their slide but knocked the breath out of him momentarily. When the Orca rolled, they both crashed against the console and then landed on the ceiling. Once again, the submersible was upside down as it revolved around an unseen drain hole that had opened up in the earth.

His mind wandered to his days as a teen when he'd survived the massive earthquake along the New Madrid Fault. He'd survived that day. He was determined to survive this one.

"Don't panic," he whispered aloud.

He closed his eyes. Just for a moment. Just to gather his thoughts. He couldn't see anything anyway. Why not? Just to think. Make sense of it all. Cherish this brief moment, amidst the turbulence that surrounded him, to hold the woman he'd fallen hard for.

He began to doze off. Suddenly, the steady circulating was calming.

He wanted to heed those words, *don't panic*. So he didn't. He didn't want to give up. Yet the feeling of helplessness seemed to overcome him.

Eventually, Mac came to a realization. He simply asked himself, *Are they even looking for me? Am I gonna die?*

He let go. The swirling motion seemed to slow

down. The Orca rolled again, throwing their bodies hard against the floor. Yet he felt no pain. He was numb. Floating. Rising upward.

To Heaven?

Maybe I'm already dead.

CHAPTER THIRTY-ONE

San Luis Reservoir
Lake California

Search and rescue teams were perched upon rock outcroppings, studying the eddy that churned in the middle of the San Luis Reservoir. A Coast Guard helicopter hovered above the vortex, prepared to drop rescue divers when called upon. A team from the Orca program was following the demise of the submersible from their offices at the USGS campus in Santa Rosa. They reported changes in movements to the on-site commander of the rescue team.

All were fully aware of the situation. The first time the Orca had been struck by a barrage of small boulders, the acoustic sensors and strain gauges of the hull-health monitoring analyzed the effects of the pummeling to determine if the hull's integrity had been compromised. Shortly thereafter, when the Orca had been caught up in the swirling eddy, analysts at Santa Rosa rang the clarion bell.

Teams sprang into action. Each was assigned a different task, from plucking the Orca out of the water to somehow lassoing the submersible out of the grasp of the eddy. Nobody had trained for this exercise in a freshwater setting. Eddies and whirlpools were typically found off the coast of Northern California and Oregon, where currents were prone to shift and merge with others.

However, the rescue task was the same. The complicating factor in this situation was the extraordinary force being exacted on the Orca by the eddy. This was an unusual phenomenon in that the eddy wasn't caused by ocean currents but, rather, by a crack in the planet surface. Currents can shift, and the eddies they create can dissipate as quickly as they were formed.

The earthquake created what could best be described as a bathtub-draining effect. The only way to make it stop was to close the drain.

A demolition team was summoned, and the

USGS freed up some of their personnel despite the earthquake activity in nearby Hollister. Everyone was committed to saving the lives of Mac and Taylor.

Unfortunately, it was deemed to be too dangerous to send the explosives team to the bottom of the lake amidst the continuing turbulence caused by the eddy. The USGS geologists were brutally frank in their assessment. The explosives could actually open the chasm even wider, hastening the descent of the powerless Orca to the bottom.

So they all waited onshore, studying monitoring screens. Commiserating about the phenomenon unfolding below them. Wondering if the chasm was large enough to swallow the submersible.

"There's been a change!" one of the analysts screamed as loud as he could. The roar from the eddy sounded like water spilling over a waterfall or dam. It was deafening and reverberated off the rocky walls surrounding the reservoir.

The members of the rescue teams didn't need to look at the analyst's computer monitor to make the same determination. The eddy gradually became smaller. The lake's surface calmed as the turbulence subsided. The rollicking waves generated by the eddy stopped battering the shoreline. Until the swirling waters stopped completely. It was over.

Everyone held their breath, staring at the eerily calm waters below, illuminated by massive lights put into place by the Coast Guard. A variety of debris began to breach the surface. Anything caught up in the eddy that had buoyancy began popping up. Inanimate objects like trees, the bass fishing boat, and other small debris littered the top of the water.

The dead fisherman and several small animals were next.

The commander gave the signal to the rescue chopper hovering above the water, its powerful propellers causing its own form of turbulence. The divers were ordered into the water. The helicopter swiftly banked and flew to the top of the ridge where a staging area had been established.

Then a specialty helicopter with a powerful winch mechanism was put into place above the surface where the vortex of the eddy had been identified. A Coast Guard team pulled the winch straps free and dropped them into the water, awaiting the divers.

The means to hoist the Orca to the surface was there. The specialists capable of opening the hatch and assisting the passengers out were in a Zodiac nearby. Medical teams were on standby, their chopper ready to race Mac and Taylor to a nearby hospital in Hollister.

All eyes were on the surface, praying the divers were able to locate the submersible. It was deathly quiet except for the thumping sound of the chopper's rotors.

Waiting.

All of a sudden, the nose of the Orca breached the surface, rising out of the water like an exuberant whale in a mood to make a nice splash.

The Zodiacs with the Orca personnel and the medical team converged on the submersible. The tension was high as the personnel on the bank walked perilously close to the water's edge. Many cried as they prayed for the lives of Mac and Taylor. Emotions swept through the crowd as they anxiously waited for the hatch to open. Begging for Mac and Taylor to be safe.

The Orca crew struggled. The battering the submersible took had dented both the fore and aft hatches. They contemplated using a torch to open the hatches, but they feared the consequences of superheating the hull with people inside. They persevered. They struggled until the hatch was opened. One stuck his head inside and immediately waved for the medical team to assist.

The Orca stabilized the submersible so it wouldn't roll while the paramedics entered through the hatch. For what seemed like hours, two trauma doctors assessed the condition of the passengers. Finally, one of them stuck her head out.

"They're alive! They're both alive!"

She could barely be heard over the sound of the whirling rotors, but it didn't take long for word to find its way to the bank. Divers held their hands over their heads to give the okay symbol. Soon, people were shouting, hugging, and thanking God for the miracle.

"They're alive!"

"Thank God they're alive!"

Stretchers were sent into the Orca. First, Taylor, who was unconscious, was extracted and immediately loaded onto a Zodiac. She needed oxygen and had lost an enormous amount of blood. She was whisked away to a chopper waiting on the other side of the reservoir.

Then Mac emerged under his own power. He crawled through the hatch and looked around at the number of people there to rescue them. He was helped onto the next Zodiac and urged to lie down on a stretcher. He refused.

Instead, he rose on his knees and waved to

everyone on the bank. He tried to make eye contact with everyone around him even though he couldn't see their faces. He forgot about being covered in blood and vomit. He ignored the pain caused by the brutal beatdown from the eddy.

He shouted, "Thank you! Thank you all so much!"

Then he looked into the clear skies and thanked God.

CHAPTER THIRTY-TWO

**Providence Memorial Hospital
Santa Rosa, California**

Dr. Jan Booher was on her sixteenth hour in the
Level 1 trauma center at Providence Memorial
Hospital in Santa Rosa. The experienced trauma
surgeon had just spent three hours repairing the
intestines of a young girl who'd been crushed by a
rebar-filled block wall. Throughout the prior evening
and into the next day, Memorial was accepting
patients from as far away as Hollister following the
M6.6 earthquake that had rocked the Diablo Range
along the San Andreas Fault. The effects of the

quake had been felt as far north as San Jose, and the injuries were widespread.

She sighed after asking for a pack of sterile wipes to clean the child's body. This young lady didn't deserve this. The team surrounding her methodically counted every instrument and towel to ensure they were accounted for and not inadvertently left inside the patient. Over the next six hours, she'd be called upon multiple times for acute trauma injuries, including the resuscitation of a paramedic whose heart stopped while he was conducting his own life-saving duties.

After cleaning up, she wanted to check on two of her other patients, the scientists from the USGS who'd almost been sucked into the earth by some kind of whirlpool in the lake. As she was working on the female patient, whose injuries were life-threatening, the paramedic from the Coast Guard opined that the earth had opened up and tried to swallow their submersible. She studied the young man as he explained his theory, and then made eye contact with her medical team. None of them bought the explanation.

After talking with the critical care nurse who'd been monitoring the young woman in the intensive care unit, she worked her way down the hallway, asking about the status of other patients she'd seen during the night. Finally, at the end, she pulled the chart. She quietly read aloud.

"Atwood, Mac. Male. Thirty-three. Head trauma. Slight concussion. Cracked ribs. Back heavily bruised. Too many lacerations and external bruises to count." She paused as she shook her head in disbelief. "And he was the lucky one."

The room was dimly lit when she entered. The television was on with the volume turned down. The local news station was providing nonstop coverage of the Hollister quake and the damages it caused.

A nurse dutifully followed her into the room and began to check the monitors attached to Mac. He'd been unconscious since the helicopter flight from the San Luis Reservoir. According to the paramedics, he'd tried to remain awake and alert before suddenly passing out.

After surgery, the anesthesiologist eased him awake. Mac immediately began asking questions for which none of them provided answers. Dr. Booher wanted him to remain calm without reminders of what had landed him in the trauma center. It was for that reason she became perturbed with the nurse.

"Why is this on?" she asked, pointing at the television suspended in the corner of the room. "The damn earthquake almost killed him. Do you think he needs to wake up to this?"

The nurse searched for the remote but was unable to find it. Flustered, she pulled a side chair beneath the television so she could reach the power cord. After unplugging it, she wrapped it around the mounting bracket, ostensibly out of reach of her patient.

"Good. Now, go hide this chair. I know men. They don't always know what's best for them. Somehow, I think this one would forget the fact he was turned into tossed salad."

As the nurse pulled the chair out of the room, Dr. Booher checked Mac's bandages and vitals. She studied his chart and was pleased the critical care team had been diligent about following up. Memorial had been a madhouse over the past several hours.

In addition to the Hollister quake, a near simultaneous although much smaller quake swarm had struck the Hayward Fault, which ran through Oakland, Berkeley, Hayward and San Jose. Several BART tracks had fallen, causing injuries to the train's passengers and the motorists below. The Bay Area Rapid Transit system had been built to earthquake specifications, which puzzled local officials as to how it had managed to fail during the unusually strong quake swarm.

Dr. Booher issued instructions to the nurse upon the young woman's return. They were both exiting Mac's room when he began to stir awake. They both rushed to his side.

"Mr. Atwood, I'm Dr. Booher. You're at Providence Memorial in Santa Rosa. Please, sir, move slowly. You've been badly injured."

Mac opened his eyes fully, and they darted around the room. He tried to sit upright to get a better look, but his bruised ribs reminded him of what he'd been through.

"Damn, that hurts."

Dr. Booher gently touched his shoulder with sufficient force to remind him to stay still. "We have you on a drip IV with some pain meds. The nurse will instruct you on how to increase the dosage, if you need it."

"Taylor?" he whispered.

"She's recovering from surgery, just like you. Both of you have been administered quite a beating."

Mac tried to push himself upright again. He winced but continued his effort. "I need to see her."

"Mr. Atwood, please. Lie down," Dr. Booher

insisted. "You can't see her at the moment. We've had to place her in a medically induced coma."

"Why?" asked Mac as he tried to stretch his arm across his body to pull out the intravenous tube and to dislodge the monitoring patches. Dr. Booher grasped his wrist and pulled it back to his side.

"Mr. Atwood, let me explain. However, please stay still. Don't make me strap you to the bed."

Mac lay back and tilted his head as he studied the trauma surgeon. He was analyzing her demeanor to determine if she was kidding. Her stern look told the story. She'd do it without hesitation.

"Okay, fine. I'll be good," he lied. He'd already concocted a plan. "What's my status, first?"

Dr. Booher smiled. She turned to the nurse and asked her to turn up the lights slightly.

"I'm having her brighten the room so I can see how your eyes adjust. You've had a concussion, but it's minor on the spectrum of concussed injuries. Technically speaking, it's a Grade 2, moderate concussion. You did lose consciousness in the rescue chopper. Fifteen minutes into the flight, you regained consciousness and then simply fell asleep."

"I feel hungover," interjected Mac.

"That's not unusual. A concussion brings on

feelings of sluggishness. That, coupled with the recovery time from the anesthesia, can make you feel groggy. How's the light? Does it bother you?"

Mac opened his eyes wide and looked around. Then he stared at the television. "No problem. Can we turn on the TV?"

"No, not yet," the doctor replied. "Now, let me tell you about the rest of your injuries."

For the next several minutes, Dr. Booher gave Mac a detailed update on his medical condition and a description of what he could expect over the next several days.

"When can I leave?" he asked.

"Well, I know we have the Fourth coming up this weekend, and you might have plans. However, I'd like to monitor you for a few more days. If all is well, then you can be released on the sixth."

Mac was about to object and argue with her. Then he caught his breath and swallowed his words. She'd tether him to the bed if she knew he planned to bolt out of there at his first opportunity.

"Okay, what about Taylor?"

"I have to ask. Are you related?"

Mac had to think quick. Before the mayhem, he seemed to recall asking Taylor to marry him. *Did she say yes? Would that count as being related?* It was all he had.

"She's my fiancée."

Dr. Booher lowered her eyebrows and viewed Mac's response with skepticism. Under the circumstances, his answer didn't matter, so she explained Taylor's condition.

"Like you, she has severe bruising and multiple lacerations. Her back took a hit resulting in a pulmonary contusion that caused significant swelling on her lungs. Fortunately, we were not able to find any indication of internal bleeding as a result of the trauma.

"However, the gash in her scalp was significant, resulting in a lot of blood loss. The location of the gash, near the temple, explains why her brain was experiencing swelling."

Mac swallowed hard. He fought back the tears. "I couldn't get the bleeding under control. It was brutal down there." Mac closed his eyes and took a deep breath. He was full of guilt.

"When did she lose consciousness? Was it when she received the gash on her head or when she hit it the second time?"

"Second time? I only remember the one that resulted in the gash." Mac became agitated. He wanted desperately to see her. He wanted to apologize for putting her in that position. He wanted to hold her. He wanted to make it all better.

Dr. Booher nodded. "Calm down, Mr. Atwood. I know you're concerned. Her head was battered at least twice."

"She was awake and alert until the end when we lost power. That's when the submersible was caught in the eddy. We began to crash into tree trunks and other things. It was ..."

Dr. Booher grasped his hand and squeezed it. She suspected he had post-traumatic stress disorder and was doing his level best to suppress his feelings.

Dr. Booher tried to reassure him. "It's over now. And you have to know Miss Reed is in good hands. The medically induced coma is simply a way for her brain to shut off while it heals. Otherwise, her brain function would stress while it instructs the body to perform a kind of radical, internal triage to repair damage. This simply reduces the amount of energy the brain needs in helping other parts of the body instead of taking care of itself.

"I would equate it to a certain young man who seems to be more concerned about the woman he loves instead of ensuring he heals himself, too. Make sense, Mr. Atwood?"

Mac's face contorted as he sighed. In that moment, he was reminded of his mother admonishing him for something when he was a boy. She was always right, as was his doctor.

"Okay, thank you. Please let me know how it's going with Taylor, when you can."

"Will do," Dr. Booher replied. She whispered to the nurse briefly before leaving.

The nurse turned her attention to Mac. She glanced back toward the door to confirm the doctor had left.

"She's telling you the truth. I can see that you're very worried about her. I promise I'll check on her constantly and let you know of any changes immediately."

Mac shifted his body to get comfortable. The nurse left him alone and lowered the lights again. He analyzed Dr. Booher's words and then tried to replay the entire ordeal in his mind. Tears ran down his cheeks as he thought about the injuries to Taylor. He blamed himself for so many things, the biggest of which was bringing her along with him.

Over the next couple of hours, he tried to sleep, but couldn't as his mind raced overtime to remember what had happened. He visualized Taylor inside the submersible, trying to hold on while stopping the blood gushing out of her scalp. She never panicked. She'd stayed strong. She wanted to survive, fighting as one injury was piled onto another.

He'd become obsessed with Taylor's condition. He had to see her.

CHAPTER THIRTY-THREE

Providence Memorial Hospital
Santa Rosa, California

After he found sleep, Mac woke up a new man, and he was on a mission. First, he tested all of his limbs and extremities to confirm his body was in good working order, although it would be painful. He convinced himself that his mind was free from the stress associated with the Orca's demise. That was ancient history now. Two things filled his mind. Taylor and San Andreas.

San Andreas had to wait. At least until he laid eyes on Taylor and saw her condition for himself. Then he'd deal with the beast below.

In the minimal light provided, Mac looked around the room in search of his clothing. He recalled using his shirt to help Taylor, and his pants had most likely been cut off him. They were covered in blood and vomit anyway.

He was wearing nothing but a hospital gown tied at the back to allow him easy access to the restroom. It certainly wouldn't do for what he had in mind. He needed something to wear.

He studied the intravenous tubing and the monitoring lines attached to his body. He needed to detach all of it. However, he was concerned that would send signals to the nurses' station and somebody would come running.

He pushed himself up and sat on the edge of the bed. He weighed his options. And then he got lucky.

Suddenly, the sound of bells and alarms filled the hospital corridor. He could hear excited voices and the clamoring of feet on the floor. They were distracted, and this was his chance.

Without hesitating, Mac pulled out the IV tube and disconnected all of the monitoring devices attached to his body. He rushed to the door and looked through the square window. To his left was the emergency exit to a stairwell. Across from his room was a utility closet with a rolling cart parked outside. The door was open, but the orderly was nowhere to be found.

Mac hustled through the door and into the utility closet. He cursed under his breath, as he'd hoped to find scrubs or any article of clothing besides the gown flapping in the breeze with every stride he took.

Then it struck him. What if the alarms at the nursing station were related to Taylor?

Without thinking about being discovered or the pain shooting through his body, he rushed down the hall toward a room not that far from the nurses' station located in the center. As he arrived, medical staff came and went. Nobody seemed to notice him standing there in his gown.

Mac inched forward and looked through the window of the large trauma recovery room. His fears were realized. Taylor was stretched out on the bed, attached to several more devices than he'd been.

Her head was covered in bandages. So much so, he could only see part of her face. Her arms were bruised, and her left hand was wrapped in bandages with a finger splint. She must've injured it during the worst of the battering the submersible had endured in the eddy. Mac pressed his face against the window. He desperately wanted to call out to

her. He wanted her to know he was near to
help her.

Dr. Booher worked with the critical care team
until she was satisfied the brief period of spasmodic
activity resulting from Taylor's temporary labored
breathing had subsided. Mac studied every move the
team made as he tried to make sense of Taylor's
condition.

"Mr. Atwood, don't let Dr. Booher see you." The
critical care nurse assigned to his room had quietly
joined him at his side. "Miss Reed is in good hands,
as you can see. Now, we'd better get you back to your
room."

Mac turned to look at her. She was sincerely
trying to help him. He reluctantly nodded and began
shuffling down the hallway by her side.

"Um, sir. You might, um, want to pull the back of
your gown together. It's kind of drafty in here."

Mac laughed. In the moment, he'd forgotten
about modesty. He slowly walked back with her until
he reached a room with an open door. He noticed
the television was turned to news coverage of the
quakes. Spontaneously, he pulled away from the
nurse and rushed in front of the TV without regard
for the woman lying in the hospital bed behind him.

"Hi," she greeted Mac without complaint. She

seemed amused by his sudden appearance. "I think you might have the wrong room."

Mac ignored her and focused on the television. The streaming video showed the destruction around Hollister and Hayward. He was hungry for the technical data behind the dual quakes. The media referred to the Hayward quakes as a swarm. Hollister was labeled an M6.6. *Bigger than expected,* he thought to himself. *Were they connected? Which came first? Related to Cajon Pass?*

His mind was filled with questions, and it demanded answers.

"Mr. Atwood, we need to get you back to your room," said the nurse.

"What's the hurry?" the female patient asked in a soft tone of voice. "Let him watch the TV for as long as he wants."

The nurse scowled when she realized Mac had forgotten to hold the back of his gown together. The patient was admiring his anatomy.

Protective of her patient, she grasped the back of his gown and pulled it together. Then, in a stern voice, she ordered him to come with her. Mac was startled by her sudden change in demeanor and left the room, craning his neck at the television as he went. Half a minute later, she escorted him into his own room.

Mac closed the door behind them and spoke. "Okay, listen. I'm fine. I need to go. I work for the USGS as a geophysicist. That whirlpool ordeal we just went through could happen again except much worse. I have to get out of here and tell them what I know."

The nurse was shocked by Mac's request. "You are recovering from a concussion. Do you know what that means? Your brain had the shit knocked out of it." She hoped being blunt would bring her patient back to his senses.

"I know. I know. Listen, I'll be careful. I won't take any risks. I just need to go."

"Dr. Booher will never discharge you. And she has to be the one to determine whether you're fully healed and recovered. I'm just a nurse, and I can tell you that you're not ready to be released."

"What if I just leave?"

The nurse had to think. "Well, it's not illegal. But it is really dangerous. There are so many things that could go wrong."

"Then I'll come back," interrupted Mac. "Please, you have to understand. Taylor is my whole world now. I want to be by her side every minute, and it kills me to think that I'm leaving her. I wouldn't if it weren't important."

She reached into her jacket and pulled out a cell phone. "Can you call them and do it? You know, your office or whatever."

"I wish. I can't help without seeing all of the internal data on these quakes. I need to get to the USGS."

The nurse pulled the phone against her chest and looked through the window. She turned back to Mac.

"I'll get fired if they find out I helped you."

"I'll never tell," Mac tried to reassure her. He pointed in the direction of the stairwell. "Where does that lead?"

"Main floor, food service entrance if you take a right at the bottom. Front lobby if you turn left."

"Is there a back dock? You know, to take food deliveries."

She furrowed her brow as she tried to visualize the hospital grounds. "Yes. There's a loading dock and a ramp leading to the dumpster enclosure that's shared by the entire hospital."

"Good. That'll work. Now, just two things, please. Let me call my assistant to have her pick me up, and, um, can you find me some clothes? I feel like a mental patient who just escaped from the loony bin on the *Halloween* movie."

"Half the staff on this floor has seen your backside," the nurse said with a laugh. She liked Mac and appreciated his concern for Taylor. Besides, she liked the subterfuge of the hall plan.

Mac stretched his arm out. "May I?" he asked, pointing toward her phone.

She handed it over to him. "Please keep it brief. I'm gonna delete the record of the call as soon as you leave. As for clothes, all I can get you will be the green orderly scrubs used in surgery. Maybe some booties or hospital socks, too. You know, so you're not totally barefoot."

"Thank you," said Mac sincerely. He began to dial his assistant, and the nurse glanced at her watch.

"I'm supposed to check you at the top of the hour. That'll give you twenty minutes before I have to report you as missing. Are you sure you wanna do this?"

"I have to. If I'm correct, this state is going to experience an upheaval like no other."

The nurse's face turned pale as she scampered out of his room. Within minutes, she'd returned with two sizes of green scrubs that she hoped fit Mac. He wasted no time slipping on the pants and then the shirt. Lastly, she provided him a pair of nonslip socks to wear.

Mac was ready. He checked the time on her phone before giving it back to her.

"Your fiancée is a very lucky lady," the nurse said as she shoved the phone in her pocket.

Mac shrugged. "She's not really my fiancée. Yet, anyway. We started that conversation when everything turned to shit down there. Besides, I don't know whether she'd consider herself lucky at the moment."

The nurse shook her head. "I don't know. She's alive, and she's got you. Be careful with your injuries."

She left first, and a minute later, he slipped out and swiftly found his way into the stairwell exit.

A few minutes later, contrary to what he'd said to the nurse, he marched directly to the front entrance. He trusted her, and she stood a lot to lose. However, he wasn't certain whether she'd have a change of heart and report that he'd left on his own via the kitchen loading dock. He knew the front entrance would be busy, and it might provide him the opportunity to hide in plain sight.

CHAPTER THIRTY-FOUR

Santa Rosa, California

Mac was the picture of nonchalance as he moseyed through the main lobby toward the large set of glass doors at the entrance. While his attire was not necessarily out of the ordinary, the bandages wrapped around his head and arms drew a second glance from several people. However, frenzied loved ones were rushing into the lobby to inquire about patients admitted following the earthquakes. Staff hustled to and fro, summoned to attend to a patient in need. A steady stream of cars pulled through the circle drive to pick up and drop off visitors. Newcomers barely noticed the man dressed like a mummy in scrubs on his way to a Halloween party.

The moment Mac exited through the sliding doors into the bright sun, a jolt of pain rushed through his head as if someone had jabbed a cattle prod into his ear. He fought the urge to scream in agony as dual security guards flanked the entrance to the hospital.

California had experienced a rash of strong-armed robberies at medical facilities by drug-crazed junkies in search of a fix. Pain medications were routinely dispensed to patients, and the desperate junkies saw the weak and infirm leaving medical facilities as prime targets. It was a trend across the state, as petty crime had reached an all-time high.

Mac fought the pain and made his way around the outside of a large column holding up the roof of the hospital's porte cochère. He closed his eyes to block the sun from invading his swollen brain. However, it only provided minimal relief. The nurse who helped him was right. He needed to spend more time in the critical care unit. Maybe he'd return in a day or so if for no other reason than to visit Taylor. For now, there was work to be done.

Suddenly, there was a commotion behind him as several orderlies rushed through the glass doors. They summoned the security personnel and shoved a photograph in their faces. There was no doubt in Mac's mind they were looking for him.

He held his position, waiting impatiently for his assistant to pull up. He took a chance and glanced around the column. The three orderlies and the rent-a-cops began searching the lobby area. One of the orderlies approached visitors and showed them Mac's photograph. Mac continued to risk being discovered in order to monitor the activity.

Then an older man who'd been sitting on a park bench, waiting for his vehicle to return from valet, was approached by the orderly. He wasted no time in pointing at the column where Mac was peering around the edge.

"Shit. Busted," he said aloud. He began walking briskly toward the parking lot. As the shouts and sounds of footsteps pounding the concrete pavement got closer, Mac broke out into a slight jog. That was when he saw his assistant's Nissan crossover. He waved her down, and she pulled to an abrupt stop.

Mac flung open the rear door and crawled onto the seat. "Go! Go! Go!" he shouted as he scrambled to pull the door closed behind him.

The Nissan lurched forward as his assistant took his words to heart. She drove out of the hospital parking lot as if her boss had just robbed a bank. She weaved in and out of traffic until they'd made their way to the westbound lanes of the Luther Burbank Highway.

Mac dared not attempt to slow her down. The determined look on her face scared him somewhat. Maybe she was wound a little too tight that day?

"Um, I think we're good," he finally said as he noticed the speedometer hit eighty. She blew through the spaghetti overpass in the center of town where the busy highway intersected with US 101.

"Are you sure? What did you do, exactly?" She looked at the rearview mirror to get a glimpse of Mac. "You look like shit."

"Gee, thanks," he answered sarcastically. Earlier, Mac hadn't really explained his need for urgency on her part. He'd wanted to keep his time on the nurse's phone to a minimum.

"As to your question, well, nothing illegal. Okay? It's just, they wanted to keep me all weekend, and I need to get back to the office."

He leaned forward between the two front bucket seats to get his bearings. His assistant turned slightly to get a better look at him.

"Were you impersonating a doctor?" she asked in all seriousness.

"No. Nothing like that. I just didn't have any

clothes." Her question served as a reminder. "Speaking of which, I need to get some real clothes. Plus, I don't have any shoes. Just hospital socks. Can you stop at a Walmart or something before we get to the campus?"

She thought for a moment. "There aren't any on the west side of town. I mean, the only thing close is probably at Stony Point Plaza. There's a Goodwill store there. Also, a Skechers."

"Goodwill?" he asked. Mac wasn't a clothes snob by any means. However, he never imagined shopping at a Goodwill for apparel. However, he only needed jeans, a tee shirt, and some shoes. How hard could it be? "That works for me. Um, I might need to borrow some money."

She laughed. "I expected as much. You still owe me for lunch last week that you said you'd buy me for working through my hour. I went and paid for it, and yours, and worked through my lunch hour, but you never paid me back."

Mac scowled. Women don't forget anything. "Okay, I'm sorry. I forgot. I swear I'll pay you back. Just run a tab for me, okay?"

She shook her head and smirked. She knew he'd forget.

The trip to Goodwill was a bust. He wanted

jeans or khakis. All of the pants in stock were either way too big or way too small. He suddenly felt like he was in the "Goldilocks and the Three Bears" fairy tale, although nothing was *just right*.

He gave up the search for clothing and decided to focus on shoes. He'd deal with the hospital scrubs later. At Skechers, he perused his options. He noticed a label on the boxes proclaiming the shoes to be vegan. Mac rolled his eyes and then showed his assistant the box.

"Who cares if a pair of shoes is vegan? I don't have a puppy. Only puppies eat shoes, and they don't give a damn if the shoe is vegan."

"A vegan does," his assistant responded with a scowl. "If you're vegan, you don't want anything to do with animals being harmed. A vegan shoe has no animal products used. No leather. No wool. No fur."

"Really?" he asked, wondering if his assistant was continuing to torture him with a line of BS.

"Really, Mac," she replied disapprovingly.

After his rant and the accompanying smack-down, he picked up a pair of boat shoes for a hundred bucks. He was pleased with the purchase, although his assistant reminded him the shoes were more than double what he owed her for last week's lunch. Mac sighed. She was worse than a bill collector.

Eventually, she calmed down and returned to her usual amiable self. She asked about his condition and Taylor's. She respected that Mac didn't want to talk about the ordeal, so she didn't press. She did offer to help him in any way she could. She could tell he was deeply concerned about what he'd discovered.

Mac paused his racing mind to consider a few practical matters. He'd lost his wallet, phone and Jeep keys in the submersible. He hoped the Coast Guard had retrieved everything for him. His assistant promised to track these items down. He wanted to follow up on Taylor's condition and asked his assistant if she knew anyone who worked at the hospital. As it happened, her niece was a nurse at Memorial who wasn't working that day but could check for him. Mac was relieved he had some form of contact there.

He closed his eyes for a moment before they reached the USGS campus. He visualized Taylor lying there, perfectly still, beautiful despite her injuries. It was going to be difficult for him to focus that day, but he had to. He was firmly convinced the state was in grave danger.

CHAPTER THIRTY-FIVE

USGS
Santa Rosa, California

Mac allowed his assistant a two-minute head start to enter the USGS building. While he waited in the car, he closed his eyes in an effort to make his head stop pounding. He needed Advil and caffeine, the first two orders of business once he reached his office. As he was about to learn, that would take longer than he expected.

Mac was well known around the USGS campus. When news spread of the search and rescue effort, many had offered to assist the Coast Guard, while most remained on campus awaiting news. Nobody, including his boss, expected to see Mac for several days, considering what he'd been through. When he walked through the glass doors into the spacious, two-story lobby, it was his appearance that caught everyone's attention first. Then the cheers rose to a crescendo.

Everybody greeted him with a hearty congratulations. A few made the mistake of hugging him and pumping his fist with a congratulatory handshake. While Mac appreciated the gesture, he wondered how his coworkers couldn't notice the bandages covering most of his exposed skin except his face.

He slowly worked his way through the crowd as more people seemed to pour out of every nook and cranny of the building. He was beginning to wonder if he'd make it to his office. It was the director of the Santa Rosa USGS offices who rescued him from the jubilant mob. She pulled him into the elevator to rescue him. Or so he thought.

"Mac," she began in the tone of voice he'd come to fear. He'd pushed the envelope many times since she took the helm of the West Coast regional office. More than once, he'd been called to the woodshed for a dressing-down for one reason or another. "I just received a call from an irate trauma doctor who plans on having you arrested for leaving her care."

Mac's eyes widened. He thought the nurse said they couldn't do that. "Wait. Can they do that?"

She lowered her eyebrows and locked eyes with Mac. "I don't know, but I can."

"For what?"

"I'll make something up. Destruction of government property. I don't know. What were you thinking? You have a concussion, she said."

Mac tried to argue as he fought the need to rub his temples. His head was pounding. "It's a minor one, she said. I figure it was one of those, you know, CYA diagnoses. I feel fine."

She rolled her eyes and looked up at the floor indicator. There were only two options. One and two. The elevator doors opened, and a crowd of people stood outside to greet Mac. His boss gave them the death stare, causing some to turn and walk away briskly. She grabbed the back of Mac's arm as if she were walking a prisoner back to the holding cell.

The reception from his coworkers became muted.

"Glad you're okay, Mac."

"Good to have you back."

"Can't wait to hear all about it."

Mac appreciated their words of encouragement

although it was the two words from his assistant that caused him to smile.

Good luck, she whispered with a smile. Mac needed her snarky sense of humor as his boss dragged him off to the woodshed.

Once they reached her office, she instructed him to take a seat before she forcibly shut the door with a bang.

"Listen, I can explain. They took away my TV, and I was in another person's room and saw the news coverage—"

She held her hand up to stop him. "Stop, Mac. I'm not gonna send you back. I look at it this way. Despite your medical condition, which, as I understand it, is serious, I think I'm probably doing this doctor and the hospital a favor. You'd be a pain in their ass. Here, you can be a pain in my ass, but I know how to deal with you."

Mac breathed a sigh of relief. He relaxed in his chair and decided to speak only when spoken to. It had always been his best tactic when he was called to the woodshed.

"Okay, now that we have that out of the way," she continued, "tell me all the details of what happened. Miss Reed's superiors at CalVO are very concerned about her. They are also of the belief that she had no business down there, a matter we'll take up later. So I'd better have a damn good explanation and reason for her life being put in danger by one of my people."

Mac took a deep breath and exhaled. "To be truthful, and I'm not gonna sugarcoat anything since you've not turned me over to the doctor—do you know she threatened to have me shackled to the hospital bed?"

"Strapped. Not shackled. She told me. I didn't say it out loud, but she made a mistake not doing it."

That was an unforced error, thought Mac. He wasn't gonna get any sympathy from his boss. He was lucky she didn't whack him on the good side of his head as punishment. He continued and stuck to the facts.

"Okay, I'm gonna cut to the chase. Afterwards, if you want a timeline of what happened, I'll give it to you."

"Finally, you're proving that you are fully aware of your surroundings." She managed a slight smile.

Mac nodded, acknowledging the seriousness of the matter. "I believe the plates are bumping into one another. They're stuck. It's possible the plates have lost the water lubricant necessary to continue their normal strike-slip movements. I don't know, but a chasm of some sort opened up beneath that part of the lake, causing a massive eddy. That's why I busted out of the hospital. I know nothing about the quake other than the epicenter was very close to where we were in the submersible."

"How would you know that?" she asked.

"Just a gut feeling and the pressure waves I felt when we were at depth."

"The epicenter was just east of Hollister, directly along the San Andreas. It measured as an M6.6."

Mac grimaced. "Something told me this event was extraordinary. Here's why. A crack in the earth is not unusual during a quake. Even one that is underwater. However, they usually fill up quickly with silt and earthen material off nearby land. This was different. It was coupled with superheated water. That's what brought me out there in the first place."

"Security logs told me you left early the day before. Miss Reed went with you, I presume."

"Yes. We went fishing and ended up in the San Luis Reservoir to try our luck. My underwater thermometers showed the surface waters to be normal, but at a hundred feet or so, the temps were twenty degrees warmer. I knew the reservoir was much deeper, so I requisitioned the submersible for after-hours use to take a look at the lakebed."

She sat back in her chair. "You went back out there yesterday to investigate the temperature anomaly. With Miss Reed?"

Mac gulped. "Yes. She came with me because, well, we're friends. I accept full responsibility for what happened to her. I'll never forgive myself." Mac showed genuine contrition for his mistake, and his boss recognized that.

"I'll speak to the people at CalVO. I'll spin it that the temperature anomaly and the recent investigation by you of the new seamount led you to believe there might be a volcanic aspect to all of this."

Mac didn't want to introduce extraneous theories along with his hypothesis about the massive tectonic plates being stuck and bouncing off each other. However, if he was correct, there might very well be a volcanic connection that made a San Andreas quake seem like tripping over a crack on the sidewalk.

"I took the submersible deeper, and the water temps continued to rise. I expected to find a seep similar to what created the seamount off the coast near Eureka. That's when all hell broke loose. The quake hit. The Orca reacted by shutting down. We got thrown about, which is what caused our injuries."

"Could you not break free of the whirlpool?"

"No. There was no way. The submersible didn't have near enough power to get free of the death grip it was under. The only reason we survived is the chasm created by the quake closed up for some reason."

His boss leaned back in her chair and swirled around to look across the lush grassy area between the building and the Russian River. While she faced away from Mac, she revealed something that had not been reported in the news because there were no injuries. The news media was focused solely on the death and destruction in Hollister, San Jose and Hayward.

"There was an oceanic eddy eight miles due west of the Golden Gate Bridge. Nobody saw it because it was dark, and fortunately there were no ships docked in the Gulf of Farallones awaiting entry into San Francisco Bay."

"How do you know?" asked Mac.

She spun around to respond, "An eagle-eye analyst with NOAA caught sight of it and provided us a pretty good idea of the size and duration. It whirled for nearly thirty minutes before it stopped."

"Similar to ours," muttered Mac.

A deathly silence came over the room as the two geophysicists contemplated the information they'd gathered.

"Mac, if I didn't need you, I'd send you back to the hospital to get medical attention. You can't mess with concussions, understand?"

"Yeah, I know. I won't lie. It really hurts."

"You lie to me all the time, and I know when."

"You do?"

"I do," she said with a smile, not revealing the fact she'd contacted Mac's mother years ago and asked her for advice on how to deal with her devious son. The two women swore they'd never let him know about the conversation. "Now, let's get you a team put together."

"And some clothes?"

"Yes, some clothes."

"Advil, too?"

She managed a smile. "Yes, Mac. Advil, too."

"Um, a raise? You know, hazard pay."

Her smile quickly disappeared. "Yeah, a raise, too. You'll need it to pay for the submersible you broke."

CHAPTER THIRTY-SIX

USGS
Santa Rosa, California

Mac was pleased to have a change of clothing and a bottle of Advil. He sucked down a couple of Red Bulls to get his caffeine fix. While he waited in the small conference room for his team to arrive, he contemplated what he'd experienced the past week. The concept of earthquake prediction was something no seismologist could keep out of the forefront of their minds. After any major earthquake, usually the second question asked after *why did this happen* was *why wasn't it predicted?*

Mac pitied the personnel who were sent out to

the media room to deal with the demands for answers. It was the same every time. If he really wanted to get into hot water with his boss, he'd explain it this way.

This isn't like predicting the weather, he'd begin. Weather is something we can all see. Heck, with advanced space satellites monitoring the Earth, we can see the weather systems and provide coordinates minute by minute. Even then, we can make weather forecasts, but they are frequently wrong.

An earthquake fault is like a wooden yardstick. You can slowly bend it. The tension on some part of the yardstick grows. The wood begins to lose its structural integrity. You know, at some point, the yardstick will snap.

But when? But where? Will it break at the exact middle, eighteen inches from either end. Will the snap be a clean break, or will it splinter?

An earthquake is not all that different. The fault strains until it breaks. Nobody knows precisely when. Sure, advanced technology can raise alarms, but never in time to make a real difference in saving lives.

A Nobel laureate in physics once said, "Prediction is very difficult, especially if it's about the future." This absolutely applied to earthquake prediction.

Yet Mac considered all the signs. The theories he'd had about earthquake weather had been roundly criticized. However, he was never dissuaded from believing the massive lake created by the ARkStorm had a profound effect on the geology of California, including San Andreas. If he was right, that these geologic signs were just a precursor to something much larger, he could issue warnings of his own. Unfortunately, he was in uncharted territory here. His only hope was to take his working theory and find the evidence to support it. There were plenty of other people in the building looking at monitors to react to the Big One. He wanted to confirm it was coming and soon.

The entire team had assembled in the room, pouring themselves mugs of coffee as they prepared for a long day and evening. Mac was a notorious workaholic, and concussion notwithstanding, he'd most likely keep them studying the data until he got the answers he wanted.

"Good afternoon, everyone. I handpicked y'all because I know two things. You're good at your jobs, and you have open minds." Mac paused as he leaned against the table set up at the front of the room. The personnel from IT, which was an archaic acronym for internet technology that had evolved into something much broader in recent years, were still setting up their workstations. He shifted back and forth to stay out of a young man's way.

He continued, "By open mind, I'm going to ask you to think outside the box, a phrase I despise. However, in this case, it's perfect. I have a theory many of you are familiar with, except those of you I requested from CalVO. The theory is a simple one.

"The weight of the water in Lake California has changed the geology under the state. This would apply to the spiderweb of smaller faults running throughout the state as well as the big ones we monitor by the minute—San Andreas, San Jacinto, and Sierra Nevada, for example.

"This week we've experienced a quake storm at the Hayward Fault, and major earthquakes at San Jacinto and now San Andreas. Different faults. Two of which, San Jacinto and San Andreas, are likely connected. The third, the quake swarm at Hayward, was possibly a trigger for the M6.6 at Hollister.

"I experienced firsthand a sudden increase in water temperature within the former San Luis Reservoir at Lake California. Prior to that, I witnessed a previously unmapped and undiscovered seamount near Eureka.

"The seep there had all the earmarks of underwater volcanic activity. Both of these facts are the reasons I've included the folks from CalVO."

Mac paused as he gathered his thoughts. He'd received clearance from his boss to reveal this newfound discovery. "And NOAA has reported a massive whirlpool just west of the Golden Gate Bridge where the San Andreas stretches across the Pacific from Point Reyes to near Daly City. This event took place near simultaneously and was of similar duration to the eddy I experienced with Taylor Reed of CalVO.

"It's easy to take these isolated occurrences, anomalies all, and disregard them as mere coincidences. However, what if they're not? As scientists, our job is to look beyond the accepted norm. We question everything. Anyone can sit behind a monitor, record data, and write a report. It's up to us to look beyond these facts and determine if there's something more. That's what a seismic detective does."

Mac studied everyone in the room. As he did, the IT team gave him a thumbs-up to indicate their workstations were up and running. After they left the room, he addressed his team.

"Is everybody still on board with open minds?"

Several responded out loud; all nodded in agreement.

"Okay, great. Let's start with a simple question. By a show of hands, who thinks the quake sequence is over?"

Nobody raised their hands. *Good*, Mac thought to himself. If they did, they could leave. He knew it wasn't over. If anything, it was just the beginning. He followed up with another question.

"How many of you think these are foreshocks? Raise your hands."

Three-quarters raised their hands; quite a few did not.

Mac furrowed his brow, curious as to their reasoning. "Okay. Okay," he began. He pointed at someone near the front. "Why not?" he asked.

"I think Hayward is unrelated," the woman replied. "True, the quake swarm was significant and occurred in close time proximity. However, I don't feel there is a connection to the others."

"Does anyone else agree with this?" asked Mac.

The remaining twenty-five percent raised their hands.

Mac pointed to a large map on the wall, indicating the location of the San Andreas Fault. He ran his index finger along the ridgeline located east of San Jose. He turned his head as he spoke.

"You're probably right. Hayward is east of San Andreas. However, let me ask, while I was, um, preoccupied last night, did Hayward continue to tremor?"

The group laughed at his reference. Everyone was fully aware that Mac and Taylor could've died in the submersible. Several members of the team relayed the cessation of seismic activity along the Hayward Fault. Afterward, the group agreed there was most likely no connection.

Mac turned to his MacBook computer, a device he jokingly claimed was named after him. He accessed a database and cropped an image of the major fault lines running through the state. He focused on the area northeast of Los Angeles where the San Andreas and San Jacinto faults nearly intersect. He returned the conversation to the southern end of Lake California.

"Okay, this is a no-brainer as far as I'm concerned, but after the hit I took, I'm only operating with half a brain," he said with a chuckle, pointing at the bandage wrapped around his forehead. He desperately wanted to remove it, but he was afraid the shaved spot on his scalp and the stitched scar might scare people. After the laughter died down, he continued.

"The epicenter of the SoCal quake was at Cajon Pass near Pitman Canyon. As we know, San Jacinto is a much smaller fault than San Andreas. There are studies that suggest the two are on the verge of merging with one another. I submit the proximity of the two faults and the epicenter of the quake are related."

He pointed to the San Andreas Fault, labeled SAF on the map, and dragged his index finger to the point where the San Jacinto Fault, labeled SJF, nearly touched the much larger fault at Cajon Pass.

"We expect earthquakes to stay in their own lane. I mean, proximity aside, these are classic geometrically simple plate boundary faults. Geology 101, right? Except the Cajon Pass quake, a considerable M7.1, could potentially transfer to San Andreas if the recent studies are correct. If it did, it would be the first evidence that these joint ruptures, or shared earthquakes, could occur."

A young man toward the rear of the room raised his hand. "Mac, I studied under Professor Oskin at Cal-Davis. We did an extensive analysis of the two recorded, multi-fault earthquakes in this region. We concluded the 1812 Ventura quake, an estimated M7.1 to M7.5, was certainly capable of jumping faults."

"If it's happened before, it can happen again," added Mac.

Every single head nodded in unison. Scientists understood a basic fact. Just because a past catastrophic event was unusual didn't mean it was an isolated occurrence. History repeats, and Mac was certain it was now.

CHAPTER THIRTY-SEVEN

Santa Rosa, California

After the Hollister earthquake, the ground stopped shaking. State and federal officials breathed a collective sigh of relief, firmly convincing themselves that the quake sequence was over. The governor thanked first responders for their efforts. He encouraged the citizens of California to help one another and understand the plight of those who were in need of food and water as they broke into stores to steal.

Unexpectedly, Dr. Booher showed up at the USGS to check on her patient. She scolded Mac but assured him she was only interested in his well-being. With his team working diligently to gather the data he requested, Mac agreed to check back into the hospital that evening so Dr. Booher could run some tests.

The trauma doctor's persistence was fortuitous for Mac. Despite his focus on the task at hand, he desperately wanted to return to Memorial so he could look in on Taylor. When Dr. Booher promised he could leave anytime and promised a visit with Taylor, he didn't hesitate to join her.

After a full examination, she adjusted his bandaging to make it appear less like a gauze head-band and more like a bandage. Earlier, he'd borrowed a camouflage cap with the USGS logo embroidered on it.

He waited an hour before he was allowed to see Taylor. Dr. Booher summoned him to Taylor's room via the same nurse who'd helped him sneak out of the hospital.

"Do they know you helped me?"

"Kinda, but it's okay," she replied. "The scrubs were a dead giveaway."

"How'd they know?"

"Security footage. So, you know, I told them you were self-conscious wearing the gown. I claimed I didn't know what your plans were."

Mac nodded. They were approaching Taylor's room, where Dr. Booher was waiting for him.

"Mr. Atwood, a couple of things have happened since you left. We made the determination that Miss Reed's medical condition has made a remarkable improvement, enabling us to bring her out of the medically induced coma."

"That's great!" exclaimed Mac. "Can I talk to her?"

"Not yet, Mr. Atwood. She's sleeping. You have to understand, a medically induced coma procedure is performed to create a deep level of sedation. I called upon the anesthesiologist to taper the medication used to sedate her, allowing her to wake up gradually. Currently, she is on a ventilator to assist her breathing. As she stabilizes, we'll allow her to breathe on her own. This is a very critical stage of her recovery and one that we monitor closely."

Mac frowned and nodded. He was dejected. "Can I at least hold her hand?"

"Yes, of course. But I must caution you against trying to stimulate her in any manner. If you would like to speak to her, do so in a very soft tone of voice. We don't want to startle her during this process."

"Okay, I promise. Oh, by the way, have you reached out to her family in Denver?"

"Denver?" she questioned. "No, we had to locate them through the State Department in Washington.

Mr. and Mrs. Reed are in Europe, at the German Embassy."

"Embassy?" asked Mac.

Dr. Booher nodded. "Yes, Mr. Reed is the ambassador to Germany."

"Wait. What? Ambassador? Like, appointed by the president?"

Dr. Booher was surprised that Mac was unaware of this fact. "You didn't know this?"

Suddenly, Mac felt stupid. He and Taylor barely knew each other. Their whirlwind romance hadn't allowed them time to talk about things like family, favorite color, and must-see TV.

"No, um, not yet. We just met, actually."

Dr. Booher glanced from Taylor to the nurse and back to Mac. "You said the two of you were engaged. Am I mistaken about that?"

Mac stammered as he responded, "Well, no, I mean, here's the thing. I did ask her to marry me while we were in the submersible. She didn't say no. In fact, well, she didn't say yes, either. She was going to, but then she teased me about the circumstances and all of that. Then everything turned to shit, and we didn't get to talk about it anymore."

Dr. Booher sighed and ran her fingers through her hair. "Your boss warned me about you. I'm going to accompany you to see her. Technically, I shouldn't because you're not family. I can tell that you care deeply for her, so I'm gonna give you the benefit of the doubt."

"Thank you," said Mac. "I really do love her."

"I believe you do, so you'll promise to keep calm and not startle her in any way, right? We'll only have a minute. Deal?"

"Deal. Thanks."

Dr. Booher led Mac inside, and his eyes grew wide as he got closer to all of the devices monitoring Taylor. He somehow found a way to equate the medical devices to the seismic monitoring equipment the USGS used to monitor its patients, the many fault lines around the world. Seismic zones, in the mind of a geophysicist, were living, breathing organisms.

A fault breathed. It ate. It grew. It argued with its neighbors. Sometimes, it got pissed off. The big difference between a medical patient and a fault line was the fault couldn't be told what to do.

Mac gently grasped Taylor's hand and leaned into her ear. He glanced at her rate monitor to make sure neither her pulse nor her blood pressure was materially altered by his actions.

"Taylor, it's Mac. I love you. I am so sorry you're

going through this. I just hope you'll give me a life-time to make it up to you. Please do a better job of listening to your doctors than I did. I'll come back as soon as I can, or whenever you wake up. I'll love you forever. That's a promise."

Mac slowly released her hand and wiped the tears off his cheeks. He looked upward and took a deep breath before exhaling. He turned to Dr. Booher and smiled.

"Thank you. She's better than I deserve, but that's not gonna stop me from showing her how much I love her."

Dr. Booher smiled and nodded. "If you'll get some rest, I will absolutely tell her what you just said."

Mac smiled and nodded to his doctor. Then he dutifully turned to the critical care nurse. "Lead the way."

CHAPTER THIRTY-EIGHT

Mojave Desert, California

It happened in the middle of the night, as these things often do. To the mother of a newborn, it's the battery dying in a smoke alarm, chirping incessantly after the infant has finally fallen asleep. To the residents of Western Oklahoma, it's the puzzling sound of a freight train coming across the prairie where no rails existed. Then the sudden realization a tornado is barreling down on their farmhouse. To the residents of Florida, it's living through the annual pilgrimage of hurricanes, many of which roar over the top of them in the middle of the night.

It was almost one a.m. on the morning of July 3

when a substantial magnitude 7.3 earthquake ruptured the earth in the Mojave Desert, northeast of Los Angeles. The temblor shook the planet surface with the energy of forty-five atomic bombs similar to the one dropped on Hiroshima in 1945.

The quake occurred in the Eastern California Shear Zone, a region that has produced some of California's largest earthquakes on record. Its epicenter was northeast of the town of Ridgecrest, a city that had quadrupled in size following the flooding of Bakersfield and other cities within the southern end of the now-flooded Central Valley.

Fortunately for residents, the quake was directed along the fault lines running from the northwest to the southeast, away from the city of Ridgecrest. With the fault directed away from the population center, the stronger ground motions occurred in the desert near Telescope Peak, the highest point within the Death Valley National Park.

First responders and the media reported damages but no loss of life. As the sun rose that morning, residents and state leaders breathed a sigh of relief.

However, a patient at Providence Memorial Hospital in Santa Rosa jumped out of his hospital bed when the critical care nurse awakened him for his morning medications. She casually mentioned that since he worked for the USGS, he might want to know an earthquake just hit east of Los Angeles.

Mac scrambled to turn on the television. The cable news station was providing footage of the minimal damage.

"Dodged a bullet," the reporter had said.

"Not as costly as the quake that hit near San Bernadino days ago," the news anchor said in an authoritative voice.

"No evidence the two quakes are connected," added the field reporter as a map of the region appeared on the screen.

"Bullshit!" exclaimed Mac, startling the nurse. She moved in his direction, and he waved her away. He didn't have to study the graphic. He immediately identified the connection.

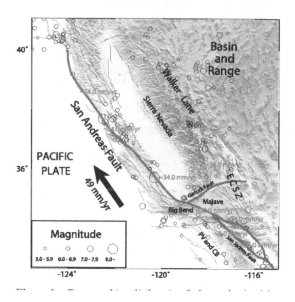

"Garlock," he said in a barely audible whisper. He suddenly turned and rushed toward the closet to retrieve his clothing. He flung off his clothes, totally disregarding the young nurse, who suddenly had a full view of his naked body.

She averted her eyes and said, "Mr. Atwood, your medications. Please."

Mac pulled on his pants and took the paper cup full of pills. He swallowed them, waving off the offer of water.

"Sir." She adopted a stern voice with Mac. "Dr. Booher will need to discharge you."

"No, she doesn't. Don't you understand? Garlock may be next. It's the damn hip bone!"

Dumbfounded, the critical care nurse stood in shock as Mac raced for the exit.

CHAPTER THIRTY-NINE

USGS
Santa Rosa, California

Mac drove faster than his concussion allowed, not that he gave his head injury a second thought. If a stranger were able to hear him mutter the lyrics to the classic children's song "Dem Bones" repeatedly, they might have suggested his brain had been damaged by the battering he took in the Orca the other day.

"The thigh bone's connected to the hip bone.

"The hip bone's connected to the backbone.

"The backbone's connected to the neck bone.

"Shake dem skeleton bones."

Mac would never forget going for beers with his first boss, an elderly geologist who dabbled in archeological digs in his spare time. He'd tried to explain the complex system of fault lines beneath California by using the well-known children's song as an example.

"Mr. Atwood," the man had begun, formally addressing Mac as if he were one of his former students at the University of California, Santa Barbara, "it would be easy to simplify this complex system of faults by naming the big ones, pardon the pun. You know, San Andreas, San Jacinto, Hayward, Sierra Nevada. However, as you have learned, in addition to these major faults, there are thousands of minor faults running below the state, some more significant than others. Many are interconnected, just like the bones in a body."

He'd taken a swig of his beer before he slowly began singing *Dem Bones*. As Mac looked back upon it, his old boss had skipped over a few major joints like the knee and hip, but that was immaterial to his point.

The fault comprising the Eastern California Seismic Zone was bordered on the north by the Garlock Fault, which ran east to west near Ridgecrest. Garlock, also a strike-slip fault, terminated near the San Andreas in northern Los Angeles County.

Mac was already suspicious of the relationship between San Andreas at the San Jacinto quake at Cajon Pass. He trusted the scientific research suggesting seismic activity could jump faults. If the theory was true, then it was possible the Mojave Desert quake could trigger a seismic event along the Garlock fault. Which, in turn, could trigger San Andreas again at the southern end of Lake California.

"Thigh bone, meet hip bone. Hip bone, meet backbone."

Mac gripped the steering wheel of his Jeep and drove recklessly through slower vehicles. He cursed the fact he'd left his replacement cell phone in his office cubicle. He hadn't even set it up yet. He needed his team to immediately turn their attention to the southern end of the Central Valley. Based upon the short period of time between the last three earthquake events, he was now certain the state was experiencing foreshocks. However, these quakes were hardly mild at, or about, M7.

He mumbled as he asked, "If these are fore-shocks, what the hell will the main seismic event look like?"

He was on the final stretch toward the USGS campus. A line of cars waited to pass through the security gates, casually showing their identification badges, driver's licenses, and smiling for the security guard. Mac didn't have time for that.

He passed the line of cars on the left and rushed through the exit. Security personnel tried to flag him down to stop. One gave chase, to no avail. Another picked up the phone to enlist reinforcements.

Mac didn't bother looking for a spot in the general parking spaces. There was no time for that. When he spotted the assigned space indicated by a sign that read DIRECTOR S. KEMP, his boss, he cut the steering wheel and pulled into it. It was as close to the front door as he could get, and he was sure his boss would understand.

He rushed out of his Jeep. Ignoring the pain shooting through his body and into his head with every stride, he made his way into the entry foyer of the USGS. A security guard was on the phone behind the reception desk, and two were manning the metal detector station at the front entrance.

Mac lowered his head and pretended to be wiping the sleep out of his eyes as he casually walked through. He didn't set off any alarms, and the two

guards were familiar with him, so they didn't question his early morning appearance.

The guard at the desk was another matter. Mac
realized the moment of recognition that came across
the guard's face. He must've received a description
of Mac's Jeep, which was legendary on the USGS
campus.

Mac cut to the side and rushed for the stairwell,
hoping the heavyset guard wouldn't give chase.

"Hey! Atwood! Hold up!"

Mac waved and burst through the door, taking
the steps two at a time. He rushed through the
upper-level corridor until he reached his team. His
assistant was already at her desk.

"Did you hear?" she asked without greeting him
good morning. He wasn't offended by that. There
were things to do on many levels. First, he needed
help with security.

"Hey. I need you to call Kemp on her cell. Tell
her I'm sorry that I'm in her parking space. Then tell
her I'm sorry I breached security."

"What? What did you do?"

"No time. I need to get security off my back. Tell
her to call off the dogs."

"What if she wants an explanation?" she asked.

Mac stopped at his cubicle to gather a few

things, including his new cell phone. By this point, he and his assistant were speaking loudly to one another, attracting the attention of everyone in the room. Heads began to pop up out of their cubicles in an effort to see what all the commotion was about.

"Garlock!" he hollered back to her. "Tell her Garlock might be next."

"Really?" asked one of the members of his team.

"Yeah, maybe," he replied. Then he paused before addressing them again. "Can y'all help me out?"

"Sure, Mac," one of them responded.

"Um, I need to ditch security. No time to explain. When they come up here, tell them I grabbed my backpack and ran down the fire escape. The last time you saw me, I was running toward the Coast Guard heliport. Can you do that?"

They responded unanimously.

"We'll sell it, boss."

"Yeah, no worries."

"Sure. Go!"

Mac entered the corridor and glanced in both directions. The small conference room where his special projects team assembled every day was on the other side of the elevators. Just as he was about to make a run for it, his assistant stood with her hand cupped over the handset's microphone.

"Mac! She said you'd better be right, or you're fired."

"Yeah, yeah."

"But she said she hoped you're wrong."

"Me too," he muttered as he walked briskly, being mindful of the telltale ding of the elevator cab arriving on their floor.

CHAPTER FORTY

USGS
Santa Rosa, California

Mac burst into the room and immediately made his presence known to his team who remained from the night shift.

"Everyone is aware of Mojave Desert, I assume," he began as he pressed the self-closing door into its frame. It was closing a little too slowly for him under the circumstances.

"Yes," responded the overnight team leader at the front of the room. He'd rarely worked directly with this young man but had been impressed by his willingness to dive into the research. "Um, I hope you don't mind, but I and one other person gathered all the data available from the monitoring center. We're now trying to see if there is a causal relationship between this tremor and Cajon Pass."

Mac was proud of the young man he hadn't spent much time working with in the past. He was clearly a self-starter.

"Good. Good. Have you reached any conclusions?"

Now the young man was on the spot, and the entire overnight team had stopped working to listen to his response. He confidently sat a little taller in his chair and jutted out his chin.

"Let me state the obvious. The two quakes are part of two wholly different fault zones. Then again, Hayward and Hollister along San Andreas are separate as well."

"All true," said Mac. "But ..." His voice trailed off, hoping the team leader would continue.

The young man laughed. He knew his boss much better than his boss knew him. "We don't believe in coincidences, do we?"

Mac smiled. *We sure don't*, he thought to himself. "Okay, I know there are a lot of circumstances in play here. Now, we need to revisit Hayward and Hollister as being interconnected. As for Cajon Pass and Mojave Desert, I don't think one triggered the other. However, there is a possibility."

"Garlock," the team leader interjected.

Mac laughed and pointed at the young man. "You go to the head of the class!"

"Um, I already am."

His response drew catcalls, boos and multiple paper wads hurled in his direction. Mac loved the comradery and devotion of his handpicked team. That was important because he was about to ask them to work overtime.

"Everyone, the day shift is on their way in. We've just doubled our research load. Can anyone stay on for a few more hours while the day team gets up to speed?"

Mac felt humbled and honored when everyone in the conference room agreed to stay as long as necessary. He exhaled and slowly stretched his back. For the first time that morning, the tension built up inside him began to subside.

He cleared the table at the front of the room. He really didn't like the arrangement because the team and their workspace were all hastily put in place. He got the sense they didn't have time to change it.

An observant member of his team had fetched him two cans of Red Bull from the USGS cafeteria.

He wasn't a coffee drinker and rarely bothered with breakfast. If there was a leftover in his refrigerator, he'd eat it. His adrenaline usually fueled his day, although the boost from the energy drink didn't hurt.

He opened his MacBook and counted more than two dozen emails from his team and other USGS departments. He tried to compartmentalize them by which quake they related to. It would be easy to get overwhelmed, so he took a deep breath and started with the most recent seismic event.

"Wow," he mumbled as he pored over the reports garnered from the Mojave Desert quake. Two dozen faults had been ruptured, further confirmation how tremors along small faults could join together to produce a sizable earthquake. Furthermore, this spiderweb-like fault zone allowed the Mojave Desert seismic event to cover a much wider area.

The door to the small conference room opened, causing the nerves in Mac's body to jolt him. He was certain the deputy dogs of the USGS campus had discovered his whereabouts and that Kemp had thrown him to said dogs. He was only somewhat relieved to see it was she who'd opened the door. He immediately stood and approached her, fully expecting to be hauled to the woodshed for the umpteenth time.

"Boss, let me explain," he began. Her arms were folded across her chest as she filled the doorway. She slowly shook her head from side to side. Then she stretched her arm toward Mac with her palm up.

"Give me your keys," she ordered.

"Um, you can't take my Jeep. I need to go to the houseboat and get some clothes."

"I'm not impounding it, which is what security wants to do," she explained. "I am, however, having it moved to a space as far away from the entrance as my secretary can find."

Mac reached into his pocket and provided her the key fob. He pressed the small, stainless button to show her how the key popped out. She took the device and rolled it around in her fingers as she spoke.

"Mac, I'm very serious about this. You've pissed off security in a big way. They said you were reckless. At some point today, you need to see these people and apologize."

Mac was contrite. "I will, and they're right. I'll make a point of doing it when I leave."

"Good. Now, about that. I take Dr. Booher's interest in your case to mean that you're not out of the woods yet. That means you need rest. You handpicked this team, so you need to trust in their capabilities."

"I do. In fact, they've done a phenomenal job in gathering data. Do you wanna see?"

"Yes, but listen to me first. You're out of here at the end of the day. Got it?"

Mac nodded, but he never verbalized his acknowledgment. He couldn't make that promise. Plus, she didn't exactly define what *end of the day* meant.

Kemp continued, "Now, show me what you have so far."

Mac gestured for her to join him, keenly aware that every member of his team had stopped their work and held their breath to listen in on the conversation. Their eyes surreptitiously followed him as he rolled an office chair next to his workspace. The thought crossed his mind that the members of his team and others within the USGS campus respected him because he bucked authority, pushing the envelope to study the most complicated seismic fault system in the world.

Once they were settled in front of his laptop, he brought up the data for her to see. He spoke as he pointed out the evidence to support his concerns.

"I suspect you're going to have to brief people outside our campus," opined Mac.

Kemp sighed. "I have three calls on my desk from the governor's office, and Reston has called more times than I can count. They don't seem to care about time zone differentials." The USGS headquarters was located in Reston, Virginia, a dozen or so miles to the west of the nation's capital

"You'll have a full report on last night's quake by noon," said Mac.

"I need the highlights now. Also, I need talking points by email as soon as I return to my office."

"Oh. Well, there's a lot of analysis to be done."

"Then say that. I need something, Mac. Our people are freaking out. The White House wants to know if warnings need to be issued. The governor's office wants to make sure nobody cancels July 4 festivities."

Mac rolled his eyes. It was always about money.

"First of all, between the two of us, I don't believe any of this activity is coincidental. I believe Cajon Pass could be a precursor of a larger quake event on San Andreas."

"A jumper?" Kemp asked.

"Yes. I believe San Andreas is the key, as indicated by the swarm along Hayward, the quake at Hollister, and the seamount forming at Eureka."

"How does the Mojave Desert quake fit in to all of this?" she asked before adding, "The governor's office will correctly point out there is a lot of real estate between Cajon Pass and that stretch of desert."

"There is also the Garlock Fault," Mac replied. He took a deep breath, leaned back in his chair for a moment to stretch, and then resumed his position over the MacBook. "Look at this. They are still experiencing aftershocks along the fault line in all directions from the epicenter. The strength of this quake cannot be overstated. It was like dropping a ten-ton rock on a frozen-solid lake in the Arctic. The cracks are stretching by the minute, as evidenced by the locations of these aftershocks."

Kemp took the MacBook and turned it toward her so she could get a better look. "Okay, I see what you are referring to. Highly unusual. However, I don't see the relationship to Garlock. Sure, the ECSZ intersects with Garlock at the north end of the Mojave. However, the aftershocks do not seem to encroach on Garlock's fault."

"It's still early," countered Mac. "So far, we've

only recorded a few dozen aftershocks. That number will grow as the day progresses."

Kemp nodded. They spoke for another moment, and then she reached a conclusion.

"At this moment, we don't have any solid evidence that another quake is imminent. We can't issue a warning until we're sure. And once we do, we can't be wrong; otherwise Californians will ignore our next one."

And that was why Mac Atwood couldn't keep his promise to leave at the end of the day. He had to be sure.

CHAPTER FORTY-ONE

USGS
Santa Rosa, California

The number of aftershocks in the Mojave Desert continued to rise, especially in the northernmost sections near Baker. Mac suspected the Garlock fault had been triggered by the Mojave Desert quake. The strong aftershocks near its intersection with the Eastern California Shear Zone continued to concern him. However, there was insufficient evidence that another quake, whether caused by the Cajon Pass or the Mojave Desert seismic activity, would occur.

Kemp poked her head into the conference room as she left for the day. She tossed Mac his keys and admonished him to *get the hell out of the building before the top of the hour*. Naturally, Mac minced her words to suit him, a practice he'd relied upon for most of his life.

The moment the door closed behind her, he whispered to himself, "She didn't say which hour."

Luckily for his boss, Mac did intend to leave earlier than planned in order to look in on Taylor before visiting hours ended. He called the hospital and learned that visiting hours were over at nine. He forced himself to leave the office that night although there had not been any additional seismic events.

With his backpack stuffed with reports and his MacBook tucked under his arm, he rushed out of the building in search of his Jeep. As promised, it was parked about as far away from the front entrance as her secretary could find. The delay in locating his vehicle caused him to race toward the hospital in a manner similar to how he'd arrived that morning. Friday evening, holiday weekend traffic complicated his drive.

By the time he arrived at Memorial Hospital, it was dark and almost nine o'clock. A steady stream of family and friends were exiting through the double doors. Mac was the only person entering at that hour. Once inside, although he knew where he was going, he checked in at the reception area, as visitors were required to do. It was time to follow some rules around here, he said to himself. That was when he was hit with the bad news.

"Hi. I just wanted to check in. Mac Atwood to see a patient. Her name is Taylor Reed."

The older woman scowled and gave Mac a disapproving look. "I remember who you are." She opened a desk drawer and pulled out a copy of his patient intake form, which included his photograph.

"Oh, yeah," Mac began to stammer. He glanced up at the clock. It was five 'til nine. "Um, I worked that out with Dr. Booher. We're good now."

She smirked at Mac and pointed her thumb over her shoulder. "Visiting hours are over, sir."

It was now four minutes 'til nine. He was regretting doing the right thing. He should've used the filled lobby as a distraction to bolt upstairs.

"I've got time to get up to her," he began before she raised her hand to cut him off. "It's not nine yet."

"No, sir. Most patient rooms fall under the nine o'clock visiting hours. ICU, however, is seven. You'll have to come back tomorrow."

Mac was about to argue his point when the elevator doors opened to his right. He thought about rushing inside, giving the gatekeeper another reason to dislike him. However, he caught a break.

"Oh, good. Just who I was looking for," he said with a smug grin to the receptionist. He turned toward the people exiting the elevator. "Hey. Um, hi, Dr. Booher!"

Mac walked away from the receptionist desk, pushing his way through the loved ones who were leaving the building. Dr. Booher stopped and allowed the crowd to walk past her.

"Mr. Atwood, I heard you left in a rush this morning. Are you here for another night?"

"No. Actually, I feel great," he said. He had improved, or so he thought. Perhaps he'd stayed so busy throughout the day he didn't have time to think about his aches, pains, and concussion.

"I seriously doubt that," she said. Mac was certain she'd never give him the benefit of the doubt.

"I came to see Taylor, and I thought I was here before visiting hours were over, but then I learned ICU has different hours," Mac rambled, hoping Dr. Booher might offer to take him upstairs.

She glanced at the receptionist and then at the clock behind her. "Karen, I need to examine Mr. Atwood upstairs. I'd rather not admit him, though."

Karen, the gatekeeper, corrected the trauma

physician. "Technically, he was never released. I just glanced at the record. He escaped one day, and the next day he just took off. Two-time escapee, Dr. Booher."

Dr. Booher chuckled under her breath. Mac was growing on her. She pulled him away from the exiting crowd.

"Let me bring you up to date. She is a warrior. Her body is responding to all treatment. She's been awake this afternoon. We even introduced some solid foods. Well, Miss Reed referred to it as Gerber baby food in a jar, and truthfully, she's not that far off base with her assessment. It's just that we need to give her body time to focus on her injuries, not digesting a steak."

Mac was elated. He tried to curb his enthusiasm but couldn't. "So I can talk to her? How long can I stay?"

As the doors opened, he forgot his manners and walked toward the opening. Dr. Booher grabbed his arm. "She's responding. That doesn't mean she's recovered. The same rules apply as when you saw her the last time. Tempered, unemotional conversation. Okay? And, I might add, do not talk shop. I've caught a glimpse of the news today. I don't need you distracting her with conversations about big quakes."

Mac scowled and sighed. "I understand." He meant it. He knew what it felt like to exit a hospital's care prematurely. He was prolonging the recovery from his mild concussion by going back to work too soon. He justified it by the unusual circumstances.

Dr. Booher invited him into the elevator, where they rode up in silence. The doors opened to a darkened, eerily silent corridor near the nurses' station.

"Here we are," she began as she led him to a recovery room similar to the one he'd occupied. Mac saw this as a good sign. "Don't forget." *One last admonishment, probably well deserved,* Mac thought.

She explained to the critical care nurse who Mac was and that he was allowed five minutes with the patient. The nurse advised Dr. Booher that Taylor was awake and had asked to see the television. She, too, was denied access to the news networks. Mac agreed that was a good thing.

The nurse escorted Mac in where Taylor was sitting somewhat upright, nibbling on shaved ice. She was attached to monitors and an IV drip. Her head was still bandaged, as were her arms in several places. The bruises inflicted on her body were various shades of purple, black, and blue.

Mac eased up to her bed as the nurse quietly left them alone. He wasn't sure how Taylor felt about him. He took sole responsibility for her condition. When she spoke first, he wasn't sure if she was addressing him in a loving way, or with a hint of sarcasm as to why she'd been placed in this predicament.

"Well, if it isn't Cap'n Mac. Have you been sailing lately?"

Mac loved her so much. In her battered, vulnerable condition, she was as beautiful as that afternoon when they first met.

Mac managed a smile, hoping she was playfully joking with him. "I think I'll be a landlubber from now on."

"You live on a boat, 'member?"

"Well, yeah. It is tied to a dock that is attached to the ground. Does that count?"

Taylor gave him a tender smile, followed by a wince. Mac imagined every move she made resulted in a painful response.

"It does in my book," she replied. "I've been asking about you."

"Because you hate me?" Mac was still unsure.

"No, because I miss you, idiot. They told me you escaped from Dr. Booher's custody."

He stood next to her. He gently took her hand and rubbed her wrist with his thumb. It felt good to touch her. She squeezed his hand in response.

"Well, there was something I needed to do on campus." He was purposefully vague.

She wasn't finished quizzing him. "Then they said you came back last night."

"I promised the doc I'd spend the night so she could monitor my recovery."

"And you ran off again. Right?"

Mac glanced toward the door. He hoped Dr. Booher was hanging around so he could tell her to read her staff the riot act just like she'd done to him. Taylor seemed to know everything about Mac's comings and goings. Dr. Booher had stepped out, giving Mac and Taylor some privacy.

"Well, I thought we were done, so I took off for work."

She chuckled. "Mac, you're such a fibber. You wouldn't have hauled ass out of here if it weren't important. I expected to see you sitting in that chair over there when I woke up. That's why I pestered the nurses for answers."

She was right. He was a fibber, and he wasn't done yet. He reconciled it by reminding himself of the doctor's orders. Don't upset the patient. He changed the subject.

"Dr. Booher said you're doing fantastic. Remarkable, actually. I'm proud of you."

She handed him the empty ice cup that had been in his left hand. She squeezed his right hand with hers. It was a firm grip. It was intentional.

"Look at me, Mac Atwood."

He did briefly before he averted his eyes.

Her grip tightened.

"Ow, they said you were weak," he complained.

"Mac, what's going on out there?" she said as she squeezed a little harder. Then she lowered her voice so only he could hear in the event a nurse interrupted them. "Before you answer, I want you to imagine something else in my hand. Something far more tender and subject to pain. Do I need to spell it out?"

Subconsciously, Mac shuddered as he squeezed his legs together. "No, I get it. Listen, she made me swear to keep you calm."

"I'll only be calm if you tell the truth," she shot back.

Mac was pleased that Taylor was showing signs of her old, before-the-Orca-ride self.

"There's been another quake swarm. Overnight, around 1:00 a.m. The epicenter was east of Ridgecrest."

"How big?"

"M7 or so. Numbers are still coming in. The aftershocks concern me. They number in the hundreds already. They are occurring in all directions from the epicenter, including north toward the Sierra Nevadas."

"Near Garlock?"

"Pretty close," Mac replied as he turned his head to check the door. He'd lost track of time and was certain he'd be kicked out soon. "Taylor, I'll know more in the morning. I promise I'll tell you everything."

"Including that you love me?"

"Yes, I love you more than life. I'm so sorry this happened."

She released her grip on his hand and touched his face. "You need to shave."

Mac smiled and laughed. "I stink, too."

Taylor continued to rub his cheek and then his neck. "I know. I wasn't gonna say anything. Are you headed home for a shower?"

"Yeah, and I can't wait to sleep in my own bed."

Taylor raised her hand and wiggled her finger, indicating that he should bring his head closer to hers. She rose slightly and kissed him on the cheek.

Then she whispered everything she'd do to him if she were in his bed.

"I love you, Mac. Get your rest, and promise to come see me tomorrow."

"It's the Fourth of July, you know," he said in response. "I'll bring the fireworks."

She lovingly touched his face again and then fell asleep. Mac desperately wanted to crawl in the bed with her. Or sleep in the chair. However, the critical care nurse came in and escorted him to the main entrance on Dr. Booher's instructions.

It was just as well. Mac was satisfied that his relationship with Taylor was on solid ground. He, too, needed sleep. The hospital setting hadn't given him a very restful bed to recover in. There was nothing like his floating house to provide the ultimate in deep sleep.

CHAPTER FORTY-TWO

KERN 96.1 FM
Ridgecrest, Kern County, California

Morning radio personality Scott Cox had been a fixture in Ridgecrest for many years. He'd worked overtime since the earthquake struck in the Mojave Desert in the easternmost parts of Kern County. Today, after thirty years in the radio industry, he'd used the occasion of his special broadcast on July 4 to announce his retirement.

"I have had many proud moments related to my career in radio. From becoming friends with then-governor Arnold Schwarzenegger to my work with Wounded Warriors and the Ronald McDonald

House. I've covered world events and significant local ones, such as the recent earthquake in the desert and, of course, the ARkStorm, which had a profound effect on all our lives.

"It's been my pleasure to bring you news, weather and traffic weekday mornings. I've tried to remain plugged in to local events of interest and concern to KERN listeners. My goal has always been to inform our listeners while mildly entertaining them with a touch of wit and humor. I hope I've succeeded on all counts.

"Many friends here at the station have asked me what's next. Well, can I say more of the same in some respects, such as charity work and a substantial amount of pleasure time on the lake. Over the years, I was able to overcome the fact that Lake California was formed during the worst natural catastrophe of our times. People died. Survivors suffered. Families were displaced, including many thousands to Ridgecrest and Kern County.

"As a result, I found a love for boating, fishing, and time with family on the water. And yes, I slather plenty of sunscreen on this cue-ball-shaped chrome dome of mine.

"So, today, as I sign off and thank our Founding Fathers for creating the greatest nation on earth, I look forward to joining friends and family on the lake. I hope that I will see all of you out there as well. Godspeed, my friends."

Cox, like other notable personalities and political icons, had urged Californians over the years to overcome the stigma associated with the newly formed lake. Lake California, a beautiful body of water on the surface, had been declared to be a graveyard. It was blamed for destroying millions of Californians' lives. Many boycotted any activity on its waters because it had been born out of death and destruction.

Over the passage of time, many Californians, like Cox, had come to appreciate the lake's beauty and the opportunities it provided for families to enjoy the beautiful vistas across the fresh water.

That July 4, the California Department of Tourism estimated nearly half a million people would descend upon Lake California's waters and shorelines to enjoy all that it had to offer.

CHAPTER FORTY-THREE

Grapevine Dam
Grapevine, California

Grapevine, California, was commonly referred to as an unincorporated community, one of many thousands that dotted the American countryside. It was too small to become a town in its own right, complete with its own government operations. It was simply a logical place to install an exit along Interstate 5, which was now mostly submerged under Lake California. The closest town of any consequence had been a few miles to the north, at Mettler.

The exit's two gas stations had been abandoned, as were the Days Inn and Jack in the Box businesses.

While Grapevine wasn't wholly drowned by the lake like so many other communities and cities in the Central Valley, it could've been relegated to obscurity, as the interstate was no longer there.

As the ARkStorm flooded the Central Valley, rebuilding efforts were contemplated. Experts at the USGS and the U.S. Army Corps of Engineers identified the gap situated at Grapevine Canyon between two massive ridges as an ideal place to construct a dam. A river had been formed following the ARkStorm that stretched from Grapevine, where it meandered through the canyons, until it reached the dry lakes surrounding Edwards Air Force Base. There it was diverted to avoid further flooding of the Los Angeles basin. The Grapevine Dam was built to prevent future flooding at Edwards as well as downstream in the areas of Santa Clarita and the San Fernando Valley.

Grapevine Dam, built hastily to protect the politically prioritized Los Angeles metropolitan area, was a 240-foot-tall earthen dam. Many chastised the government for allowing the earthen dam to remain in place. Originally, it was planned to build a massive concrete dam just below Grapevine once the earthen dam was completed. However, environmental issues arose, delaying its approval. Plus, the state, with limited resources, had to focus their water-retention efforts elsewhere.

After the earthquake event in the Mojave Desert, the U.S. Federal Energy Regulatory Commission, or FERC, contacted the director of the California Division of Safety of Dams. The division was not only responsible for approving construction of new dams and subsequent annual inspections, but they were also focused on safety, as many of the earthen dams were under stress from the weight of the water.

The director was ordered to begin releasing water into the canyon in order to reduce lake levels. The upper portion of the dam was in need of repair. After the earthquake, regulators feared another seismic event might put too much stress on the dam.

That morning at nine, the usual two-person crew who monitored the dam operations had been expanded to four. They expected to work a few hours before shutting off the spillover. It was a holiday, and none of them wanted to be there. However, the short, three-hour shift that paid them a full day at double-time rates was attractive.

"So what's the deal?" asked one of the normally

off-duty engineers who'd volunteered for the short shift.

His supervisor shrugged as he began the process of opening the spillway. "Here's what I was told," he began. "FERC's afraid of another quake. They think if we open the spillways, the water levels will drop enough to take the pressure off the top of the dam."

"Do they think that's gonna make a difference?" another man asked sarcastically. He pointed toward the main body of the lake, which was already filling up with motorboats of all sizes. "Do they not realize how many millions of gallons of water is over there. What did they say? Twenty-two Mississippi Rivers or some such?"

"Dude, I don't know," his supervisor replied. "I guess they're spooked about what happened at Devil's Gate during the other big one. Supposedly, they don't think the dam and the Grapevine Reservoir will survive a 7.2 quake. Anyway, this is what the bureaucrats want, so we're gonna give it to them."

The other engineer on duty questioned the decision, regardless of the fact his arguments were being ignored. "I don't disagree that this dam is already past its prime. It should've been replaced years ago." He paused and took a deep breath. "Here's the thing. When we start the flow over the spillways, if an earthquake were to hit, it would be a worst-case scenario. I mean, we'd be talking about an uncontrolled release of water that would be like trying to put the proverbial genie back in the bottle. We couldn't stop it."

The supervisor shrugged as he started the four-hour-long process. "Listen, I've lived in Cali all my life. We've had three hella-big quakes this past week. There's no way we're gonna get a fourth. It's never happened before."

With a rush, the spill gates opened, and thousands of gallons of water began flowing over the dam. Water in all directions was sucked toward the opening, following the pull of gravity, seeking the lowest point in the surrounding terrain.

Water always seeks its own level, so they say.

CHAPTER FORTY-FOUR

Near Mettler, California

Eighteen miles beneath the surface of Lake California, near the former town of Mettler, the Garlock Fault curves from the Mohave Desert to the town of Frazier Park, where it intersects with San Andreas. Over many thousands of years, the force exerted by the Garlock Fault on San Andreas caused the most famous fault in the world to bend into a lazy S pattern. The power exerted by these two faults on one another compressed rocks upward to form parts of the San Gabriel Mountains north of Los Angeles.

The Garlock Fault had been considered relatively dormant, as the San Andreas and San Jacinto faults frequently relieved the stress on the seismic system. However, geophysicists considered it to be a sleeping giant beneath the lake. Just because it was slow didn't mean it wasn't dangerous. It just meant the seismic event would last longer than most, making it more destructive.

Following the quake in the Mojave Desert, thousands of aftershocks had been recorded. Immense pressure was being exerted on the Garlock Fault, so much so that a part of the fault slipped as it was squeezed. The fault's creep, as it was known, was not visible to satellite imagery, as it occurred under the lake. The lack of seismometers in the area meant the USGS had no data on the slow movement of Garlock.

The creep resulted in both sides of the fault rupturing. In modern times, the fault remained locked through friction. Now, there'd been a combination of the Mojave Desert quake exerting pressure from the east coupled with the Cajon Pass seismic event terminating where Garlock intersected near San Andreas to the west.

The breaking point was at Mettler, just north of the Grapevine Dam. The Garlock Fault succumbed to the immense pressure. It was squeezed until it was forced apart. An enormous rift stretching three miles along the fault was formed. The earth opened and belched.

It was the beginning of an M8 earthquake that would be felt in Oregon, Nevada, Arizona, and Mexico. Shortly thereafter, it set off a chain reaction resulting in an unparalleled catastrophic event.

CHAPTER FORTY-FIVE

Mount Vaca, California

By the time Mac had crossed the Mount Vaca ridgeline leading to his floating house, he could barely keep his eyes open. Feeling exhausted as he left the hospital, he pulled back the top of his four-door Rubicon and rolled down all the windows. The fresh air revived him. That and his sense of euphoria after visiting Taylor. Then fatigue set in.

He hadn't been home since the morning following their fishing outing. He could still sense her presence in the houseboat. The two plates in the sink. Two napkins. Two glasses left on the table. He wondered if she could envision herself living there.

At least, when she was called to the Santa Rosa

campus, anyway. The problem was that Taylor rarely was called to Santa Rosa. Granted, it was a large complex of buildings, but Mac had never seen her before that day at Eureka.

He'd tried a long-distance relationship once. It had been a disaster from the start. He wanted something more with Taylor. Something permanent. That necessarily required one of them to give up their job or relocate in order to be together.

Mac's head was filled with the events of the last few days and his approach to a possible future with the woman he'd just met. He set his jaw and imagined the snide remarks about their whirlwind relationship. He didn't care. He loved Taylor, and he now was convinced she loved him back. He vowed to sit down with her and discuss ways to make it work as soon as she was discharged from the hospital.

In the meantime, Mac stripped off the clothing that had been purchased for him. He had every intention of taking a shower. Instead, he pulled out a pair of gym shorts and a corny tee shirt his family had given him for Christmas the year he received the offer from the USGS. It depicted two cartoonish tectonic plates sliding against one another. The face on one had a pair of *oops, sorry eyes,* and the other had its mouth wide open in agony. In between the graphic, the shirt read:

One tectonic plate bumped into another and said
SORRY, MY FAULT

The white tee was tattered and torn from many days on the lake and crawling around geologic formations in search of clues to what was happening underneath the Earth's surface. He vowed to keep it until it literally fell off his back.

Comfortable, Mac made himself a drink. He made his way to the bed and slid his sore body under the covers. Sitting upright in bed, in the dark, he sipped the whiskey and allowed it to soak into his body. For the first time, he was truly relaxed.

The next day was the Fourth, a holiday. Although not for him. He'd go into the USGS campus to continue his research on the quakes that had struck the state in rapid succession. His mind wandered to what could happen next. Then, after the last sip of whiskey, he fell into a deep, restorative sleep.

This morning, Mac continued to sleep well past

the normal hour he stirred awake on his own. A partly cloudy sky coupled with him pulling the blackout curtains closed in his cabin prevented the morning sun from waking him as usual. Mac, like many people who kept an established routine, was used to waking up at a specific time or related to a specific event, like sunrise. This time was different. He was still recovering from the mild concussion and associated injuries surrounding their experience in the Orca. The ordeal had taken an emotional toll on him as well. That, and the stout whiskey before bed, allowed him to slumber until just past ten o'clock that morning.

He was awakened by his floating house rocking back and forth. In his half-sleepy state, Mac thought he'd heard the roar of a boat pass his dock. It would be the logical cause of the wake that subsequently shook his house. For a brief moment, he considered rushing onto his dock to curse the asshole responsible for disturbing his home. Instead, he rolled over and found a comfortable position to sleep some more. It was too early and probably just a gust of wind, he surmised. Besides, the alarm on his phone would wake him at seven.

Except his old phone had gone missing during the extraction from the Orca, and he never set up the new one. Mac was wholly unaware of the time or what was happening underneath him.

Until seconds later when another large wave rolled underneath his floating house. The nose of his floating house, where his cabin was located, abruptly dipped downward. Then it lurched upward. This was followed by a loud series of cracks that resembled the reports of a hunting rifle.

Mac scrambled out of bed. In his haste to enter the main cabin, he tripped over the threshold separating his bedroom from the open living area. He sprawled onto the floor, tearing open carpet burns on his knees. After hurling several expletives, Mac scrambled to the sliding glass door and pushed the louvered blinds to the side.

His eyes grew wide, and his mouth fell open. Momentarily, he froze. Unable to move. He finally recovered and pushed the door open. Mac rushed onto the deck, where he was immediately thrown backwards, crashing hard into the door frame. He crawled forward again, struggling against the unexplained, massive waves rocking his houseboat. He grabbed the stainless-steel railing and used all of his strength to pull himself up. Still, he struggled against the forces roiling his home.

"What the hell?" he mumbled.

CHAPTER FORTY-SIX

USGS
Santa Rosa, CA

The USGS campus exploded with activity that morning, as an unprecedented fourth major earthquake in the last seven days had shaken California to its core. A steady stream of vehicles stood in line at the security gates, a process made more complicated by the number of media vehicles attempting to access the facility. Some, like Mac had done a couple of days prior, entered through the exit, using their high-level administrative status to cut in line. Unlike the other day, however, security personnel were checking identification. The scene was reminiscent of the mass evacuation measures undertaken during the ARkStorm, except in reverse.

Inside the building, harried scientists rushed in all directions, carrying their laptops or reams of printed reports under their arms. Coffee machines were emptied and quickly refilled. Chitchat around the water cooler was kept to a minimum. Nobody complained that it was America's Independence Day. In their minds, it was the day the Big One hit California. Or so they thought.

Director Sierra Kemp had arrived moments before the Garlock Fault reawakened. She'd been haunted the night before, finding sleep near impossible, as she contemplated Mac's theories on the connection between the Mojave Desert quake and the one that had occurred at Cajon Pass several days ago. It was far-fetched, to be sure, but scientifically plausible. Far-fetched, yet here they were.

Her family had planned a day on their boat and were disappointed when Mom begged off of the festivities. Instead, her husband took the family into the recently reopened Oracle Park, the San Francisco Giants baseball stadium. The previous stadium overlooking the bay had been swamped during the ARkStorm. Team officials had managed to procure higher ground with a view of the Golden Gate bridge.

Kemp was summoned to the monitoring room when the first data came in from the few Mettler seismographs in operation. The tiny foreshocks along the Garlock Fault began to accumulate. The geophysicists raised the alarm just after ten o'clock that morning. Minutes later, the fault ripped itself open, and the room erupted in nervous excitement. She managed to calm the floor supervisor and pulled the twenty-year veteran aside to get an update.

He took a deep breath and wiped the perspiration off his brow. His face was red with anxiety. Kemp had seen this type of reaction before. Most members of the USGS team were dedicated to earthquake prediction and, therefore, saving lives. However, not unlike the news media who'd gathered around the building, there was a feeding frenzy of sorts within the USGS when something of this magnitude unfolded.

"The swarm began just before dawn," he began before taking a deep breath to regain his composure. "We detected between two hundred and two hundred forty minor quakes. Truthfully, the timing and magnitude was not that much different than what we've been monitoring at Hayward.

"Anyway, just minutes ago, we registered an M7.8 with an epicenter—"

Startled, Kemp reared her head and shoulders back from her slightly slouched posture. "Say that again," ordered Kemp.

"That's correct. Magnitude seven-point-eight. The epicenter was near Mettler. Um, at least, where Mettler once was."

"You've absolutely confirmed this?" she asked. "The Garlock Fault only stretches a hundred and sixty miles."

"Yes, ma'am, that's true. However, it's the longest in duration this week. It's also four to five miles deeper than both Cajon Pass and Hollister."

Kemp wandered away from the geophysicist and ran her fingers through her hair. She raised her index finger to the bearer of the bad news, indicating for him to wait a moment. She pulled her cell phone out of her jeans pocket and called her secretary.

"Check security logs and see if Mac Atwood is here. I haven't seen him this morning."

Kemp waited for a moment as the secretary pounded away on her keyboard. She paced the floor, periodically looking up at the monitors, which revealed seismic activity across the state. She lowered her eyes as something caught her attention.

Her secretary updated her. "No, Mrs. Kemp. He's not in yet. I can call him if you'd like."

"Yes. Get him in here, now!" She disconnected the call. She found it odd that Mac wasn't there first thing. She knew him to be an early riser. She turned her attention back to the monitoring center supervisor on duty.

As she spoke, she pointed to blips appearing on the screen in a concentrated area along California's coast. Along a purple line labeled San Andreas Fault. "When did this start?"

The supervisor walked closer to the screen. He spun around. "Collins! Hamlin! Give me the data on this activity near, um." He studied the large projection screen that depicted the state of California with the major faults marked in a variety of colors. "Parkfield."

"On it!" one of the analysts replied.

"Parkfield? What else is new?" asked Kemp.

Her questioning the analyst was not inappropriate. One of the places where scientists have intensively studied the San Andreas Fault is the small community of Parkfield located in southern Monterey County. Local officials had proudly declared the town to be the Earthquake Capital of the World. Geophysicists descended upon the region where small to moderately large earthquakes occurred with regularity, a phenomenon that was considered unusual for seismic zones around the world.

The Pacific and North American plates slip past each other at an annual rate of two and a half inches per year. At that rate, Parkfield community leaders determined Los Angeles would slip past San Francisco in thirty-one million years, making Parkfield a seaside town.

Kemp and the supervisor stood side by side, arms folded in front of them, watching brightly illuminated blips appearing on the screen. At Mettler, aftershocks were rocking the lakebed in all directions. At Parkfield, a new quake swarm was unfolding. Their thoughts were interrupted by an analyst at the back of the room.

"I've got reports from first responders. You're not gonna believe this."

CHAPTER FORTY-SEVEN

Pine Mountain Club, California, USA

Over the years, many locations in Southern California had been declared to be the *Playground of the Stars*. The famed Sunset Strip was the place to be seen for Hollywood starlets and playboys alike. Then the rich and famous discovered Palm Springs. The oasis in the desert attracted the likes of Bob Hope, Jayne Mansfield, and Johnny Carson. Decades later, anybody who was anybody in Hollywood had a place around the ski resort community of Mammoth Lakes.

The ARkStorm changed all of that. Sunset Strip and Palm Springs were flooded. The snowpack at Mammoth Mountain was too deep for operators of the ski resorts and businesses to function. It took years for the area to reopen.

However, new enclaves for the rich and famous opened up on the shores of Lake California. One location in Southwest Kern County was known as Pine Mountain Club. Once a quaint mountain town known for hosting hikers and campers, the northern edge of the Tecuya Ridge now offered a miles-long, pristine view of Lake California.

Magnificent mansions were built, many taking years to construct, along the bluffs overlooking the water. Elaborate trails and winding boardwalks led to the shore, where pavilions were built to host parties. That day, an aging actress was turning sixty. Determined not to let the milestone rain on her parade, she decided to throw a party for a large contingent of her friends from prior film and television projects.

Melissa Alano had just dropped a fortune at her plastic surgeon's office for the occasion. She wanted to look good for the governor and his entourage, who promised to make an appearance later that day. Even one of California's U.S. senators and his partner planned on attending.

The early morning party featured a spread of breakfast delectables and a never-ending supply of cocktails. Namely, mimosas and bloody marys. When the foreshocks around Mettler began, they all joked about how wonderful it was to be so close to nature. The magnificent view of the mountains. The pristine water. Even the reminder that their glorious planet was a living, breathing organism.

Then the energy from the massive Mettler earthquake, barely twelve miles away from the grand party, ripped the planet open. The initial shaking knocked the guests to the ground. Most had experienced earthquakes in the past. When the ARkStorm hit, Hollywood stars had fled for Las Vegas or the mountains of Colorado. A few of the actors had appeared in big-screen disaster films made using artificial intelligence. In their minds, they were no stranger to catastrophes.

"Everyone! Please don't be alarmed," Alano cried out as the massive quake continued to rumble underwater, sending shock waves in all directions. "Let's get back to the house. It's been built to withstand an earthquake."

The dignitaries pushed and shoved to reach the boardwalk leading up the bluff. Those who arrived at the platform walkway first were greeted by boulders and rocks tumbling down the side of the ridge. Some were killed instantly. Others were trampled as the guests ran away from the deluge. In less than a minute, the wooden boardwalk was destroyed under the weight of the rocks pummeling it.

Now they were trapped on the man-made sandy beach as the ground continued to shake.

Alano tried to play the role of field general to defend her guests from the onslaught of rubble. "Everyone, this way! Let's get away from the cliff. Hurry! As far away as possible. By the water!"

Her distinguished guests lost all sense of decorum as they reversed course back toward the shoreline. A few, however, took a relaxed, lackadaisical approach to the disaster. They began to swig champagne out of the bottle and take videos of the unfolding catastrophic event.

Now huddled against the shore, they watched in fear as the rocks continued to tumble. The sheer volume of boulders tumbling down the bluff concerned them, as the beach was beginning to shrink before their eyes. Then their moods lightened somewhat as the shaking stopped and the rollicking boulders became fewer in number.

A loud creaking sound could now be heard emanating from above them. All eyes were directed up the bluff.

"Um, Melissa, is your home gonna stay up

there?" one of her guests asked. A legitimate question in the minds of nearly everyone. The stately mansion was perched as close to the edge of the cliff as the engineers would allow. It seemed to be teetering on the brink of collapse. It was easily four times the size of the beach they stood on.

"Absolutely," she said with conviction. "I wouldn't have spent forty million dollars to build it if I thought it might tip over some day."

Her braggadocio joke drew laughter from her pals. The mood relaxed, but their eyes remained affixed on the house, still a considerable threat, hovering nearly a hundred feet above them.

They were looking in the wrong direction.

As the Mettler earthquake unfolded, the Garlock Fault pushed open. Within a minute, the north side of the fault jutted upward, and the southern side sheered downward. The energy generated at the epicenter raced away in all directions. Much of the shock wave's energy was trapped along the steep rock walls bordering the lake.

On the surface, the water followed a similar pattern. A pulse of water pushed outward from the epicenter as if the lake had been hit by a comet or an asteroid. The waves caused by the disturbance began to build. Ten feet quickly grew to thirty feet as it approached the coastline. By the time the inland tsunami hit Pine Mountain Club, it was twenty feet above the shoreline.

The party was over.

The powerful tsunami crushed everything in its path against the rocky bluff. People were killed instantly by the massive blow. Those who survived the initial wave were sucked back into the lake, only to be forced against the rocks a second time as the surrounding mountains on the southern end of Lake California created a large *seiche*, a sloshing back and forth against the enclosure akin to water movement in a bathtub before it was drained.

CHAPTER FORTY-EIGHT

USGS
Santa Rosa, CA

"We have tsunamis!" the analyst exclaimed, drawing the attention of the entire USGS team.

Kemp walked briskly toward the young woman's workstation and studied her monitor. "Thirty feet? Am I reading that correctly?"

"Yes, ma'am. Ridgecrest is flooding. The water is rushing toward the Temblor Range at an estimated speed of eighty miles an hour."

"Issue a warning!" she ordered.

"Ma'am, there isn't one. An inland tsunami

warning system was never set up for Lake California. We still haven't finished the ShakeAlert."

"Dammit!" Kemp yelled as she turned away from the monitoring station.

She retrieved her phone and found the governor's office in her contacts. She placed the call and received the switchboard. Nobody in the executive office was working that day. She asked to be connected to Cal OES, the California Governor's Office of Emergency Services.

After getting the highest-ranking official in the office, she identified herself and then simply said, "Get everybody off the lake and away from the shoreline!"

Naturally, the official questioned her, and she screamed at him, reflecting her sense of urgency.

"Do it! We have massive tsunamis approaching the southern shoreline. This will likely cross the entire lake before it's over. Do you understand?"

"Holy shit!" exclaimed a geophysicist, who suddenly jumped out of his chair. Startled, Kemp fumbled her phone, and it dropped to the floor. The OES manager on the other end tried to get her attention, to no avail.

"What now?" Kemp asked.

"Parkfield! Wait." A hush grew over the monitoring center. The man's arm was raised in the air as he hunched over his computer monitor. "M7.3."

"Concur!" shouted another. "Epicenter is a few miles north of Parkfield, east side of the fault."

While Parkfield boasted the distinction of being the Earthquake Capital, it had never experienced a major quake compared to the northern and southern ends of San Andreas where the fault locks up, accumulating stress and strain.

"Garlock intersects near there!" shouted one of the analysts, stating the obvious, at least to the people in the monitoring center.

"Where's my phone?" shouted Kemp, who searched her pockets.

The center's supervisor returned to where they'd been standing and located it. He handed it to her as more analysts were calling out the data from the quakes. She called her secretary again.

"Where the hell is Atwood?"

Still no answer, her secretary explained.

"Confirming aftershocks," an analyst in the front row announced. "Just south of Mettler, twin mag fives struck both sides of the canyon. It's gonna squeeze the dam."

"Grapevine Dam?" asked an analyst who stood

in the back of the room. "Are you referring to the Grapevine Dam?"

"Affirmative," the earth scientist who'd trained at NASA replied.

"I was copied on an email from FERC. They were scheduled to open the spillways at Grapevine today. That will expose the weaker, more permeable layers of the earthen dam. Without the water adding stability, the upstream slope will not be able to absorb the stress waves from the aftershocks."

Kemp walked toward the earth scientist. "What happens when the tsunami hits the dam?"

A geophysicist near her interjected, "By my calculations, it already has. Because of its close proximity to the epicenter at Mettler, the tsunami would be in the twelve-to-fifteen-meter range. Well, eighteen to twenty feet."

"What about that? Eighteen feet?" asked Kemp. Her mind was racing. If the Grapevine Dam were to potentially suffer a structural failure, evacuations would need to be ordered at Edwards Air Force Base and into Santa Clarita. Maybe more.

"Most likely, the dam will suffer a hydraulic failure caused by the overtopping of the dam. With the spillways open, there is a drawing of the lake toward the canyon opening already. This would add speed to the tsunami. It's kind of like a hurricane arriving in a coastal region during high tide. Flooding is exacerbated by the tides.

"Also, a structural failure is likely as the upstream face and shoulders, the sides, would be crushed under the enormous weight of the water. The sudden drawdown by the dam engineers coupled with the tsunami effect would be devastating to the structural integrity."

Kemp held her phone and looked for her recent calls. She had to warn Cal OES again. She quickly placed the call to the overwhelmed staff of Cal OES in San Francisco. They relayed to her that Ridgecrest was practically underwater from a thirty-two-foot tsunami wave.

Kemp closed her eyes and sighed. For decades, the state had prepared itself for the so-called *Big One*. The ARkStorm, dubbed the *Other Big One*, had proved the state was threatened by more than seismic activity. Now, a biblical flood was once again going to be unleashed on Southern California. All the rebuilding efforts would be threatened by a wall of water that rivaled the deluge caused by the ARkStorm.

Yet, thus far, the quakes had struck in sparsely populated areas. Mettler was underwater, and Parkfield was in an isolated part of the mountains with a population of eighteen.

Kemp wanted to find a bright side. The epicenters of the two recent quakes were isolated. Property damage from the ground shaking would be minimal. Loss of life could've been far worse. She expected Lake California to stabilize, eventually. She began to wonder, *Could the Big One actually be several large ones equal to a single, massive Big One?*

As her mind wandered, she was knocked off her feet.

CHAPTER FORTY-NINE

Mac's Floating House
Mount Vaca, CA

It had happened so fast. Maybe forty-five seconds in duration. But in that short period of time, the earthquake along the Green Valley Fault that ran ten miles east of NAPA underneath the Vaca Mountains had threatened to destroy everything he owned.

And him.

One by one, the rollicking waves thrashed underneath his floating house, causing the dock lines to be stretched. The continuous pulling and tugging yanked the cleats free of the floating dock. In a matter of seconds, the houseboat had been ripped away and tossed wildly on the surface of Lake California as more massive waves rolled underneath it.

Mac regained his footing in time to view another wave smack the side of his fishing boat, tossing it onto the dock momentarily, until the Boston Whaler was pulled free of its cleats. The boat turned on its side, spun around, and then was thrown onto the shore, where it crashed hard into a stand of trees.

As his houseboat was being pulled away from land, he became mesmerized by the shoreline being eaten up by the massive waves that swallowed it in large chunks. His Jeep began to slide down the muddy embankment until it, too, succumbed to the onslaught of water.

Mac lost his focus and his grip on the railings. His floating house was adrift, wholly at the mercy of the tsunami generated by both the Mettler quake and the one that had just occurred nearby.

He slid down the water-soaked decking toward the entertainment deck of his boat. He desperately grabbed at the polished, stainless railings that protected passengers from falling overboard. The shaking was too violent. He couldn't get a grip. He slid to the back and almost flew off the stern before he managed to grab onto a loose dock line.

With all the strength his battered body could

muster, Mac held on. His mind raced as he fought for his survival. He tried to calculate whether he'd be better off in the water, using his excellent physical conditioning to swim ashore. Or should he stay on board until the tsunami subsided?

Mac gripped the rope tighter. He'd take his chances on the houseboat. He looked toward the shore, desperately searching for his boat. Like his Jeep, it was now gone. He glanced behind him as the waves bashing his house tried to dislodge him. It was a monster. A devilish creature in search of lives to extinguish.

"Not mine!" Mac yelled. With a herculean effort, he pulled himself upright. He gripped the railing once again and tugged himself toward the open sliding doors. Once he reached the opening, he was not surprised to see his living area filled with water.

He pulled the door shut and locked it to keep the demon outside. His rooftop solar panels managed to continue delivering power to his generator. The combination of his body's fatigue and the cool air that continued to spill out of his air-conditioning vents caused him to shiver uncontrollably.

He tried to walk into his bedroom in search of his phone and a towel. The waves rolling under the house made him look like a drunken sailor in search of his bunk. Two steps forward, three steps to one side or the other.

Locating a towel to dry off was easy. The cell phone was nowhere to be found. Anything not permanently attached to the floating house had been thrown about. Picture frames with photos of his family had been knocked to the floor. His empty glass of whiskey was shattered. The dresser drawers had been thrown out and emptied.

Mac sat on the bed, resigning himself to remaining on board and adrift. The turbulent waters would've most certainly pulled him under or crushed him against a larger object like a tree or the remains of his dock. As he tumbled back and forth on his bed, he tried to make sense of it all.

He was aware of the studies by the USGS at Lake Tahoe regarding the potential for inland tsunamis. While Tahoe had never experienced a quake capable of generating a tsunami, the science supported the possibility. Naturally, the thousands of faults under Lake California would certainly generate a tsunami. But this one was massive.

Another wave rolled under his house, pushing it farther away from shore. Then came another from a different direction. Puzzled, Mac began walking around the interior of his house. He pulled the curtains away from the windows and tried to establish a pattern to the waves. He'd been pushed past the point on a ridge that once overlooked Vacaville. In just that short period of time, he'd been drawn away from shore by nearly a mile.

"It has to be the Green Valley Fault," Mac said aloud as he walked through the house and studied his surroundings.

There were four major faults in Northern California primed for a major earthquake. The Green Valley Fault, which ran between Fairfield and Napa, a mile or so from where Mac's floating house was once docked, was one of them.

He searched the floor for his Xero Barefoot shoes. The grippy soul was ideal for his excursions on the boat, and he'd even practiced swimming in them. After he slid them on, he made his way back onto the deck to get a better look at the ridge running along Mount Vaca.

Once outside, he could hear an aftershock that struck the ridge. It began as a slow rumble and then grew louder as the sound carried across the water. It echoed off the ridge, across the cove, and seemed to reverberate longer than the mainshock had lasted.

Mac gasped as he saw the destruction wrought

by the new quake and its equally destructive after-shock. The ridge was collapsing. Massive boulders crashed through the pines. Toppled trees slid toward the bank, followed by more rocks. It was marvelous and frightening at the same time.

The little-known Green Valley fault had always been recognized as having the potential to pack a significant punch. There were three fault segments loaded with enough tension to produce quakes of M7 or greater. Depending on the initial quake's length and duration, the dams and aqueducts north-east of San Francisco could be impacted. Even if the quake was confined to the fault running between Fairfield and Napa, the ridge below Mount Vaca could be altered considerably, as Mac was witnessing.

"What about the other side?" he shouted. He ran to the edge of the railing closest to his former dock. He stared at the top of the ridge. On the other side was Santa Rosa. Near the base of the ridge was Providence Memorial Hospital.

And Taylor.

CHAPTER FIFTY

Mac's Floating House
Lake California, CA

Inexplicably, Mac's home picked up speed as it floated aimlessly above the former town of Vacaville. At first, after it had been ripped from its dock, the house spun in circles, periodically dipping its stern or bow into the lake. Then it was pulled farther from shore as massive tsunami waves rolled underneath it. Now the floating house, which had no engine and no propeller, was picking up speed.

In that moment, Mac cursed the decision not to purchase a more conventional houseboat. One with a

hundred-and-fifty-horsepower outboard at a minimum. One that was somewhat capable of getting him
out of this disaster.

As the water seemed to carry him away from
shore and toward the center of Lake California, he
began to panic. It was making his task of swimming
to shore near impossible. Under perfectly still, early
morning conditions, he was capable of swimming to
shore from where Vacaville once stood. With the
waves rolling in all directions, he was uncertain
whether he could make it halfway, if that.

He'd resigned himself to waiting for help. A
rescue boat of some type. Or a floating chopper.
Surely, they'd be searching for stranded people like
himself, floating uncontrollably in their house. Mac
rolled his eyes at the thought.

Moreover, he'd have to trust that Taylor was safe
within the confines of the hospital. He tried to think
of how old Memorial was. Was it built to the most
recent earthquake standards? She was on the second
floor. It would be easy for her to evacuate, if need be.
He'd made the escape down the emergency stairwell
twice. It didn't take long.

Suddenly, his house was forced to a stop. Mac
was thrown off balance and crashed hard against the

side, smacking his head on the window. Then the floating house was turned as if it were on an axis. It was pushed toward the south. Toward where the Grizzly Island Wildlife Area once was. He recalled the stories of grizzlies making their way toward Los Angeles during the ARkStorm. Their swimming ability was now legendary. Mac's decision to stay out of the water was justified for this reason alone.

The house was being pulled around the bluff. Mac made his way inside again and searched for his binoculars. He kept a set on both his fishing boat and inside his house. *There!* he exclaimed in his mind. He rushed to the front of the house and studied the terrain that he knew so well from fishing its banks.

"That's odd," he muttered as he scanned the remains of the ridge that ran north and south from Fairfield past Mount Vaca. He continued to mumble aloud, "The water level is dropping. And where did this communication tower come from?"

A small ridge stood alone between Fairfield and Vacaville. Its elevation of eight hundred feet was easily underwater after the ARkStorm. Sitting atop the ridge was a communications tower once utilized by emergency responders in the area. Now a small portion of the lattice-style tower had breached the lake's surface, revealing the myriad of antenna equipment.

The house lurched forward again, knocking Mac to his knees. The sudden, quick movement made no sense. The waves were still rolling past him, but they were smaller now. The effects of the inland tsunami were starting to dissipate.

He visualized a scene from the movie *Jaws* in which the massive underwater beast had taken a hold of a dock line and began towing a group of hapless souls across the water. He was beginning to feel hapless as well.

Subconsciously, he scanned the water in search of a dorsal fin. He broadened his search toward the south where Fairfield had been submerged under the lake. His body tensed, and he straightened his back. After removing the binoculars from his eyes, he blinked rapidly and looked through them again.

He screamed at the turbulent waters ahead of him, "No freakin' way! Not again. No way!"

A massive whirlpool had formed in the lake that dwarfed the eddy he and Taylor had been caught up in. He'd never survive this one. At least the Orca was watertight. Mac's floating house would be ripped apart after the first trip around the whirlpool.

He had to think fast. All of his predictions were

coming to fruition. Perhaps it was karma for thinking up such awful shit and telling people about it. Regardless, there had to be a rift at Garlock that had caused the tsunami activity. There had to be a smaller rift at Green Valley, obviously near Fairfield, to create this massive whirlpool.

However, the lake levels were dropping precipitously. Were there more than two earthquakes? Had San Andreas erupted into the Big One that everyone feared? At the moment, none of that mattered. Mac had to abandon ship. It was his only hope.

He tore off his clothes and shoes. Naked, he ran into his bedroom in search of the Speedo swimsuit he despised so much. It didn't matter. He needed to be sleek. He'd need to be able to pump his legs with all of his strength to avoid the gravitational pull of the vortex exerting its force on the lake's surface.

He rushed onto the deck and took a final glance at the whirlpool to confirm he wasn't overreacting. It loomed large on the horizon. He smacked the side of his floating house with his palm and said goodbye.

Mac ran toward the stern and got his bearings. The closest parcel of land was the top of the small ridge overlooking Fairfield. He could use the communications tower that rose above the peak as a point of reference.

He didn't waste another second as he ran toward the water and pushed off the edge of his floating house. Using the overhead swim stroke that had propelled him hundreds of miles during his years living on the ridge at Mount Vaca, he never looked back to watch his home swallowed by the earth.

CHAPTER FIFTY-ONE

Lake California

As the tectonic plates moved away from each other, the Earth's crust and upper mantle stretched and pulled apart. Under Lake California, numerous deformations appeared near the Mettler epicenter, along the coast below Parkfield and now southeast of where Vacaville once stood. Some of the chasms ran parallel to the San Andreas and Garlock Faults. However, due to the chain reaction caused by the massive quake at Mettler, the chasms splintered off, perpendicular to the larger faults.

The most pronounced rift along the Garlock Fault stretched for miles between Mettler and Ridgecrest. The rift was being pulled in multiple directions at once as the deformations ran both parallel and perpendicular to the fault.

The planet surface was being torn to shreds, a phenomenon that gave rise to a superplume. As the rift widened and became deeper, huge rising jets of hot, partially molten rock originating deep beneath the earth found their way through the upper mantle.

These superplumes were much larger than those associated with the Hawaiian Island chain of volcanoes. The molten rock, at the Earth's core, measured around eight thousand degrees Fahrenheit. As it rose upward and met the seventy-two-degree water of Lake California, it cooled. However, not before it had a boiling effect.

For miles, the superheated water caused visible bubbling across the lake's surface. Any creatures or plant life underwater were killed instantly.

Nearby, a duck boat, a floating vehicle capable of navigating on the lake as well as driving on a street, had been taking tourists on a tour of the stars' hilltop homes. They were traveling along the top of the Garlock Fault when the quake hit. Their proximity to the fault prevented them taking the brunt of the tsunami that was created. However, they were unable to avoid the boiling water that followed soon thereafter.

At first, the tour operator tried to calm his passengers when they first noticed fish popping to the surface around them. The partially boiled skeletal remains were nauseating for even the strongest stomachs. But then the surface water began to boil, sending the cruisers into a full-blown panic.

They urged the driver of the duck boat to go faster. They begged him to head toward shore. When he countered the tsunami might tip them over, they argued they'd take their chances.

"What about the heat?" a man asked.

"No worries," came the response. "The aluminum hull is rated to three hundred fifty degrees."

The water was approaching four hundred degrees. The vessel's propellers had failed, leaving the duck boat at the mercy of the rollicking waves and boiling water. Soon, the aluminum hull began to expand and oxidize. Its strength was compromised. A heavyset man standing in the middle of the boat suddenly fell through the floor and into the water. He screamed in agony as he reached for help, only to end up boiled alive.

Within minutes, as the vessel capsized, everyone suffered the same fate. Their bodies would never be found.

CHAPTER FIFTY-TWO

Providence Memorial Hospital
Santa Rosa, CA

Taylor had just been visited by a critical care nurse and was settling in for a nap when the ground started to violently shake beneath Memorial Hospital. Everything on tabletops or near the monitoring devices was knocked to the floor. Her bed was dislodged from the wall and began to slide across the floor. The television, disconnected by doctor's orders, careened off its bracket and crashed onto the windowsill.

Taylor fought the pain and made her way to the window in an effort to gauge the amount of damage the tremor was causing. It lasted nearly forty seconds, rattling the ceiling tiles out of their grids and loosening the fluorescent light fixtures until they swung by their metal electrical conduit.

Shouting was heard from the hallway as well as feet carrying frantic hospital personnel in all directions. Fire alarms were blaring. Medical monitoring equipment was beeping. The electronics were having a fit.

Until they stopped.

The hospital had lost power. When the emergency power generators kicked on, some of the devices came back online. However, because they needed to be reset, they simply emitted loud, incessant beeping that annoyed Taylor.

She pulled the plug on all of the devices and then unhooked the monitoring lines from her body. Just as she made her way to the door to enter the corridor, the plate-glass window shattered and broke into hundreds of pieces. The building was being twisted and turned by the force of the quake.

Then, inexplicably, the backup generators stopped delivering power. The entire building went dark except for the ambient light filtering in through the broken window.

Outside her room, mayhem ensued. Two

patients were being pushed on gurneys toward a freight elevator that was no longer working. At the far end of the corridor, frantic nurses argued over the best way to assist those on life support. They were the patients with no living will who had little hope of recovery. Sadly, their death sentence had just been executed.

The nurse who'd just checked in on Taylor ran past her. She was shouting to everyone who could hear her.

"All visitors! Leave the building now! Please, through the emergency exits at either end of the hallways. Patients who are ambulatory, please make your way to the emergency stairwell."

Taylor started toward the emergency exit and then stopped. She owed it to the medical team in the intensive care unit to help. They'd saved her life and kept her comfortable.

Wearing cotton pajamas and hospital socks with grippy soles, she moved to the nurses' station at the middle of the ICU. Several hospital personnel were gathered around, using a triage method to determine which patients should be moved out first. Their voices were hurried but not panicked.

"ICU patients won't stand a chance without

their ventilators or infusion pumps for their IV thera-
py," a second-year resident warned.

"We have no power," added a nurse. "There's no
power out there, either. We don't have a choice but
to hope the genny comes back online."

"Okay, agreed. We have to escort the patients out
in wheelchairs. We'll roll them backwards down the
emergency stairs."

"Where are the orderlies?"

"They're downstairs, I think."

The women fell silent for a moment until the
head nurse spoke up.

"Okay, I have the list for the first patients out.
Let's start there."

"Who will watch the others?"

The three nurses looked at one another.

"I will," interrupted Taylor.

"What? Miss Reed, right?" asked the nurse
who'd just looked in on her.

"Yes. I can help. Just tell me what to do."

"You need to leave, young lady," ordered the
oldest nurse. She ran her finger down the list of
patients on their floor. "Geez! You have a concussion. One of you help her. Go now!"

"I won't," Taylor responded stubbornly. "I'm
fine. Please let me help."

One of the nurses leaned into the oldest nurse and whispered, "She could help keep the patients calm and show them how to protect themselves. That will free us up to evacuate the others."

"Dammit! I don't like it. Booher will have my ass if this one injures herself further."

"I'll say you didn't know," offered Taylor.

The head nurse sighed. "Fine. However, you proceed slowly and deliberately. No sudden moves. No heroics. Got it!"

She means business, Taylor thought to herself. "Got it."

Taylor was pulled aside and instructed to visit each of the critical care recovery rooms. She was to advise the patients a nurse would be by to see them and they'd be evacuated soon. In the meantime, if they were bedbound, they should cover their head with their pillows and stay under the covers in case there was an aftershock. For those who could move, if they could, exit the building. If they weren't strong enough to evacuate on their own, they needed to get under a desk or stand in the doorframe leading into the bathroom or hallway. Windows should be avoided.

She began to systematically move from room to room. She provided a comforting word or prayer to everyone she met. They thanked her profusely until she had to pull away to assist another patient.

Throughout, she ignored the pain radiating through her body. *The threat posed by the earthquake is simply a test of my mettle*, she thought to herself. Taylor believed in signs, very much like a geophysicist had a gut feeling an earthquake swarm might develop into something much larger. She felt like this was the first opportunity in her lifetime to make a real difference.

She continued her work, emboldened by the words of appreciation from the other patients. She noticed the ICU floor was gradually being emptied by the nursing staff and a few orderlies who'd returned from the first floor.

Only the patients on ventilators and monitoring devices were suffering. She'd learned the generators had been damaged by a collapsing wall. There was no hope for those patients. They were carried out on stretchers and taken to the ground level, where ambulances from other medical facilities awaited them.

Taylor had lost track of time, only focusing on the task at hand. Methodically, the floor was being emptied of patients and personnel. She reached the last room at the east end of the corridor. An elderly woman had rolled out of bed and fallen to the floor. Her body was wrapped in her covers. Apparently, in the chaos and darkness, the nurse who checked this room didn't notice what had happened.

Taylor rushed to the side of her bed. She flung open the blinds so some daylight could enter the room. She tried to rouse the woman but was unsuccessful. Then, reluctantly, she checked for the unthinkable. She held her fingers to the woman's wrinkled skin near her carotid artery. There was no pulse.

Taylor's chin dropped to her chest. She began to sob. She'd never seen the woman before and knew nothing of her condition. She was another patient, just like her, in their most vulnerable state. They had looked into the eyes of strangers, pleading for help. Begging doctors to perform miracles to keep them alive. And they had.

Taylor, like this woman, had survived whatever had beset them. They were in recovery. The next step was discharge. For this woman, it probably meant a loving husband of many years and children and grandchildren and her church and an annual cruise.

For Taylor, it meant she could spend a lifetime with the man she barely knew but whom she'd quickly fallen in love with. She began to say a prayer for the woman and then closed her eyes to thank God for her own good fortune.

Then the ceiling fell on top of her, and the east wing of the hospital crashed to the ground with her in it.

CHAPTER FIFTY-THREE

Lake California

Mac's conditioning took over. He forced himself to eliminate the peril created by the nearby whirlpool. His entire focus was on the protruding communications tower and its multiple radio masts that were remarkably intact over the years. Because the rebuilding effort following the ARkStorm demanded so many state and federal resources, the task of cleaning up what was under the surface of Lake California had not yet begun. Unlike the building of new lakes, such as when the Tennessee Valley Authority began to build dams, California wasn't able to eliminate potential subsurface hazards.

As the water receded, ostensibly sucked into the

chasms created by the earthquakes, both natural and man-made features began to reveal themselves. The communications tower provided Mac a landmark to swim towards as well as a potential resting spot before he made the final leg of his swim toward land.

Despite his adrenaline being at its highest levels, Mac remained calm and relied upon his training to steadily propel himself through the water. His elbows high, his toned arms alternated circling through the water to pull his body along. His legs kicked in perfect rhythm, not overexerting or attempting to push him toward an unsustainable pace.

He glanced back only once. His house was gone, not unexpectedly. Several boats were about to succumb to the same fate. They swirled around and around. Slowly at first. Then, as they dipped below the surface, their speed picked up until they disappeared. Mac caught his breath and continued swimming, satisfied that he'd cleared the powerful tow of the whirlpool's circular motion.

He was half a mile from the tower when he heard the faint roar of a boat motor approaching. He stopped for a moment and kicked his legs to raise his upper body a little higher out of the lake. He was able to get a look at the surface water near the communications tower.

Traveling from right to left was a jet ski effortlessly skimming across the lake's surface. The watercraft's lone rider appeared to be hunched over the steering wheel to lessen the drag his body created. Mac had seen many jet skis during his childhood and his days on Lake California. This one was small, maybe a one- or two-seater, and traveling at a high rate of speed.

His first inclination was to stay where he was so the reckless driver didn't run over him. Then, as the watercraft got closer, Mac considered hitching a ride.

He swam as if he were on the final leg of a two-hundred-meter freestyle event in the Summer Olympics. He forgot about pacing himself. He urged his body to find the strength to pick up speed, giving it his all to reach a point where he could get the jet ski driver's attention.

His right arm sliced into the water, coupled with a furious kick. Then the left arm did the same. Mac kept his head down, like the jet ski driver, to minimize the drag as he sped across the lake's surface.

He was close to a point where he thought the jet ski driver could see him. Mac stopped and kicked furiously to raise his body off the surface, wishing he had a powerful tail fluke like a dolphin uses to dance on water. He waved his arm back and forth with each effort. He shouted as loud as his tired lungs would allow.

With one final effort, he kicked his torso upward, waved, and shouted, "Hey! Over here!"

It worked!

The driver suddenly rose from his hunched-over position and turned to look in Mac's direction. Distracted as he focused on Mac, he drove into the center of the lattice-like steel structure. He was decapitated by the supports holding the antennas, and his body was knocked off the jet ski by the steel tower supports. The jet ski continued forward until it stopped, aimlessly turning in a circle as the motor shut down.

"Oh, sweet Jesus," said an astonished Mac. His attempt to seek help had killed the young man, who became distracted by Mac's shouting and waving. "His head. Dammit! I killed him!"

Mac was overwhelmed with horror and then grief. Tears flowed down his face as he forced himself to tread water amidst the horrific experience. His mind tried to help him by denying what he'd just seen. Maybe he was wrong. Maybe the man had simply been knocked off.

Mac began swimming furiously toward the communications tower, having convinced himself the driver was simply knocked off. *He might be unconscious*, Mac told himself. He had to prevent the driver from drowning. Getting to shore and Taylor never crossed his mind. Now Mac had become a one-man version of a search and rescue team.

As he reached the tower, the well-being of the rider revealed itself immediately. Near the antenna array, the teen's head bobbed and rolled in the water. His lifeless eyes would point toward Mac before the still-choppy water turned it in the other direction.

Mac spontaneously vomited. He retched over and over again. He used his arms to push himself away from the contents of his stomach, which seemed to be floating toward the man's bloody head. The thought of the two merging into one pile of floating scum caused him to vomit again.

He finally found his way to one of the steel supports to hold onto. He turned his upper body away from the head and his vomit. He focused on the shoreline and the jet ski rocking back and forth on the surface. Mac's breathing became shallow and fast. He was panicking.

Don't panic!

Internally, he argued with himself as to whether panicking was justified considering a severed head was floating a dozen feet from him.

Dammit, Mac! Don't panic!

He stopped breathing, a dangerous technique that would draw the ire of any physician. For Mac, it was the only way to force himself to calm down. He held his breath for fifteen seconds. Then twenty. He'd counted thirty potatoes before he let out a deep exhale. As always, his technique worked.

Mac wiped the tears from his eyes and caught his breath. He put the ordeal out of his mind for the moment. His body ached from the furious swim toward the tower. He'd need to rest before he started for shore. He glanced across the surface of the water, and his eyes became affixed on the jet ski.

"You're such an asshole, Mac Atwood."

He cursed himself. However, he knew what he needed to do. He began swimming toward the watercraft. It was no longer running, which was not surprising. Most riders wrap a cord around their wrist that is attached to the jet ski's key. In the event the driver is thrown off, the key is easily removed, and the jet ski comes to a halt.

Mac had to make sure that was the case. He arrived at the Sea-Doo and lifted himself out of the water to search for the key. It was missing. Instantaneously, he became sick to his stomach again. The key was most likely attached to the dead rider's wrist.

He had to find the body.

A corpse initially sinks to the bottom of a body of water as water replaces the air in its lungs. Then, as the body decomposes, it will float back upward. Mac didn't have time to wait for the corpse to decompose. He had to find it now.

He swam back to the tower and looked for a way to climb up. Even if it was five or ten feet, it would give him a view of the lake and what was just below the surface. He was an accomplished diver and was able to hold his breath for long periods of time. If he could catch a glimpse of the corpse as it slowly descended, he could retrieve the key.

Mac reached the tower and found a footing on a steel support just below the surface. It was a longshot, but he had to try. He crouched down and jumped upward with his arms extended in an effort to grab ahold of the next support.

He got it. Both hands were firmly grasping the support as his legs and body swayed just above the water. He set his jaw and held his breath, willing his body to respond to his brain's commands. He did a pull-up until he could wrap his arm around the support. Then he swung one leg onto it before catching his breath again. Seconds later, he'd pulled himself up completely and slid on his butt to the upright support.

Mac was now standing and had a clear view of the water around the communications tower. It was murky due to the series of tsunami waves that had rolled past this part of Lake California. To Mac, it seemed like hours ago since his house had been ripped from his dock. In fact, it had been more like fifty minutes.

He covered his eyes from the blinding sunlight. He looked for any shadow that seemed to indicate something floating just below the surface. For minutes, he desperately searched. He glanced toward shore and estimated the distance.

Maybe the jet ski isn't necessary, he thought to himself. Then he recalled how the lake stretched around the ridge at Mount Vaca until it made its way into San Pablo Bay to the south of Santa Rosa. He could save hours of walking if he could find the key.

He redoubled his efforts and focused all of his senses on the water.

There! Something bright white. Mac closed his eyes and forced himself to replay the moment the driver's body had been torn from the jet ski's seat.

The young man had been wearing white swim trunks with red and blue stripes. He had been celebrating the nation's independence when he'd died.

Mac didn't hesitate. He dove off the steel support, and his body sliced through the surface. Once underwater, he opened his eyes and searched for the flash of white he'd just seen.

He couldn't find it. He was now fifteen feet underwater, holding his breath, and using his arms to turn in circles. He turned and swam in the direction of the communications tower to look again. In his haste, he crashed headfirst into the torso.

Mac was startled and spontaneously yelled while under water. Several small fish ran into him as they approached the bloody corpse in a frenzy. Mac set aside his terror and reached out for the corpse, grabbing the young man's ankle. He pulled himself forward, feeling his way along the body, fighting back the urge to vomit underwater.

His hand ran up the still warm body until it reached the neck. Mac felt the goo where the driver's head had been removed. His stomach convulsed, and he vomited into the water. Mac was saved from drowning that day because he'd already emptied the contents of his stomach earlier. The smooth stomach contents came out quickly and allowed him to recover without inhaling the lake water.

He reached the man's wrist and found the rubber stop/start safety lanyard. He wrapped it around his own wrist and propelled himself upward. When he breached the surface, he gasped for air and then promptly vomited again.

CHAPTER FIFTY-FOUR

Lake California

Mac treaded water for a moment and then swam to the tower. The severed head and his earlier vomit had sunk below the surface, leaving the water mostly clean. He took a chance and cupped his hands to fill them with the warm lake water. Just as he brought it to his nostrils, he detected the smell of sulfur. He was puzzled as to why he hadn't noticed it before or why it was being released now.

When fresh water smells like sulfur, there can be a variety of reasons. Ordinarily, it's because of pollutants being dumped into the lake. That rotten-egg odor is created when hydrogen sulfide is released into the water, creating a foul-smelling gas.

Mac looked around the surface of the lake in search of bubbles. A geophysicist knows the presence of sulfur gases could result from magma being present in the groundwater. As the magma rises, the sulfur reacts with the water to create hydrogen sulfide.

This puzzled Mac. The closest volcano to the Bay Area was two hundred seventy miles to the southeast at the Long Valley Caldera. He shook off the thought of what that meant. He wasn't a volcanologist although he was aware of the science. Taylor, however, would certainly be interested in this discovery.

Taylor. The task at hand.

Mac had a newfound sense of purpose. He discarded the water and dove back into the lake. He swam furiously toward the jet ski. Getting to Taylor was foremost on his mind, but the rapid drop in the lake's levels might affect his ability to make his way through the straits into San Pablo Bay.

He pulled himself up onto the rear deck of the Sea-Doo and settled onto the seat. He grasped the handlebars and turned them left to right to get a feel for the jet ski. He clipped the tether key to just below the handlebar and pushed the red Start/Stop button.

The jet ski started easily. Mac didn't hesitate to

apply full throttle to the Sea-Doo. It had been a while since he'd zipped across the lake on a rented Yamaha WaveRunner, but the watercraft were similar, and the principles were the same. He followed the shoreline in order to keep his bearings. He was used to fishing in the coves along the base of the ridge, but now the terrain had changed.

The water had receded, exposing thirty or forty feet of muddy shore. Structures like small cabins or utility buildings appeared here and there. Trees were still standing, devoid of foliage, creating an eerie boneyard along the exposed base of the ridge.

Mac suddenly became mindful of the potential threats just below the surface. The closer he got to the Carquinez Strait, the more likely he was to encounter bridges and jetties on both sides of Suison Point.

He never bothered to look at the fuel gauge. He needed some good luck, and if he ran out of fuel, at least he'd be closer to Santa Rosa. He tried to visualize the shoreline on the north end of San Pablo Bay. A dam had been built near Sears Point, the home of the famed Sonoma Raceway.

The purpose of the dam was to keep water from approaching Santa Rosa. He hoped the quake hadn't damaged the earthen dam at Sears Point. The floodwaters would certainly reach downtown Santa Rosa thirty miles to the north. *Although,* Mac thought to himself, *the lower water levels might keep the lake within its natural boundaries before the ARkStorm hit.*

He focused on the lake's surface directly in front of him to avoid any hazards. Although, his curiosity got the best of him once he entered Grizzly Bay and made the turn toward the straits. Parts of the land that he'd never seen since the biblical rainstorms had beset the state were reappearing. The light posts that lined the Benicia-Martinez Bridge rose above the surface.

Mac's heart raced. He was getting closer. He easily dodged a submerged barge that had landed on its stern and turned its bow toward the sky. It was now protruding above the water. On both sides of the straits, buildings began to appear that had once been buried in an underwater graveyard. Another communications tower appeared on his right. He made a point to steer clear of it. Also, on his right was the Training Ship *Golden Bear,* a five-hundred-foot freighter that had been turned into a classroom for the California State University Maritime Academy. It was still tethered to its dock although it was listing to port.

There were fires burning on the Santa Rosa side of the bay. It was common to experience fires following a large earthquake. The movement of the earth breaks gas pipelines. Flammable liquids can be spilled from their aboveground containers. Other combustible material can be ignited as buildings are damaged.

Mac had witnessed it all. However, not this close to home. Even his experience as a teen when the New Madrid Seismic Zone came to life hadn't come this close.

He passed the naval shipyard, now underwater but gradually coming back to the surface. He was on the final stretch, so he hunched over the handlebars and squeezed the throttle to its max.

Sears Point came into view. The dam was still intact. He was almost on dry land again. Thirty miles to Taylor. It seemed like an insurmountable distance until he considered what he'd just gone through.

"Piece of cake," he muttered to himself as he beached the Sea-Doo near Sonoma Raceway.

CHAPTER FIFTY-FIVE

**Providence Memorial Hospital
Santa Rosa, CA**

Taylor just lay there for a moment, not that she had a choice. She'd been awakened by the earth shaking again. Small pieces of concrete and a cloud of crumbled stucco dust had fallen onto her head. Most got caught in her hair. Some invaded her eyes, nose and mouth. Her brain warned her not to move. *Don't make matters worse*, it admonished her. *Get a handle on things before you act rash*, it continued, echoing her father's words when she'd gotten in trouble as a teen.

Don't panic. Mac's voice filled her head. She

wanted to open her eyes. See his face peering through the pile of rubble that had crashed upon her. She wanted the voice she heard in her head to be coming from his lips.

The events that had led her to the darkness that surrounded her came back in a rush. She was helping others. Going room to room, offering words of encouragement and prayer. Then, just as she was about to leave, she'd checked one last room. A room that others had disregarded as being empty. She could've done the same. Simply entered the emergency exit at the east wing of the hospital and moseyed out into the sunshine to join everyone else.

Something had been amiss. She had to investigate. Because that was who she was. She just had to know. Her gut was right. She'd found the woman who'd rolled out of bed, hidden from sight to anyone who didn't explore the entire room. Taylor had found her. She'd prayed over the woman's dead body. And now, here she was. Buried under the building, which had collapsed with her in it.

She recalled the building shaking violently for the second time. An aftershock. Or the mainshock. She hadn't had time to count Mississippis or potatoes or the seconds.

When the ceiling began to fall apart and the tiles

fell on top of her, she wasn't sure if she could crawl out of the room. She tried to scramble under the hospital bed, but there was no room. By the time she extricated herself from the stainless-steel bed frame, the tile floor covering a concrete slab began to crack and sink. It shattered like glass, in huge hunks of concrete tied together by rebar. She curled into a fetal position and buried her head in her arms as she rode the rubble to the ground floor.

Then came the rest of the east wing of Memorial's intensive care unit on top of her. The ceiling was followed by the walls falling inward. She tried to scramble away from the debris and then rolled over to avoid a steel roof support that came crashing down. She ended lying flat on her back, legs stretched out and her arms tucked against her body, when the rest of the upper levels fell upon her. That was when she blacked out.

Apparently, Taylor thought in hindsight, all of it covered her. It was almost completely dark. She didn't know if it was the millions of particles of dust swirling around or if she'd passed out and slept until evening. Or maybe there was so much debris on top of her that she was many feet away from daylight.

She kept her eyes closed despite the urge to open them and search her surroundings. She realized it was a fruitless exercise. Besides, the few particles that had already struck her eyeballs were causing them to itch. She desperately wanted to scratch at them. Rub the concrete dust from her eyes. If only she could free her arms from the remains of the hospital's east wing that pinned her down.

Taylor thanked God she wasn't claustrophobic. For, if she were, between the joyride in the Orca and now the building collapsing on top of her, she'd certainly have a panic attack that would result in heart failure.

Don't panic. Mac again.

"Yeah, yeah." The words were barely audible. However, hearing them aloud was somehow comforting to Taylor. It confirmed she was alive.

This brought a smile to her face. Maybe she was a cat? *I survived twice this week. Once, when I was in high school. When I found myself in the wrong place at the wrong time, much to the chagrin of my father, the former chief financial officer of Mercedes-Benz USA.* When he retired, he was rewarded for his generous political donations with an ambassadorship to Germany. Taylor chuckled. Germany, of all places. Imagine that.

That was her senior year in college, when she dated a guy who was a little on the crazy side. There was a party. The adults were out of town. There was drinking and weed. Her boyfriend was the host and a bit of a showoff. He was playing around with his parents' handgun in the backyard, shooting at beer cans stacked on the family's fence. That was when a stray bullet sailed over the fence and shot one of their friends who'd wandered into the woods to relieve himself.

The party was over, and Taylor's life was thrust into turmoil. Everyone at the party scattered except for her. She was loyal to a fault. She agreed to stay with her boyfriend until the police arrived. She took the gun from him and forced him to calm down. He was beyond distraught. He asked to be left alone for a minute. So Taylor went inside the house and waited.

When she heard shouts outside, she greeted the police, who'd been called by a neighbor. It was more like a SWAT team. They burst through the door, slammed her to the ground, and took the gun out of her hand. Moments later, she was under arrest.

"Why?" she'd asked. "My boyfriend shot the gun, not me," she'd explained.

"What boyfriend?" the officer had questioned. "There's nobody else here but you." She'd been abandoned to take the fall.

Now she was lying flat on her back, covered in concrete and steel and medical devices. Alone. Abandoned. Forgotten. It was the same sickening feeling she'd had that night as a teen. And that evening in the Orca. And now.

Except this time around, there was a guy named Mac Atwood. She was certain he wouldn't leave her alone. Even as another aftershock rattled the building that threatened to crush her.

CHAPTER FIFTY-SIX

Sears Point, CA

Mac was greeted by an aftershock that knocked him off his feet into the muck. His eyes had been studying the terrain just below Sonoma Raceway as he searched for the best way to get into Santa Rosa. Distracted, he immediately lost his balance as the ground shook, and he fell backwards. The landing wasn't hard because of the muddy conditions as the lake receded. However, it reminded him of something he'd lost sight of. He was practically naked.

Mac was only wearing the Speedo that was his swimwear of choice when he was distance training. The back of it was now covered in brown goop, which might lead someone to believe he'd lost control of his bowels for some reason. Well, there were several reasons, but Mac was not of the mindset to explain.

He'd hoped to hitch a ride into town. The way he looked, he doubted anyone would dare slow down, much less allow him in their vehicle.

Mac knocked off the excess mud and began the trek up the hill toward the entrance to the road course. He'd tried to count the seconds of the tremor. Without the aid of data, he was still capable of differentiating an aftershock from a strong earthquake.

"It doesn't mean it's over, pal," he mumbled to himself as he found the gates to the track locked. While he was atop the hill, he glanced up the road toward Santa Rosa. There were several small vineyards and wineries in sight. He'd take them one at a time until he had clothes and maybe transportation.

Barefoot, Mac began to jog up the slope away from the lake. In the distance, toward Santa Rosa, he saw black smoke trailing into what was otherwise a gorgeous Sonoma County day. The natural beauty of the area, including nearby Napa Valley, was what had drawn Mac to his cabin in the first place. To be sure, there were plenty of places to live closer to the original USGS campus at Sacramento when he started his new job. However, the woods and rural surroundings reminded him of home.

Mac approached the first winery with trepidation. It was a Victorian-style, two-story home perched on a hill. From a distance, Mac couldn't determine if it was a hundred years old or new. Regardless, near the highway, the winery had a store that was open to the public. Well, not anymore.

He presumed the first quake had been respon sible for its demise, as the aftershock he'd just experienced wasn't sufficient to pancake the building like this. The entire roof system had fallen in, blowing the four walls of the rectangular structure outward. It was possible the store was a converted barn or other form of outbuilding belonging to the Victorian home. It certainly wasn't built to the earthquake standards prevalent throughout California.

Mac was relieved to see that there were no cars in the parking lot. If customers had been inside, they would've likely died. He stopped to look at the demolished building and then past it toward the house. Up the road, there was another winery with a vineyard surrounding it. There were several undamaged buildings with better opportunities for clothing and a ride.

The minutes ticked away as Mac headed toward

town. He jogged when he could before his feet began to bleed from stepping on small pieces of asphalt and occasional bits of glass. He arrived at the next property. The winery retail building was intact, and Mac was amazed to find it unlocked. He politely knocked. He didn't want to be on the wrong end of a shotgun blast.

"Hello? Can anyone help me?"

With no answer, he slowly turned the knob and pushed the double-Dutch door inward. A bell rang above his head, causing him to instinctively jump back.

Mac laughed nervously. Anybody observing him would be more afraid of him than he was of them.

He slowly stepped inside. Warm, stale air struck his nostrils. The smell of wine, ordinarily pleasing to the palate, reeked in the enclosed space. Dozens of bottles had been knocked out of their racks, crashing hard on the wood floor. They'd broken and spilled through the cracks, leaving broken glass throughout the store.

The air-conditioning system and lighting were not working because the power had been knocked out. The shadows were growing long as the light of day faded. It gave him a new sense of urgency that would require him to take some risks.

"Hey! Anybody! I'm Mac Atwood with the USGS. I need your help."

Still no answer.

Mac was careful as he proceeded through the store, looking for clothing of any kind. He did find black tee shirts bearing the vineyard's logo on the front. He wasn't quite sure if the yellowish-gold insect was a bee, a moth, or a murder hornet. Regardless, he found an extra-large tee shirt on the floor that was larger than what he'd ordinarily purchase. He hoped it might cover his Speedo. It didn't.

As he was about to exit the store, he noticed a display that included a beach bicycle. The bottles of wine were still mostly intact, as they'd been crated. The labels depicted a beach cruiser bicycle that matched the actual bike on display.

Mac approached the display, keeping an eye on the floor for glass. He felt the tires of the Chatham Beach Cruiser. The orangish-brown color of the tires matched the brown leather seat and handlebar grips. He smiled as he squeezed them to check the air pressure.

He examined it further. There was a basket attached to the handlebars. At the rear, a flat rack was affixed above the wheel to match the sunflower-yellow frame. To top off the beachy design, a whirling sunflower would spin furiously as the rider took to the streets.

Mac actually debated whether to use the bicycle. He wasn't necessarily concerned about the looting aspect. He was certain the winery would be filing a substantial claim with their insurance company.

Rather, he tried to visualize his appearance as he sped up the streets leading to Memorial Hospital. Between the yellow color, the basket in front, the spinning sunflower in back, and the Speedo, he was certain he'd look like somebody cruising down Castro Street in San Francisco.

"Screw it," he said with a laugh. He grabbed a bottle of the wine and studied the label. He laughed as he read it. "Enjoy the ride."

Whatever it takes.

CHAPTER FIFTY-SEVEN

USGS
Santa Rosa, CA

Director Sierra Kemp rushed into the monitoring center the moment the shaking stopped. It was abysmal throughout the USGS building, but especially so inside the monitoring center. The generators only allowed enough power to operate emergency lighting and anything plugged into an outlet. Namely, computers. Telephone service in Santa Rosa had been knocked out, and cell service was spotty, as most of the towers lined the ridge on both sides of Mount Vaca.

"Talk to me, people!" she shouted the moment

she crossed the open door's threshold. Her established protocols in all aspects of operations on her campus were to follow the proper hierarchy, the chain of command. She'd always been a very hands-on administrator. In a crisis like this one, she circumvented her own policy and addressed all the geophysicists and analysts directly.

"Definitely an aftershock, ma'am," responded one of the scientists assigned to a cubicle. "Not near as strong as the mainshock."

"Sure felt like it," mumbled one of the analysts on Mac's team.

"It's a function of proximity," the monitoring station's supervisor on duty responded. He immediately asserted control over his team by fielding Kemp's questions. He stepped to one side and led her toward the front of the room. He directed her attention to the large screen in the center of the wall. "Please bring up the Green Valley mainshock and an overlay of the aftershocks, please." His demeanor was calm, likely one of the reasons he'd been promoted to his position.

The screen brightened considerably, causing several in the darkened room to quickly close their eyes until they adjusted. They'd been working in near darkness due to the power issues and to avoid excess heat being emitted by the lighting.

The supervisor stepped forward and pointed toward the ten-foot-diagonal monitor. "The epicenter of the Green Valley mainshock was here, just northwest of the old town of Fairfield, at the base of Mount Vaca. This aftershock, far less severe at M5.9, occurred closer to Napa, just up the ridge from Santa Rosa."

"Did we have someone monitoring Green Valley?" asked Kemp.

The supervisor gulped before responding, "No, ma'am. Not specifically. All eyes were on Mettler and Parkfield at that point."

Kemp sensed he felt negligent in failing to monitor other fault zones along San Andreas. "Listen, we don't have the staff to monitor all of them. Never have, never will. That's why we have to rely upon our seismographs and warning programs."

Kemp turned to the monitoring team. "Who's prepared to give me probabilities?" Undoubtedly, the governor's office would be ringing her phone off the hook if the lines were open. Fortunately, the USGS campus had Starlink satellite internet so they could operate. That also meant her email inbox would be flooded with inquiries.

"I can." A young woman on Mac's team raised her hand.

"Go ahead," said the supervisor.

"My area of responsibility is to monitor the seismograph data from that part of Lake California where installation was complete. Because we've not covered the area due east of San Jose toward old Modesto and Mammoth, I have to extrapolate data from the San Andreas Fault Zone in the Bay Area and apply it to the surrounding region." She paused to catch her breath.

Kemp walked closer to the analyst so she didn't have to speak as loud. The stuffiness in the monitoring center was causing most everyone to sweat profusely and also made breathing difficult at times.

"Please continue," she said in a hushed tone. The young woman nodded her appreciation.

"The ground is moving enough that we're not seeing anything below magnitude 3, which means less severe foreshocks and aftershocks may not have been noticed. That said, after the intense quake at Parkfield, and the fact the seismic jolt spread to and from other fault zones, Garlock and Green Valley, it's safe to say additional quake activity could occur on parallel and regional faults extending under the lake."

"They're jumping," mumbled Kemp.

"Yes, ma'am. Or it's a heckuva coincidence." She shook her head as she reflected her doubt in the coincidence theory.

"They're jumping," Kemp reiterated.

The analyst nodded and continued, "I believe the chance of another M5 to M5.5 is approaching certainty, especially at Cajon Pass where the faults intersect."

"And greater than that?" asked Kemp.

"After what we've experienced with these three quakes. You know, chain reaction, rapid succession. I'd wager that an M6 or equivalent is fifty percent, and I'd be prepared to make a preliminary estimate of another quake near M7 at about ten percent. If there is any upside, both Garlock and San Andreas released a lot of energy over a large swath of real estate during the past week. That may alleviate the stress on the plates. For now, anyway."

"Well, every quake has a one-in-twenty chance of being followed by an even bigger one," observed Kemp. That was what she planned on telling the governor's office just so they'd be vigilant. She fully expected her team to get thrown under the bus when it was time to address the media. "If only the USGS had given us advance warning," he'd say. Kemp sighed before her thoughts were interrupted.

The supervisor stepped in with an observation. "As we are seeing at Garlock, especially in the Ridgecrest area, and all along the mountainous region at Parkfield, aftershocks in the M3 to M4 range may continue for weeks. The same is likely here, although the Green Valley is much shorter, which will limit activity somewhat."

Kemp wandered back to the large projection screen to study the overlay of the various quakes that had tormented California. It was updating continuously with different-colored dots with an accompanying magnitude estimate. It was as if somebody were using a plastic gun tethered to a video game controller in an elaborate game of *Duck Hunt*. Only the targets were seismic zones.

Her mind wandered to Mac. They had been unable to reach him before the Green Valley earthquake struck Mount Vaca and the surrounding areas. His home was on the other side of the ridge and might have been impacted. Plus, she'd been monitoring reports on the emergency broadcast channels regarding the precipitous drop in the lake levels. His theories were not as farfetched as his fellow geophysicists claimed.

Kemp was also concerned by the discovery of the warmer water seeping into the Pacific at the newly discovered seamount. The data from the submersible registered potentially scalding one-hundred-forty-degree temperatures at the Orca's lowest point of descent the day the eddy formed. If the heated water escaping meant the plates were stuck in that region, then quakes could develop toward the east. Toward Mammoth and the Long Valley Caldera.

"Where are you, Atwood?" she mumbled as she left the monitoring center for her office. It was time to face the powers that be.

CHAPTER FIFTY-EIGHT

Santa Rosa, CA

Mac was astonished, and relieved, that very few people gave him a second glance as he pedaled furiously toward the hospital. His feet were still bleeding, leaving droplets along the pavement and splatter marks on the back of the yellow frame. The whirling sunflower held on for dear life, as Mac didn't let up, closing the thirty-mile gap between where he'd stolen the bike and Taylor as fast as his exhausted legs allowed.

When he arrived at the hospital, he was shocked to view the scene. How could part of a hospital collapse? The modern structure had to have been built to the highest level of earthquake requirements.

He was certain it was meticulously maintained and inspected. Yet the wing located on the east side of the hospital, behind the emergency room, had collapsed into itself.

Mac slid off the seat of the bike and left it leaning against a monument sign with the hospital's name on top and directions to the emergency room below it. He took in the chaos as he tried to determine where to begin. Surface parking was limited around the facility, as it was set in a densely populated area of homes as well as off-site medical offices.

Temporary triage tents had been established along Montgomery Drive in front of the hospital and in a parking area adjacent to Santa Rosa Creek. Yellow tape was wrapped around the front of the building and the entrance to the parking garage to warn people away from the structure. Remarkably, he didn't notice any fire and rescue crews on scene to search for missing patients. It appeared the hospital staff was on their own at the moment.

Without regard for his appearance, Mac began searching the triage tents. He'd poke his head in, say her name, and immediately get run off by a trauma surgeon trying to save lives. Mac wanted to respect the injured. He also needed to find Taylor.

One by one, he repeated his search efforts, only

to be rebuked by medical personnel. He refused to leave until he examined every patient under their care to confirm it wasn't her.

Several Memorial ambulances were parked near the emergency room entrance. Their lights were flashing and engines running as critically injured patients were being loaded. Mac approached the first one in line.

"Where are you taking these patients?" He had to shout his question over the ruckus.

"Petaluma," the driver replied brusquely. His eyes assessed Mac. "Stand back, please." The doors of his ambulance were slammed shut, and the orderlies smacked the back door twice to indicate he was authorized to leave. He turned on his sirens, which threatened to burst Mac's eardrums, before he wheeled away from the emergency room exit.

Because Taylor had been recovering in the critical care unit, he presumed she might be one of the patients being evacuated. So he searched and questioned everyone he came in contact with.

He approached a paramedic. "My friend was in the ICU recovery. Her name is Taylor Reed. Have you seen her?" Mac's eyes plead with the paramedic for help.

"These are ER patients, sir. ICU left first." The

man waved for the next patient to be brought to the back of the waiting ambulance.

"Have you been here the whole time? Do you remember Taylor Reed? She has long brunette hair. A bandage wrapped around her forehead from a concussion. Very pretty." Mac added that last part spontaneously.

The paramedic turned to Mac. "Listen, I've been bouncing all over the place. I don't remember anyone who looks like that, and I have no idea what their names are. We don't have time to get acquainted, you know? Try over there." He pointed toward the entrance where groups of patients were huddled around folding tables. Hospital administrative personnel had notebooks in front of them as they responded to inquiries.

Mac rushed to the table and was immediately scolded for cutting line. He was pointed by several of the loved ones seeking information to the rear of the line, some twenty-five people deep.

He waited impatiently for ten minutes or more. He grew aggravated with the people in front of him. Even though their inquiries had been answered, if it wasn't what they wanted to hear, they remained in place to badger the administrators. On several occasions, Mac was prepared to step in and tell the others to get out of the way.

Finally, Mac was able to speak to someone. "I'm looking for Taylor Reed. She was on the second floor, critical care recovery. Her doctor's name was Booher."

Over her glasses, the woman looked disapprovingly at Mac. "Are you a relative?"

"Yes, um, brother," he lied. Based on the woman's attitude, he didn't think fiancée would suffice, especially the way he was dressed.

She scowled. "I show the next of kin as her parents. No mention of a brother on her visitor list."

Mac suddenly understood why the people in line before him were perturbed. Now was not the time to follow health care privacy protocols to the letter.

"Visitor list? Okay, do you see Mac Atwood? That's me."

She ran her finger down the page until it landed on Mac's name. He reached over the table and pointed to it.

"Stand back, sir," she demanded as she pulled the three-ring binder off the table onto her lap. "Don't make me call security."

Mac looked around. There wasn't any security. Just mayhem.

"That's me," he repeated with a huff.

"Do you have identification?" she asked, her eyes studying him from head to toe.

He wanted to flip the table and lose his mind on this woman. "No, I don't. Obviously. I told you who I am."

"Well, sir, I don't have any information on Miss Taylor. You'll have to check back later."

Mac slammed both hands on the table, causing several people to scream. He gave the woman a death stare and then left, immediately regretting his outburst.

He felt helpless. He didn't know what to do. So he joined the chorus of others who were similarly frustrated. He began to shout her name as loud as he could.

"Taylor! Taylor Reed! Taylor, are you here?"

CHAPTER FIFTY-NINE

**Providence Memorial Hospital
Santa Rosa, CA**

Taylor tried to be patient. She tried to heed the warnings of the two most important men in her life. She didn't want to make things worse, and she vowed not to panic. The problem was nobody was coming to find her.

Once the aftershock subsided, she yelled to anyone who might hear her pleas. "Help! I'm trapped! Does anybody hear me? Help!"

Taylor began coughing uncontrollably. Dust seemed to coat her entire throat. No matter how much her body tried to clear the foreign objects, the dust seemed to increase in volume with each breath she took.

Regardless, she repeated her shouts for help. Each time she called out, she inhaled more of the concrete dust and floating debris. She became dejected when no one shouted back in response.

The sirens, shouting and screams of agony seemed miles away. Strangely, there were no other shouts for help. There wasn't the sound of a rescue team pulling away the rubble. There weren't the groans of injured people buried nearby. All she could hear was the sound of the debris continuing to find its way to the ground, following the path of least resistance through gaps created in the rubble. The rest, the sounds of a rescue effort, seemed to be in another world. Outside. Away from where Taylor was buried alive.

Taylor was determined not to be left behind. She wasn't going to be the subject headline from several days from now that read *Gruesome Discovery Made Beneath the Rubble at Memorial*. She was not a quitter. However, she also hadn't given up on Mac or a rescue team finding her. She needed to do her part, too.

The first thing was to conduct a self-assessment of her body's condition. She tried to make light of the fact that she'd already been beaten half to death in the submersible. Now, it seemed every piece of concrete had bounced off her once concussed head. Every piece of electrical conduit and rebar had found its mark where a deep bruise already existed. Naturally, the initial blow when she'd hit the ground floor had smacked her back in the exact place she had been pounded in the Orca.

She hurt so much it was impossible to determine where the pain was the worst. She started by wiggling her fingers and toes. Not paralyzed, that was a good thing. Then she flexed her muscles in her thighs, calves and arms. She was able to move her head from side to side. Again, a good thing. Finally, gently at first and then with more vigor, she shimmied her hips and shoulders simultaneously, visualizing what an earthworm might do to get the hell out of the pickle she was in.

Now for the hard part. She needed to clean her face off without the use of her pinned-down arms. Her skin had an odd, abrasive feeling. It was if she'd been locked in a room with a sandblaster for hours. She imagined the same coating of debris covered her face.

She did a quick exhale through her nose, forcing air out through her nostrils to clear the airway around her nose and upper lip. Then she slid her jaw to the right and blew air through a small gap in her lips, much like she used to do as a child to remove her too-long hair bangs from around her eyes.

A cloud of dust was sent upwards and found her face again.

"Okay, okay," Taylor mumbled without opening her mouth. She had to refine her approach.

She turned her head to the side and tried again. This time, the dust flew away and landed somewhere below her. She turned her head the other way and repeated the technique. More success.

Taylor smiled. Wash. Rinse. Repeat.

After several attempts, she was confident enough to open her eyes. A few specks of dust found their way onto her eyeballs. She blinked rapidly, allowing the moisture of her tears to do its job. Taylor tried to force herself to cry, thinking the tears would flush the dust out. She couldn't do it and didn't want to take the time to conjure up some reason to let the water-works flow.

She decided to just deal with it. At least, she was better able to assess her predicament now. The dust had settled, as they say, and she was able to see rays of sunlight filtering into the pile of rubble that surround her. She was able to lift her head slightly to see what pinned her down.

"Well, shit," she mumbled aloud. "Not good."

Two steel trusses had come to rest on top of the hospital bed that had followed her to the ground floor. The stainless-steel frame of the bed and its mattress had been crushed under the weight of the ceiling trusses. There was no way she could move it.

Taylor turned her head the best she could to see what was behind her. There were large sections of the exterior wall piled inward. The drywall had crumbled, leaving the exposed steel studs. All of that was attached to the sheathing and stucco finish products. There was a slight gap that she could push toward if she could only get free of the pile of roofing material.

She pressed her feet as if she were mashing the gas pedal in her car. She hoped to find something solid to push off of. She grunted and pushed.

She moved slightly. She was certain of it.

She wiggled her body back and forth. Then she pushed again. Her toes barely reached the solid surface of a concrete slab. However, it was enough to force her body toward the collapsed exterior wall.

Taylor turned her shoulders in an attempt to pull an arm free. This earned her a face full of dust and bits of concrete.

"Dammit!" she shouted, resulting in her mouth being filled with the same dust and debris.

Don't make matters worse, Taylor.

Sure, Dad. Easy for you to say.

Taylor didn't bother to clear her face again. She gave up on pushing with her feet. Instead, she wiggled her shoulders again and focused on freeing her right arm, which had a little more room to maneuver.

"Yes!" she shouted before having a coughing fit. Her exuberance stirred the concrete dust, which immediately entered her airway. She controlled her cough and then spit out the concrete dust the best she could. Then, with a slight sigh of relief, she used her free hand to wipe off her face.

That was when she was able to cry tears of joy. She happily pounded the back of her right fist against the metal frame of the bed. She shouted yes again, as she felt the progress would be just the first step in extricating herself from the rubble.

With the last exuberant blow of her fist against the frame, a piece of metal broke loose. It quickly recoiled and cut a gash in her forearm. Warm blood oozed out and mixed with the concrete dust.

Taylor had just made matters worse.

CHAPTER SIXTY

**Providence Memorial Hospital
Santa Rosa, CA**

Mac wandered the grounds, checking with groups of patients huddled under trees to get out of the sun. He asked anybody who'd make eye contact with him if they'd seen Taylor. He continued to be disappointed. Finally, a man with tears in his eyes pointed toward the parking garage on the east side of the building.

"I found my wife over there," he said in between sobs. "They, um, they set up a temporary morgue."

Mac closed his eyes. He welled up in tears, not

only for the grieving man, but for entertaining the thought that Taylor might be dead.

He wiped his face and ran across the parking lot, pushing wandering loved ones out of the way. A policeman stood guard near the yellow caution tape that was wrapped from tree to tree in front of the garage entrance. Just inside, Mac could see body bags lined up on the concrete ramp. Several nurses and hospital personnel mingled about, making notes on clipboards.

The security guard saw Mac approaching and moved in to intercept him. He raised his hands in front of him in an effort to stop Mac from busting through the caution tape. "Sir, this is off-limits to everyone. If you are searching for someone, you need to see the hospital staff at the entrance—"

"They're incompetent idiots!" Mac shouted as he tried to dodge the guard's grasp and run under the caution tape.

The guard was too strong and quick for Mac. He grasped the back of the tee shirt he'd stolen and pulled the collar, arresting Mac's forward momentum. His feet flew out from under his body, causing him to land hard on the pavement. It was a blow to his back that he really didn't need.

Pain shot through his body as he lost his breath.

He rolled into a fetal position, gasping for air. The guard towered over him, talking into his radio. Mac was stunned by the blow to his back, but the guard still made the call asking for backup.

Two of the nurses working in the temporary morgue noticed the commotion and walked into the sun. Mac recognized one nurse as the young woman who'd helped him escape the hospital the first time.

He crawled onto his knees and sat back on his heels. He dared not move. The guard had his right hand on his stun gun. If Mac looked like he'd lost control of his bowels before, he'd certainly let loose this time. He lifted an arm and waved to get the nurse's attention.

"Hey! Do you remember me? Atwood. Mac Atwood. From the USGS."

She shielded her eyes from the bright sun. "Of course, Mr. Atwood. Um, where are your clothes?"

Both nurses giggled at his appearance. Mac looked down at his swimsuit and noticed the Speedo logo had been covered in crusty mud.

"This is a swimsuit," he shot back.

"Sure it is, buddy," said the guard. "You stay put. We've got a place for you to sleep it off."

"Sleep what off? I'm not drunk or high!" Mac objected.

"Sure. Whatever you say. Stay still."

The nurses approached. His previous partner in crime addressed the security guard. "He's telling the truth. He's a patient of the hospital."

"I am?" Mac blurted out the question before he swallowed his words. He was ruining the ruse, except it wasn't one.

"Yes, you are. Dr. Booher never released you."

Mac started to stand. He put his hands on his hips defiantly as he spoke to the guard, a former football player who'd pulled him down with a perfectly executed horse-collar tackle. "See, I'm a patient. Now, call off the dogs." Mac nodded toward the two Sonoma County deputies hustling in their direction.

The guard looked from Mac to the nurses to the deputies. He shrugged and walked toward them, leaving Mac alone.

"Mr. Atwood, are you all right?" she asked.

Mac nodded. "Yeah, long story. Listen, have you seen Taylor? Taylor Reed? She was in one of the recovery rooms."

The other nurse replied, "Oh, yeah. She's wonderful. She helped us keep the patients calm while we evacuated the more critical ones. Very nice, too."

Mac looked around. "I've been looking everywhere for her. The people at the admin desk were no help. She wasn't in any of the tents. I started hollering for her. Nothing."

"Some patients were evacuated to Petaluma," the other nurse offered by way of explanation.

Mac's nurse interjected, "Her condition wouldn't warrant a transfer on a box." Mac's bewildered expression caused her to add, "An ambulance, sorry." In the EMS world, an ambulance was often referred to by a variety of slang terms. Medic, unit, rig, ambo, among others. In the Bay Area, box was the most prevalent since an ambulance was a truck chassis with a box on the back.

Mac pressed them as he noticed a hospital administrator approaching. "So where else could she be? When was the last time you saw her?"

The nurse pointed over shoulder toward the rear of the emergency room. "We had finished up evacuating the critical care patients. Taylor was assisting us in checking all the rooms. Then ..." Her voice trailed off.

"What?" asked Mac anxiously.

His nurse replied, "The power was out, so we were using the emergency exit that brought us out in front of the ER entrance. Come to think about it, I don't remember seeing Miss Reed when the last of us came out."

"Then the east wing collapsed," added the other nurse.

"Is that what you're talking about?" asked Mac. "Was that part of the ICU?"

"Critical care recovery," his nurse replied. "We'd cleared those rooms already. Unless she went to double-check?" Her words hung in the air as the faces of the two nurses revealed their fears.

"Shit!" Mac yelled. "Are they searching for patients or staff?"

"No. I mean, not yet. With the earthquake, the fire department is overwhelmed. We didn't think anybody was left on that end of our floor. Below us, in the ER, every patient had already been relocated into the temporary tents."

Mac walked toward the corridor that connected the ER with the parking garage. Just beyond it, a pile of stucco and rubble sat off to the side. An opening remained to the main part of the hospital, revealing broken concrete and bent rebar protruding out. The particles of debris and dust still hadn't completely settled following the collapse.

He felt faint. Mac bent over and rested his hands on his knees. He began breathing rapidly. *Don't panic,* he thought to himself. *She needs you. Don't yell. That won't accomplish anything.* As concern overtook him, he fought it.

"Don't panic," he said aloud.

"What was that?" the nurse asked.

Mac was suddenly lucid. "She may be trapped in there. Get help, please. Now!"

Then he burst through the caution tape and carried it around his waist for thirty yards as he sprinted toward the collapsed building.

CHAPTER SIXTY-ONE

Providence Memorial Hospital
Santa Rosa, CA

Taylor let out a deep exhale. She just added bleeding to death to the list of ways she might die that day. She brought her forearm close to her face to determine how bad the cut was. Her entire body was in pain, so her brain didn't register the new wound. The blood dripped off her arm onto her chin before rolling down her throat. She stretched her arm to pat the wound against her forehead. The bandage protecting the wound to her temple was still in place, albeit dusty. For the moment, Taylor hoped to stop the bleeding. The wound was already filled with dust and whatever other building materials had been pulverized during the earthquake.

The bleeding stopped, and Taylor was ready to help herself again. The number of people wailing in agony had dwindled to just a few. The sirens continued, but seemed to trail off as if an ambulance was driving away from the hospital. A few shouts of people's names managed to filter through the rubble.

But not hers.

Taylor was undeterred. If she could free one arm, she could free a second.

She started to dig out the dust and small rocks from underneath her back. She worked her way down towards her thighs, pushing away as much as her reach would allow. She wiggled back and forth. Next, she arched her back and tried to slide her shoulders. She did everything she could imagine to create a larger space than the one she'd been pancaked into by the roof of the hospital.

After a while, she tried to slide her body to the side so she could fall into the void she'd created by her one-arm excavation project. If she could just lower her body, then her other arm could be freed.

Taylor moved her shoulders to the right. Her lower body remained hopelessly stuck. She tried to bend sideways at her waist, pulling her left arm away from the death grip the pile of debris had on her.

There was some success. She grinned but tempered her emotions. She didn't need a gash on both arms.

She continued for several minutes until, suddenly, her left arm was free. She pulled it out quickly, moving it away from the side of her body as if some creature lurked in the rubble, intent on snatching it back.

"Two arms free! Screw you, you pile of crap!" She managed a laugh, and then she became suddenly quiet. A thought struck her as her wounded forearm began to burn.

She lifted her shoulders in a partial crunch and tried to get a better look at the stainless-steel bed frame. She recalled how the piece had broken loose, resulting in the wound.

"What if I can break off a piece?" she asked. Speaking to herself aloud seemed to comfort her. It confirmed she was alive and not in some in-between state.

If she was successful, she'd smack the frame until somebody heard the racket. Taylor carefully reached around in search of the loose piece. The entire bed had been crushed by the heavy steel truss from above. It was the bed's rigidity coupled with the mattress that prevented it from hitting her body.

With her right hand, she tried to find the piece of metal. Her mind strained to remember whether the piece was still attached or if it had fallen on her. She was puzzled as to why it wasn't within her reach.

Taylor gave up the search on the right side. She bent her body to the left as far as her surroundings allowed. She reached into the darkness with her left hand, looking for any piece of metal strong enough to pound on the bed. Surely, she thought, steel pounding on steel would get somebody's attention out there.

She clawed through the debris, blindly turning over pieces of concrete, searching for anything whether it was part of the bed or a piece of rebar. What she found was unexpected.

Her outstretched hand found the leg of the deceased woman she'd discovered in the room. Taylor recoiled from the corpse and screamed. It was primal. An intense release of fear that shook Taylor to her core. Finding the woman dead in her bedding was one thing. Grabbing the cold corpse under these conditions was something else.

"Help! Help! Can anyone hear me!" she began shouting, much louder than before. Somehow, being buried alive with a corpse was worse than her state of mind earlier.

She stopped to listen for a response.

Nothing.

Taylor began another coughing fit. She alternated between coughing and blowing the dust off her face. She tried shouting again with no response. There had been so much yelling and crying around the hospital that people were immune to it. She needed to try something different.

She turned her body again to find the loose piece of bed frame that had cut her. It had to be there. *It must still be attached*, she thought to herself. As she groped around in the dark, she began to wonder if she'd even be able to pull it loose.

Taylor grunted as she stretched as far as her restrained body would allow. Her hand found the sharp end of the steel support of the frame. It had been broken off on one end.

She wrapped her hand around the piece and pulled as hard as she could, hoping to tear it off the frame where it was attached. Her dust-covered hands started to slide, causing Taylor to lose her grip.

CLANG!

Taylor's eyes grew wide as the loud noise pierced her eardrums.

"Hell, damn, yeah!" she shouted at the top of her lungs. Naturally, she started coughing, not that it mattered.

She reached forward and found the piece of metal. She tugged it toward her and then released it.

CLANG!

Taylor was giddy with excitement. She reached for the piece again.

She cut open the palm of her hand. It didn't matter. She let out a laugh. Almost maniacal. She pulled and released her grip.

CLANG!

She kept pulling the piece of the bed frame with a little more caution and care. It continued to emit the loud sound of metal on metal.

Taylor made a promise to herself. She wasn't going down without a fight. She'd do this until she heard the sound of somebody else's voice besides her own.

CHAPTER SIXTY-TWO

Memorial Hospital
Santa Rosa, CA

Mac was incredulous. For one thing, the hospital had not kept up with the whereabouts of their patients. Also, they had no business disregarding Taylor's injuries and putting her to work. He imagined it had been hectic, and there had been a genuine concern for the infirm. That was fine. However, Taylor was recovering from a concussion and other serious injuries. Just because she was feeling better didn't mean she was well.

He reached the pile and assessed the arduous task of digging through it while avoiding the risk of it collapsing further. He was no expert, but he quickly realized extracting the wrong piece of concrete or collapsed support could result in a crushing blow to anyone trapped underneath it.

As he walked around the pile of rubble, he fought to restrain himself. He wanted to start removing hunks of stucco and concrete. Surely, there was something he could do until the trained search and rescue team arrived.

Mac studied the debris pile, looking for voids or pockets where he might be able to see in. The sun was setting on the other side of the building, making it darker. They'd need flashlights or those large, halogen temporary lights.

Frustrated, he ran back toward the temporary morgue, where he addressed the hospital staff. "Did you call the fire department? Are they on their way?"

A hospital administrator approached him, as well as the chaplain, who'd been consoling loved ones who'd lost a friend or family member.

"Sir," the administrator began in response, "we're told by Santa Rosa Fire their units are focusing on putting out the many structure fires in the area. They've summoned assistance from the Sonoma County Fire District and Petaluma, both of which should be here soon."

"Taylor could be dying under your building! How could this even happen?" Mac was beside himself.

The administrator tried to mollify him. "Sir, we don't even know if she was in that part of the building. The nurses don't believe she was."

"Then where the hell is she? I've checked every part of that mess over there." Mac pointed toward the organized chaos that was growing in size, as the media had arrived. Onlookers were now muddling the process of helping family members locate patients.

"Mr. Atwood, is it? I'm Reverend Brooks. Would you like to sit and talk for a moment? I understand you're still recovering from a serious head wound."

Mac stared at the clergyman for a moment. He restrained himself before responding, "No, I don't want to talk. I want to rescue Taylor. Do you wanna help me dig her out until help arrives?" Mac was surprised by his response.

"Yes, of course. Lead the way."

Mac gave the hospital administrator a dirty look and turned his attention to Reverend Brooks. He took a deep breath and exhaled. "Reverend, I apologize. I was being flippant. You don't have to help."

"Mr. Atwood, I want to. Now, they may need me

to console a grieving family member from time to time."

Mac smiled. "Of course. Thank you, and please call me Mac."

The two men walked side by side to the rubble. Mac explained his appearance and what he had gone through to get there. Reverend Brooks made an accurate observation that God had played a hand in Mac's ability to make it to the hospital. Perhaps it was to save Taylor, the reverend believed.

The two men worked together, pulling away large pieces of the pile while carefully observing the collapsed building for signs it might drop further.

Within minutes, more people showed up next to them. The nurses had spread the word to other hospital staff about Taylor's volunteer effort and the fact she'd gone missing. Now, she was one of their own and deserved their help. Any staff member who wasn't assigned a specific duty made themselves available to Mac. Bystanders who'd descended upon the hospital to watch the events unfold also came to lend a hand.

They worked quietly, forming teams to pick at the rubble and safely remove it from the pile. Periodically, Mac would call out Taylor's name but never received a response.

The excavation effort continued, digging deeper into the debris. The exterior walls had been mostly removed. The cinder blocks that made up the walls of the emergency exit were tossed to the side. A piece of medical equipment revealed itself, indicating they'd reached the inside of the hospital rooms, although nobody was certain if it was part of the ER or the ICU.

Then one of the volunteers waved her hand over her head. "Stop! Everyone, please stop."

The group laid down their debris and remained perfectly still. Mac approached the location where the woman was standing.

"What?"

"Bend over and listen," she replied.

Mac took a deep breath and squatted down on a slab of tile-covered concrete.

CLANG!

His heart almost leapt out of his chest. His eyes teared up as he looked around at the yearning faces of the people who'd spent their time with Mac as he searched for Taylor.

Was the search over? Was that her sending a message?

CLANG!

CHAPTER SIXTY-THREE

**Memorial Hospital
Santa Rosa, CA**

"Taylor! It's Mac. Taylor! Is that you?"

The entire group had closed around Mac and remained deathly quiet as he awaited a response.

"Mac? Mac, I'm okay." Her voice was weak and breathless. She'd been trapped for hours and was approaching dehydration. Yet she'd managed to keep her wits about her and continued to pull the stainless-steel bed support.

Outside the rubble, the more than twenty volunteers erupted in cheers. They exchanged high fives and hugs. Tears flowed as they joined in the exuberance of finding a woman they'd never met and most likely wouldn't see again. They'd helped save a life, and that was worth cheering.

However, their work wasn't over. On Mac's command, they began to remove the rubble in the area where Taylor's voice came from. They worked quietly so Mac could continue to talk to her and offer her words of encouragement.

"I love you, Taylor! Hang on. We've got to do this slowly."

"I love you back. I knew you'd come for me."

"I'm here, and there are two dozen others, including a Methodist minister to help."

"I'm Catholic," her weak voice responded jokingly.

Reverend Brooks's smile almost broke his face. Tears of joy flowed out of his eyes. "We're all God's children," he yelled to her.

Taylor fell quiet for a moment, which immediately concerned Mac. Reverend Brooks backed away from the pile to allow Mac to get closer.

"Taylor, are you okay?" he asked.

She responded. *CLANG!*

"She's probably weak, Mr. Atwood," offered his nurse. "I carefully listened to her voice. It was strained and raspy. She's most likely inhaled some of this dust."

"Crap," said Mac, concerned his desire to talk to Taylor might've made her condition worse. He turned his attention back to her. "Taylor, don't try to talk unless I ask you a question. But if you see us, beat the pipe again. Okay?"

CLANG!

That was all Mac and the volunteer rescuers needed. They worked quickly and methodically to remove more of the debris. Periodically, Taylor banged the steel together to give them a point of reference. As an opening was created, she pulled the pipe more often. Eventually, she said the words they all needed to hear.

"I see you!"

Mac leaned into the hole they'd created. "Does anyone have a flashlight?"

"I do," a woman replied. Her voice was familiar to Mac.

Mac crawled back out and turned around. It was Dr. Booher.

"Oh, hi. Um, Taylor's in there."

"I heard. I straightened a few people out for allowing this to happen. I'm sorry, Mr. Atwood. We should've done better." She handed him the flashlight.

Mac smiled at her and mouthed the words *thank you*. His appreciative eyes spoke volumes. He crawled back on his belly to the opening. After powering on the flashlight, he slowly panned the opening.

There she was. Her perfectly angelic, innocent, dust-covered face. Taylor blinked rapidly to see Mac but quickly shut her eyes.

"Dusty down here. I think I'd like to get out now."

"We've got you," said Mac, excitement in his voice. He wiped away the tears. He had to remain focused and not rush the process. If they removed the wrong piece of rubble, they risked further collapse. He backed out of the void and addressed Dr. Booher.

"Do you know anything about the fire and rescue people? I understand the locals are busy. What about the units from Petaluma or even the Bay Area."

Dr. Booher sighed. "They're stretched too thin, kinda like our hospital."

Mac stood to relieve the tension in his back and shoulders. As he did, his nurse arrived by his side. She handed him a stack of folded pants and shirts.

"One of our nurses lives within walking distance. You're about the same size as her husband. As soon as she was freed up, she ran to her condo and got you these."

Mac pulled the jeans on over his Speedos covered in dried mud. Then he laughed when he slipped on the Oregon State Beavers football tee shirt. He was glad to trade the fighting beaver logo for the gold-colored murder-hornet-looking logo from the winery. The sneakers she provided were a little too large but were workable.

"Tell her thanks," said Mac. Then he added, "I was tired of showing my backside to everyone."

"You've been showing your ass since the moment you arrived in our hospital, Mr. Atwood," interjected Dr. Booher.

Mac scowled. He wasn't a hundred percent certain how she meant that statement. When she began smiling, he felt better.

And reinvigorated. He got to work digging out Taylor. She no longer pulled the pipe, opting instead to provide Mac information on the condition of the rubble around her. She was fully aware it could collapse further if the volunteers were overzealous. She relayed to Mac that she was injured but not seriously. There was no rush, she assured him, other than the fact she wanted out of there.

They finally reached her. A small, wiry man agreed to crawl in headfirst to dig out the debris and dust under Taylor's body. This allowed her to shimmy out from under the collapsed ceiling. Then Mac crawled into the hole and grasped her by the arms. They stared in each other's eyes as two burly orderlies slowly tugged on Mac's legs. As he was pulled back out, he dragged Taylor with him. Finally, amidst the cheers and celebration of the volunteers, their joyful reunion began.

CHAPTER SIXTY-FOUR

**Memorial Hospital
Santa Rosa, CA**

Mac wanted to hold her forever. Taylor's head and face were covered in dust. Her bandage was bloody. The wounds on her arms continued to ooze blood. However, he smiled, and happy tears erased any concerns Mac had about her physical condition or mental state. Like him, Taylor had endured an ordeal that should've killed her. Again.

Naturally, Dr. Booher insisted that both of her patients accompany her to a temporary medical treatment tent. There, the nurses worked expeditiously to clean their wounds and provide fresh bandages. Against Dr. Booher's better judgment, but upon her patients' solemn promise to take it easy and avoid trouble, she finally discharged both Mac and Taylor from her care.

After they were provided some privacy to clean up, the two of them got dressed in the clothing given to them, except for the shoes that were ill fitting. They were given booties and hospital socks for footwear. When they left, the clothes hung on them, as the sizes were too large for their bodies. Every few steps, they were forced to grab the waistband of their pants and hike them up to avoid dropping them around their ankles.

As they walked away from the medical tent, Taylor wrapped one arm through Mac's while she held up her pants with the other hand. He leaned into her, his voice reflecting his concern for her injuries, especially her head.

"Are you sure you don't want to spend more time being observed by a doc? I can take you to another hospital nearby."

Taylor looked back over her shoulder at the collapsed portion of the ICU. "Um, no thanks. Let's just go to your place, okay?"

Mac grimaced and swallowed hard. "Oh, um,

about that. It appears I'm homeless again. Plus, my land is no longer waterfront."

"Whadya mean?" she asked as she pulled him to a stop.

"Well, I don't know all the details. What I know is based upon eavesdropping on conversations. It appears a massive quake at Mettler near the Grapevine dam started it off. Soon afterwards, another hit Parkland, followed by the one nearby, most likely at the Green Valley fault."

"So your house got hit?" she asked, still confused. She turned to face him as she awaited an explanation. "It was on the water."

Mac shrugged and began to talk rapidly. "Taylor, my house got ripped from the dock and began floating toward the center of the lake. It had to be an inland tsunami. Anyway, while I was floating out of control, my house was being sucked toward a whirlpool. Just before it got sucked under, I jumped overboard and swam to a communications tower that was no longer underwater. From there, I got ahold of a jet ski. I don't want to talk about how. Not yet. I drove the jet ski to near Sonoma Raceway and then rode that yellow bike over there to get to you."

Taylor's eyes grew wide and darted back and forth as she studied Mac's face. She suddenly burst out laughing, so hard she doubled over in pain from the shaking of her body.

"Ow! Come on, Atwood. If you didn't want to take me home with you, you could've just said so. You didn't have to make up all that elaborate shit."

Mac's voice rose to a higher pitch. He raised his hands to his sides. "It's true. I swear. All of it. And the lake's draining. The water levels had dropped at least twenty to thirty feet by the time I hit the shoreline at the racetrack."

Taylor rolled her eyes and walked in a complete circle until she was several feet away. She laughed as she spoke while counting each of Mac's assertions on her fingers. "Let me get this straight. One, we've got three more earthquakes. Two, we have an inland tsunami that carried off your house. Three, another whirlpool, this time big enough to swallow said house. Four, you swam until you came across a jet ski that happened to be waiting for you. Five, you rode that yellow bicycle with the whirling daisy on the back to rescue me."

"It's a sunflower," he interjected.

This caused her to laugh even harder. "Oh, six, to sell the ruse, you correct me and call a daisy a sunflower. Did you even ride that bicycle here?" She raised her eyebrows and folded her arms in front of her. Her grin had stretched across her face.

"I'll prove it," said Mac defiantly. "There's a bottle of wine in that basket that has an exact replica of this bike on it."

"Nope. I call bullshit." She shook her head side to side.

Mac marched past her and reached into the basket. It was empty. He turned toward her and then looked around. "What? It was here. I swear it. I brought a bottle of wine back to celebrate our engagement."

"Now I know who needs to have their head examined!" she said playfully. She turned toward the hospital. "Dr. Booher. Paging Dr. Booher. Please take this man in for a psych eval. He's totally lost all sense of reality. He thinks we're engaged, too."

Mac was not finding any of this humorous. "You said you'd think about it."

"I didn't say yes, which means we're not engaged."

Mac was exasperated. He glanced past Taylor and saw the bottle lying in the grass next to an oak tree.

"Okay, let's make a deal."

"Maybe? What is it?"

Mac was gonna gain the upper hand. "No maybes. Here's the deal. I'll prove to you that I rode that bicycle and brought you a bottle of wine. If I do, you have to say yes."

"Yes to what?"

"Not gonna tell you. Do we have a deal?"

Taylor furrowed her brow and thought for a moment. She enjoyed teasing Mac, but she didn't believe the story about the bicycle. The rest of the tall tale was pretty far-fetched, too. In the end, she decided she had nothing to lose by agreeing to his deal.

"Fine. But if I win, man, you have no idea what it's gonna cost you. I mean, if all that BS fiction you just spewed is true, then you'll have a fat insurance check coming, and I want my cut."

"Why do you get a cut?"

"I get a cut because you made me listen to your BS fiction. Now show me the receipts."

Mac hustled to the base of the oak tree and retrieved the wine bottle. He was angry to find it empty, but the fact he had the evidence she asked for would suffice.

He held in front of her. "Here, see the label? Same as the bicycle. It's a sunflower, too."

Taylor folded her arms in front of her chest and shook her head side to side. "It's empty. You lose."

"No, I don't! I'm telling the truth. Now you have to say yes."

Taylor clenched her mouth shut and shook her head. She grunted her response. "Uh-uh."

"I'll tickle you," said Mac childishly.

She repeatedly shook her head although her attempt to stifle her laugh was unsuccessful. "So big deal. The bike part was true."

"You have to marry me!" Mac insisted. He dropped to a knee and presented the empty wine bottle as if it were an engagement ring.

She laughed and looked into his eyes. "Of course I'll marry you, Mac Atwood, you idiot. I swore it to myself while we were swirling around in the submersible. I just wanted to make you work for it." She held her arms out for him to embrace her. Mac didn't hesitate. He lifted his aching body from kneeling and wrapped his arms around her. He twirled her around and around, oblivious to the crowd of people who had gathered nearby to listen to the odd proposal.

He set her down and studied her face to make sure it was real. Then his loose-fitting jeans immediately fell to his ankles, revealing his mud-stained

Speedos. The crowd roared its approval as Mac's battered face turned beet red. Taylor stepped back, pointed at the soiled swimsuit, and laughed until the tears flushed her eyes of any dust particles.

It was a fitting end to an extraordinary sequence of events. It was also the beginning of a new life together, one filled with laughter, excitement and new discoveries.

EPILOGUE

Aboard the USAF AW139
Above the San Andreas Fault, CA

"I hate long goodbyes," muttered Mac as he pressed his nose against the glass. The USGS campus at Santa Rosa became smaller and smaller until it was obscured by the coastal fog rolling into San Francisco Bay. It was a near daily phenomenon in the summer months for foggy conditions to cover the region, keeping temperatures unseasonably cool. Then it burned off by afternoon, revealing sunny, clear skies. For years, Mac had taken the time to sit back and smell the roses, as they say, by parking his Jeep atop a bluff at Mount Vaca to watch the fog arrive before he descended into Santa Rosa for work. Those days were over.

Taylor leaned over and ran her arm through his. She laid her head on his shoulder and spoke into the microphone of her headset. She wanted to whisper in his ear, but he'd never be able to hear her aboard the Air Force's helicopter, the same AW139 that had transported them from Eureka to the USGS the day they met. That ride had been romantic as the pilot expertly skirted the shoreline, allowing them to take in the crashing surf as well as a glorious sunset. She'd fallen in love with Mac that day, something others might never be able to comprehend. She knew her feelings then and had only confirmed them since that moment.

"It's been a crazy week since the Green Valley quake. But I understand why we had to wait."

Mac nodded and turned his seat to face Taylor. "We could've left earlier. I was immediately approved for my two-month LOA. Heck, I had so much vacation time built up I didn't need to request the formal leave of absence."

"Kemp had your back on that one. The way things worked out, you'll get paid for the accrued vacation time and get paid while you're on leave. It's a win-win."

Mac dropped his chin to his chest and chuckled. He leaned over and kissed Taylor. "This is why I'm a winner." He was holding something back from her, and it was making him nervous. She had a knack for seeing into his soul. It was unsettling.

The two cuddled as the fogbank surrounding the Bay Area passed underneath the chopper. Monterey Bay and then Big Sur came into view. They marveled at the beauty of a state that was fraught with threats from below the ground and those invading from the Pacific Ocean, like the ARkStorm.

The pilot continued to hug the coast until he approached the no-fly zone around Vandenburg Air Force Base. The nation had been on high alert due to the continuing saber-rattling between Washington and Beijing over Taiwan.

Ironically, and not by Mac's instructions, the pilot followed a route taking them above San Andreas. Mac and Taylor were able to observe the damage around Parkfield and Cajon Pass. Their low altitude afforded them a clear view of what used to be Lake California. Mostly drained, it was now a muddy graveyard that had been disturbed, resulting in everything buried being exposed.

As the pilot cruised along the former western shoreline of the lake, capsized boats and the remains of submerged homes littered the landscape. Silt and debris from years of mudslides following the ARkStorm had covered the roads and most buildings. A few had managed to avoid total destruction, standing eerily in the muck.

The chopper turned away from the coast and moved inland along the Mettler Fault. The remains of the Grapevine Dam were on full display, as now a small lake shimmered in the morning light at its base. Mac quickly pointed out the twenty-foot-wide chasm that stitched the earth near Mettler. After a week, the muddy lake bottom had begun to dry under the intense July heat. It created an eerie, cracked surface until the edge of the chasm left a dark void.

Geologists and geophysicists had already descended upon the epicenter of the Mettler quake where the Garlock Fault had created the small rift. Similar openings had occurred south of Fairfield where Mac's floating house had succumbed to the strength of the powerful whirlpool. Others, smaller in width but longer in length, ran toward the east away from San Andreas.

After a long moment of quietly enjoying the ride and their time together, Mac said, "They're gonna have their hands full. There's a lot to unpack, and to say the least, Kemp is somewhat paranoid about what's to come."

"Are you?" asked Taylor.

Mac laughed. "Paranoid? Nah. It is what it is. I do have concerns, however. It goes back to that silly 'Dem Bones' song. I've always looked at San Andreas, as did my mentor, as being the neck bone, backbone and hip bone. You know, the main skeletal structure of the whole."

"Okay." Taylor stretched out the word as she tried to follow Mac's logic.

"What if that assumption is wrong?" he asked. "What if the hip bone is Garlock? It's the connector. A complex joint lying at the center of two legs. And the two legs are San Andreas on the left and the other is the Sierra Nevada Fault on the right."

Taylor laughed. "Well, one leg is certainly longer than the other. The Sierra Nevada got cut off at the knee at some point."

Mac smiled and lowered his head. His nervous anxiety was beginning to show. "Um, there's something I need to tell you."

"Oh no. What? Another quake coming? Where?"

"No, nothing like that. I mean, I hope not, anyway."

"Are you gonna go somewhere else during your time off?"

Mac allowed a coy smile. "Well, you know I'm homeless, right?"

"Duh," said Taylor.

"Um, my leave of absence is two months, but it's leading to a transfer that Kemp got approved."

Taylor leaned back in her seat and folded her arms across her chest. "What kind of transfer?"

Mac turned to her and took her hands. "Kemp has approved a USGS satellite office in Mammoth Lakes. My LOA may be temporary, but my move to Mammoth Lakes is permanent."

Taylor set her jaw and shoved Mac. When he sat upright, she did it again, followed by her pounding his thighs with the backs of her fists.

"Don't you mess with me, Mac Atwood! Is this real? Are you really not going back to Santa Rosa? Is that why you were all sad about saying goodbye?"

Mac laughed as he held his hands up, expecting another onslaught of punches. "Yes, to all of the above. Kemp has tasked me with finding new office space for my team and, drum roll please, yours. CalVO and the USGS will merge to share staff, facilities, and a new monitoring center."

"You're lying."

"No, I swear. It's all true. That's part of why it took a week for me to start my LOA. You were right when you said Kemp had my back. She's set up a sweet gig for me. For us."

"Us? There is no us, asshole. I retract my previous yes based on the stupid bet you came up with. You've been holding back on me. So you have to start over."

"Whadya mean?" Mac asked as he studied her face.

Taylor's back stiffened. Her mood defiant. "A proper courtship. I'm talking flowers. Chocolates. Dates for lunch and dinner. Walks in the park. I want the whole nine yards."

"Okay, I can do that." Mac extended his hand to shake hers. He was ready to seal the deal until Taylor upped the ante.

"And no sex."

"Wait. What? Come on."

"You heard me, mister. No sex. Plus, you have to ask the ambassador for my hand in marriage. He and Mom arrive the day after tomorrow."

The blood flowed out of Mac's face. For some reason, the thought of meeting her father frightened him. "The ambassador, um, your parents will be here in two days?"

Taylor smiled and nodded. "Yup. You'd better shape up, Atwood. You're looking a little haggard."

Mac thought for a moment. He leaned forward so he was kneeling between the pilots. He pretended to push the button on the headset that would allow him to speak directly to them.

"Fellas, we've got a change of plans. Um, we'll be dropping Miss Reed off at Mammoth, and I'll be coming back with you to Santa Rosa."

Taylor grabbed him by the shirt and yanked him back into his seat. "Okay. Okay. Yes."

"Yes, what?" asked Mac.

"Yes to the original proposal. No change to the deal."

"No courtship?"

"A little one, please?" Taylor's tone had changed completely.

"Okay. How about the sex part?"

"We'll see how you behave. And you'd better not be a slob in my cabin. Your place looked like a frat house."

"Okay, deal. I'll even ask the ambassador for your hand in marriage."

Taylor had a hearty laugh. "I'll be peeking around the corner with my mom when you do it. Good luck, Atwood!"

The pilot took them on a wide turn around Mammoth Mountain as he approached the Mammoth Yosemite Airport in Mammoth Lakes. The beauty was something to behold. It was what lay underneath the adjacent Long Valley Caldera that kept volcanologists up at night.

THANK YOU FOR READING FRACTURED!

If you enjoyed it, I'd be grateful if you'd take a moment to write a short review (just a few words are needed) and post it on Amazon. Amazon uses complicated algorithms to determine what books are recommended to readers. Sales are, of course, a factor, but so are the quantities of reviews my books get. By taking a few seconds to leave a review, you help me out and also help new readers learn about my work.

Sign up to my email list to learn about upcoming titles, deals, contests, appearances, and more!

Sign up at BobbyAkart.com

VISIT my feature page at Amazon.com/Bobby-Akart for more information on my other action-packed thrillers, which includes over forty Amazon

#1 bestsellers in forty-plus fiction and nonfiction genres.

READ ON to see what's coming next and to learn the backstory behind the writing of this novel. Also, I have some news media excerpts related to the story that might be of interest. They're the types of stories you don't ordinarily see. If you did, you might be stocking up on the basics because you never know when the day before, is the day before. Prepare for tomorrow.

MAMMOTH, a standalone disaster thriller in the CALIFORNIA DREAMIN' universe.

California is a state shaped by its explosive past.
In recent years, the state's been flooded and then ripped apart by tremors.
Now, the earth's crust is heaving like the chest of a gasping beast.
The ground has grown restless around Mammoth Mountain as the world waits.
Will the fire-breathing beast relieve the pressure?

A standalone disaster thriller from international bestselling author, Bobby Akart, one of America's favorite storytellers, who delivers up-all-night thrillers to readers in 245 countries and territories worldwide.

"Akart is one of those very rare authors who makes things so visceral, so real, that you experience what he writes."

California had experienced back-to-back catastrophic events. First, an ARkStorm, a thousand-year flood event led to another catastrophic event, a series of earthquakes causing the rupture of the famous San Andreas fault.

USGS geophysicist, Mac Atwood, and volcanologist, Taylor Reed, survived being swallowed by the Earth during the earthquake swarm. They returned to the ordinarily peaceful and serene environs surrounding Mammoth Mountain and the Long Valley Caldera.

"Bobby Akart is a genius at creating disaster scenarios."

When a series of seemingly minor earthquakes take place in the Sierra Nevada Mountains, Mac the seismic detective, expresses his concern to Taylor. Her skills as a volcanologist will be tested as it appears the Long Valley Caldera, the second largest supervolcano in the U.S. behind Yellowstone, is awakening.

Mac and Taylor lived through the devastation wrought by the earthquakes at San Andreas. They proved earthquakes have the ability to transfer between faults. They believed the complicated geology beneath California had changed after the ARkStorm.

Now, they believe the geologic formations surrounding Mammoth Mountain and the Long Valley Caldera have been fundamentally changed. For the worst.

"You are there. Feeling what they feel. Anger, joy, love, mourning. You feel it all. Not everyone can write a book like this. It takes a special writer to make you feel a book."

The ARkStorm had been dubbed the Other Big

One and a San Andreas earthquake was known as the Big One. The eruption of the Long Valley Caldera would be more than a flood or knocked down buildings. It could result in the end of the world as we know it.

"Edge of your seat thrilling!"

This modern-day, fact-based novel will have you whispering just one more chapter until the end.

Available on Amazon by clicking here.

AUTHOR'S NOTE

July 2023

When I laid out my writing schedule for 2023, my wife Dani asked, "Did California do something to piss you off?" I looked at her funny and then laughed as I outlined the synopsis of each novel I planned on writing this year.

Let me assure my dear readers, California didn't *piss me off*. On the contrary, I find the state incredibly beautiful. The eight-hundred-forty miles of exquisite coastline along the Pacific Ocean, the numerous mountain ranges, forests, and even the three main deserts in the state are phenomenal.

I suppose, the one thing you won't hear me praise are the state's large cities. It's unfortunate what has become of Los Angeles in many respects. It's down-right criminal what the local political leaders have allowed to happen in parts of San Francisco. These are all people problems that can be fixed.

Setting aside the man-made destruction of an exquisite state, I wanted to bring my readers' attention to the natural catastrophes that could result in the end of the world as they know it, or the acronym —TEOTWAWKI.

My California readers inundated my inbox around Thanksgiving of 2022 when I announced ARkStorm. I've been accused of having a certain prescient nature to my fictional stories. Few had heard of the term, ARkStorm. In fact, the terminology atmospheric river wasn't used all that often by the media.

Until the winter of 2022 – 23. Then, the deluge of rain brought by the atmospheric rivers and the massive amount of snowfall dropped on the mountains caused some to refer to last winter's precipitation as biblical in nature. When, in fact, it was nowhere close to what could happen, as I portrayed in ARkStorm.

While conducting research for ARkStorm and interviewing geophysicists at the USGS, I learned the correlation between the newly formed Lake California, the fictional body of water in my novel, and the impact the water's weight would have on the geology of the state. I was astonished.

Our mighty planet is fragile in many respects, including the myriad of fault lines that stretch underneath the Earth's surface. Adding that much groundwater (twenty-two times the volume of the Mississippi River) to the Central Valley of California would alter the composition of rock, soil, and therefore, seismic zones.

As I explained in the book through the characters, namely Mac Atwood and Taylor Reed, the major faults of San Andreas, San Jacinto and Garlock would be directly affected by the massive weight of the lake. My analogy using the *Dem Bones* song came as I wrote the chapter in which it first appeared. Who knows? The *Dem Bones* illustration might make its way into a Geology 101 course somewhere.

Now, for a few tidbits in the story.

I follow this maxim when I write a novel. *Every character has a story to tell.* In my disaster thrillers, a major character is nonhuman. In this case earthquake faults. Without question, the most recognized fault in America, if not the world, is the San Andreas. There have been countless movies made referencing this fault. My goal was to remind all of us that lesser-known seismic zones can be just as devastating. Hence, the reason I incorporated major quakes at San Jacinto and Garlock. If you wanna read about another lesser-known seismic zone in America that could bring the entire nation to its knees, I'd be honored if you'd read my novel—*New Madrid Earthquake*.

We also have heroes, heroines and villains in every story. To be sure, an overactive seismic zone makes for a good villain. Taylor Reed made for a great heroine. You'll see more of her in my next novel, *Mammoth*, a story about America's second most active supervolcano located in the Sierra Nevada Mountains. The Long Valley Caldera may not be as large as Yellowstone, but its potential for destruction is comparable.

Our hero, and this novels title, has been on the drawing board since 2015 when I began writing. After my success writing a novella for Amazon's Kindle Worlds, Dani began to outline a story of her own to write. The title of the novel would've been *Fractured* and its hero was to be Mac Atwood. At the time, the *Boston Brahmin* series was a huge success and Dani abandoned her own writing dreams to support me, just another one of the sacri-

fices she's made enabling me to bring you these
stories.

Mac Atwood patiently waited his turn to appear
in a story. Those of you who've read *New Madrid
Earthquake* might remember the attorney, Jack
Atwood, who found himself in St. Louis, far away
from his Memphis family, when the world turned
upside down as the New Madrid Seismic Zone
roared to life. Jack was one of several heroes in that
story and I didn't feel like that particular character
was appropriate for the singularly important role
Mac Atwood would play.

So, I introduced him in *Fractured* as a seismic
detective, related to Jack in the same small town of
Dyersburg in West Tennessee. He turned out to be
an outstanding leading man and waiting eight years
to tell his story was worth it. By the way, you'll see
more of Mac Atwood in my upcoming standalone
novel, *Mammoth*.

Here's another couple of names readers of my
Yellowstone series should remember—Ashby
Donovan and Rita Charles. They were volcanologists studying the Kilauea Volcano in Hawaii before
being called to study the Yellowstone Caldera. I do
these things as a wink and a nod to my loyal readers.
I try to make the characters' roles as consistent as

possible with their story in my other novel. Here, I had a little fun with the interaction between the quirky Rita and Mac. I threw in a dating connection between Mac and Ashby just for grins and giggles.

On occasion in my previous sixty-five books, I've had the opportunity to include characters based on real people with real names. In this case, it was the fictional Dr. Jan Booher who saved Taylor and Mac's lives only to later hound Mac as he continuously slipped out of the hospital. The real Jan Booher is a member of the Daughters of the American Revolution, an incredible organization of women who are lineal descendants of Patriot ancestors who aided in our nation achieving its independence. Jan made a very generous donation to a DAR charity to earn the right to be named in the story. I truly enjoyed bringing her character to life.

In Chapter 44, I made reference to Mac's tee shirt that read *Sorry, My Fault*. Every time I start a novel, I manage to accumulate items, whether apparel or tchotchkes, that provide me inspiration as it relates to the story. As a collector of antique books, Dani scoured online bookstores in search of books related to San Andreas and especially the 1906 San Francisco earthquake. *San Francisco's Great Disaster* by Sydney Tyler was published immediately following the massive April 1906 quake. The personal accounts of those who survived, and the old photographs are fascinating.

Sorry, My Fault was one of three tee shirts for this California Dreamin' universe. As I've written *ARkStorm, Fractured,* and *Mammoth,* I've alternated between the *Sorry, My Fault* tee, a *California Dreamin'* tee shirt, and a vintage tee shirt from 1989 promoting a concert event for the victims of the Loma Prieta earthquake. The concert, attended by twenty-two thousand people in three cities around the Bay Area, raised more than $2 million dollars for the relief effort. The blue tee shirt read—*It's everybody's fault.* Headliners at the concerts included Santana, Neil Young, Eddie Money, Bonnie Raitt and Crosby, Stills & Nash, among others. Bob Hope even showed up at the San Francisco event. It's tattered and torn but continues to be well-worn.

Now for a solemn and more serious matter. The stories I write are full of scientific facts and sometimes extraordinary technological advances are used to create realism. When I sent Mac to the bottom of the Pacific Ocean and later, to nearly the center of the Earth while caught in a large eddy, I needed to accurately describe an underwater vessel for him to pilot. I studied many options and settled on the Titan submersible built by OceanGate. As a way of introducing readers to this technological marvel, I originally wrote the story with the submersible being named Titan. During the editing process, I followed the story of Titan's descent into the darkest depths of the North Atlantic to view the wreckage of the Titanic. I can only imagine the excitement of the five men as they slowly embarked on this momentous journey. Then, something went horribly wrong. The Titan submersible imploded, and all passengers were killed.

Out of respect for those who perished, I changed the name of the submersible to Orca. Once it was finally announced that Titan had likely imploded many days before it was made known to the public, I cursed our government for hiding this salient fact from the friends and families of those on board. For days, they held out hope for the rescue and return of their loved ones. I hope and pray the men onboard Titan were able to accomplish their dream before death. Please remember them and their families in your prayers:

Stockton Rush, the CEO of OceanGate

Paul-Henri Nargeolet, a French deep-sea explorer and Titanic expert

Hamish Harding, a British businessman

Shahzada Dawood, a Pakistani-British business-man; and

Dawood's son Suleman.

Rest in peace, explorers!

Okay, I'd like to end on a whimsical high note. In Chapter 56, Mac entered a winery's retail shop wearing nothing except a Speedo covered in muck. Can you imagine how he looked? You know, like he pooped his pants. Anyway, Mac was in search of transportation and clothing. The winery's logo, as I wrote, was something akin to a *yellowish-gold insect ... a bee, a moth, or a murder hornet.*

So, I'm sure the winery would be insulted by my inability to identify the bug on their apparel. My apologies for that. My readers, on the other hand, might recall the cover art Dani created for a never-to-be-written story we imagined at April Fool's Day in 2021. That said, at times, I furrow my brow and consider giving you, dear readers, this epic tome.

Much love to you all!

AUTHOR'S NOTE

A BRIEF OF HISTORY OF THE SAN ANDREAS FAULT

California's sleeping giant, the San Andreas Fault, marks the slippery yet potentially sticky boundary between two of Earth's tectonic plates. Historically, it's been responsible for the biggest, most destructive earthquakes in state, up to at least a magnitude 8.1.

Beginnings

Viewed from space, the San Andreas looks like a long, narrow valley where the North American and Pacific tectonic plates meet. This narrow break between the two plates is called a fault. In actuality, when viewed up close, there are many fractures and faults that make up the seismic zone where the two plates slide past one another. In places, the boundary is a zone of several smaller faults, one or more of which may break during an earthquake. Sometimes it is a single fault that is ruptured.

On the ground, the San Andreas Fault is recognizable by looking for landforms it created. For example, sharp cliffs called *scarps* form when the two sides of the fault slide past each other during earthquakes. Chasms or small rifts occur in places, oftentimes filled by water to create a stream.

One of the most fascinating aspects of San Andreas is the continuous movement of the enormous tectonic plates. On the west side of the fault sits most of California's population, riding the Pacific Plate northwest while the remainder of California, east of the fault, rests on the North American plate which inches south. The Pacific Plate is moving to the northwest at three inches each year, and the North American Plate is heading south at about one inch per year. Over time, Los Angeles and San Francisco will be side-by-side.

The San Andreas Fault was born about 30 million years ago in California when the Pacific Plate and the North America plate first met. Before then, another oceanic plate, the Farallon plate, was gradually disappearing beneath North America at a subduction zone, another type of plate boundary similar to Cascadia. The new configuration meant the two plates slid past one another instead of crashing into each other, a boundary called a strike-slip fault.

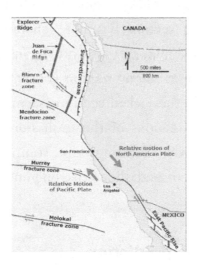

NorCal vs. SoCal

At eight-hundred-miles long, the San Andreas Fault stretches from the Mendocino coast south to the San Bernardino Mountains and the Salton Sea. Geologists divide the fault into northern and southern segments, separated in the middle by a curiously quiet portion that *creeps*.

The northern segment runs from Hollister north

through the Point Reyes National Seashore, then eventually moves offshore. The southern segment stretches from Parkfield south through the Salton Sea.

The central, creeping section includes everything from Parkfield to Hollister. In historical times, this creeping section has not generated powerful earthquakes similar to those on the *locked* sections. Although, the creeping section slowly, continuously moves, while the locked sections seem to get stuck. These stuck sections of the fault store energy like springs, slowly building up strain until they suddenly unzip and slide past one another causing an earthquake.

Earthquake prediction

The San Andreas Fault was the site of a massive effort to drill into the Earth's crust and investigate a fault at depth. In 2004, work began near the town of Parkfield to drill nearly two miles into the fault.

Parkfield, in central California, pops off a moderate earthquake of around M6 every fifteen to twenty years, and is a well-known center for earthquake research. It was the site of the first official earthquake prediction by the USGS.

Earthquake history

The largest earthquakes in California since European settlers arrived struck in 1857 and 1906 on the San Andreas Fault. On Jan. 9, 1857, the Fort Tejon earthquake near Parkfield in southern California was an estimated M7.9. It rerouted stream channels by as much as twenty-nine feet. The USGS estimates that a similar-size earthquake today, in the same location, would damage half the buildings in Los Angeles, destroy the city's water supply and injure or kill more than fifty-thousand people.

After the Fort Tejon quake came the April 18, 1906, San Francisco earthquake, which triggered deadly fires in the growing city and killed over seven-hundred people. The earthquake was an estimated M8.3 on the Richter scale and broke the Earth's surface along a two-hundred-fifty-mile length from San Juan Bautista to Cape Mendocino.

The San Andreas Fault has been unusually quiet since the two big earthquakes in 1857 and 1906. Recently, studies looking at the fault's past earthquakes suggest that instead of popping off big earthquakes on a regular, somewhat predictable schedule, the fault seems to release its pent-up energy through earthquakes that vary in size and timing. Scientists now think the San Andreas Fault needs time to build up a critical stress level before it breaks again.

The question that nobody can answer with certainty is when.

THE SAN ANDREAS FAULT IS SLEEPY NEAR LOS ANGELES

~ New York Times, June 6, 2023

A new paper in the journal Nature offers an explanation for why the major fault line is overdue for the Big One.

It has been about three centuries since the last great earthquake on the southern San Andreas Fault, the most treacherous seismic hazard in California. For decades researchers have puzzled over why it has been so long. The average interval of large earthquakes along that portion of the fault has been 180 years over the past 1,000 years.

While seismologists agree that Southern California is due for the Big One, a group of researchers published a paper on Wednesday in the journal Nature that offers a reason for the period of seismic silence along the southern San Andreas, the tension-wracked meeting point of the North American and Pacific tectonic plates.

The theory hinges on the idea that while the friction of tectonic plates is the primary driving force behind earthquakes, there are other factors, including the weight of large bodies of water. Building on prior research, the scientists drew a link between the occurrence of large earthquakes and the filling of a lake that has grown and ebbed across the centuries. The authors of the study found that major earthquakes along the southern San Andreas fault tended to happen when a large body of water, in this case, Lake Cahuilla, was filling or was full with water from the Colorado River in what are now the Coachella and Imperial valleys.

The lake has drained over the last three centuries and all that remains is the vestigial Salton Sea. The authors of the paper believe that the process of the ancient lake's emptying and disappearance stabilized the fault to a certain degree. Impounding more water in the region would likely trigger seismic activity.

The earthquake will happen, probably sooner rather than later.

CALIFORNIA FLOODING EXPANDS HISTORIC "GHOST LAKE" TO ALMOST SAME SIZE AS LAKE TAHOE
~ *USA Today, May 23, 2023*

History rising ... a once dead lake is back.

Once the largest body of freshwater west of the Mississippi River, Tulare Lake dried up in the early 20th century after its tributaries were diverted for irrigating crops and municipal water use.

Now, the once-dead lake is back: a surprise effect of the massive amounts of runoff from the winter storms that blanketed California.

Just how big has the lake grown? Tulare Lake has expanded over 180 square miles—nearly the same size as Lake Tahoe. And while some of the wet conditions have been a welcomed relief in the drought-ridden state, the unexpected rise of the

"Ghost Lake" could result in unforeseen consequences below the surface of the planet. The geologic impact, while still unknown, could reveal itself in an more activity in California's many seismic zones.

EXPERTS ON RED ALERT FOR MEGA-EARTHQUAKE OFF THE U.S. COAST
~ *UK Daily Mail, April 14, 2023*

After discovering a crack in 600-mile long fault line at the bottom of the Pacific, experts fear the hole may be leaking 'fault lubricant' that reduces stress on two plates. As a result the fault could unleash a magnitude-9 earthquake along America's West Coast.

This geological feature is capable of unleashing a magnitude-9 earthquake in the Pacific Northwest - and the hole could be the fuel it needs.

The leak was first observed in 2015, but a new analysis led by the University of Washington suggests the chemically distinct liquid is *fault lubri-*

cant. This liquid allows plates to move smoothly, but without it, "stress can build to create a damaging quake," researchers said. Loss of fluid from the offshore megathrust interface through these strike-slip faults is important,' the statement notes, 'because it lowers the fluid pressure between the sediment particles and hence increases the friction between the oceanic and continental plates.

DRAINAGE OF A LAKE BY AN EARTHQUAKE
~ *Scientific American, January 29, 1953*

From the archived articles of Scientific American.

A singular phenomenon lately occurred in California, by which Lake Merced, a sheet of water, covering about thirty acres, and which is situated seven miles distant from San Francisco, threatens to become dry ground.

A shock of an earthquake took place during the night, and in the morning, it was discovered that a portion of the lake's boundary had been swept away, and a passage forced by the rushing waters about three hundred yards in width, and ten or twelve feet deep, opening on the seashore to the width of a mile.

Subsequently, a sort of mid-channel had been formed, commencing a short distance below the origin of the outlet, narrower and much deeper than the first, down which the water seems to have rushed with much velocity, until the lake has been emptied at least thirty feet below its previous surface. This mid-channel has gradually deepened in the centre, forming an outlet down which the waters are yet flowing into the ocean.

And now that the outlet has been forced from its abrupt sides may be seen flowing the gaseous fluids which succeed earthquakes among lofty mountains. It is supposed that the bed of the Lake may have been instantly uplifted, and as quickly have returned to its customary level; thus forcing an outlet through the heavy alluvial by which it was formerly confined.

ACKNOWLEDGMENTS

Creating a novel that is both informative and entertaining requires a tremendous team effort. Writing is the easy part.

For their efforts in making this novel a reality, I would like to thank Hristo Argirov Kovatliev for his incredible artistic talents in creating my cover art. He and my loving wife, Dani, collaborate (and conspire) to create the most incredible cover art in the publishing business. A huge hug of appreciation goes out to Pauline Nolet, the *Professor*, for her editorial prowess and patience in correcting this writer's same tics after sixty-plus novels. Thank you, Drew Avera, a United States Navy veteran, who has brought his talented formatting skills from a writer's perspective to create multiple formats for reading my novels.

ACKNOWLEDGMENTS

Thank you, Andrew Wehrlen, an incredible talent who returns to perform the audio narration of my stories.

As I mentioned in my Author's Note, a big thank you to Jan Booher, a lineal descendent of the patriots who fought for our independence during the American Revolution and a member of the Daughters of the American Revolution. She won a raffle at a DAR fundraiser earning her a spot as a named character in *Fractured*.

Now, allow me to acknowledge the professionals who helped make this novel possible. Accurately portraying an earthquake swarm across the State of California and the aftermath required countless hours of never-ending research as well as interviews of some of the brightest minds in the world of geophysics.

Once again, as I immersed myself in the science and history, source material and research flooded my inbox from around the globe. Without the assistance of many individuals and organizations, this story could not be told. Please allow me a moment to acknowledge a few of those individuals whom, without their tireless efforts and patience, ARkStorm could not have been written.

Many thanks to the preeminent researchers

and engineers at the United States Geological Survey and the team at Oregon State's VIPER Research group for their research and earthquake models. I began working with some of these folks back in 2018 as I wrote the *Yellowstone* series and again in 2019 as I outlined my standalone novel, *New Madrid Earthquake*. They are brilliant scientists.

The following individuals assisted in the research of all three novels in the *California Dreamin'* universe.

A shout-out must go to Jeffrey Mount, a senior fellow at the Public Policy Institute of California. He is an emeritus professor of earth and planetary sciences at the University of California, Davis. A geomorphologist who specializes in the study of rivers, streams, and wetlands, his research focuses on integrated water resource management, flood management, and improving aquatic ecosystem health.

This story couldn't have been written without the research done by Dr. Lucy Jones and Dr. Daniel Swain.

Dr. Lucille Jones is one of the foremost and trusted public authorities on earthquakes, Jones is referred to by many in Southern California as the *seismologist-next-door* who is frequently called up on to provide information on recent earthquakes.

She is currently a research associate at the Seismological Laboratory at Caltech and chief scientist and founder of the Dr. Lucy Jones Center for Science and Society. She was previously at the USGS from 1985 to 2016, where she conducted research in the areas of foreshocks, seismotectonics, and the application of hazards science to improve societal resilience after natural disasters.

At the USGS, she was also part of the team of scientists that developed the Great Shakeout Earthquake Drills, during which millions around the world participate in annual earthquake safety drills.

Dr. Daniel Swain is a climate scientist in the Institute of the Environment and Sustainability at the University of California, Los Angeles, and holds concurrent appointments as a Research Fellow in the Capacity Center for Climate and Weather Extremes at the National Center for Atmospheric Research and as the California Climate Fellow at The Nature Conservancy of California.

Dr. Swain studies the changing character, causes, and impacts of extreme weather and climate events on a warming planet—with a particular focus on the physical processes leading to droughts, floods, and wildfires. He holds a PhD in Earth System Science from Stanford University and a B.S. in Atmospheric Science from the University of California, Davis.

Finally, as always, a special thank you to my team of loyal friends and readers who've always supported my work and provided me valuable insight over the years.

Thanks, y'all, and Choose Freedom!

ABOUT THE AUTHOR, BOBBY AKART

Author Bobby Akart has been ranked by Amazon as #25 on the Amazon Charts list of most popular, best-selling authors. He has achieved recognition as the #1 bestselling Horror Author, #1 bestselling Science Fiction Author, #5 bestselling Action & Adventure Author, #7 bestselling Historical Fiction Author and #10 on Amazon's bestselling Thriller Author list.

Mr. Akart has delivered up-all-night thrillers to readers in 245 countries and territories worldwide. He has sold nearly two million books in all formats, which includes over forty international bestsellers, in nearly fifty fiction and nonfiction genres. He has produced more #1 bestselling novels in Science Fiction's post-apocalyptic genre than any author in Amazon's history.

His novel *Yellowstone: Hellfire* reached the Top 25 on the Amazon bestsellers list and earned him multiple Kindle All-Star awards for most pages read in a month and most pages read as an author. The Yellowstone series vaulted him to the #25 bestselling author on Amazon Charts, and the #1 bestselling science fiction author.

Since its release in December 2020, his stand-alone novel, *New Madrid Earthquake*, has been ranked #1 on Amazon Charts in multiple countries as a natural disaster thriller.

Mr. Akart is a graduate of the University of Tennessee after pursuing a dual major in economics and political science. He went on to obtain his master's degree in business administration and his doctorate degree in law at Tennessee.

With nearly two million copies of his novels sold in all formats, Bobby Akart has provided his readers a diverse range of topics that are both informative and entertaining. His attention to detail and impeccable research has allowed him to capture the imagination of his readers through his fictional works and bring them valuable knowledge through his nonfiction books.

SIGN UP for Bobby Akart's mailing list to learn of special offers, view bonus content, and be the first to receive news about new releases.

Visit www.BobbyAkart.com for details.

OTHER WORKS BY AMAZON CHARTS TOP 25 AUTHOR BOBBY AKART

The California Dreamin' Disaster Thrillers

ARkStorm (a standalone, disaster thriller)

Fractured (a standalone, disaster thriller)

Mammoth (a standalone, disaster thriller)

The Perfect Storm Series

Perfect Storm 1

Perfect Storm 2

Perfect Storm 3

Perfect Storm 4

Black Gold (a standalone, terrorism thriller)

The Nuclear Winter Series
First Strike

Armageddon

Whiteout

Devil Storm

Desolation

New Madrid (a standalone, disaster thriller)

Odessa (a Gunner Fox trilogy)
Odessa Reborn

Odessa Rising

Odessa Strikes

The Virus Hunters
Virus Hunters I

Virus Hunters II

Virus Hunters III

The Geostorm Series
The Shift

The Pulse

The Collapse
The Flood
The Tempest
The Pioneers

The Asteroid Series (A Gunner Fox trilogy)

Discovery
Diversion
Destruction

The Doomsday Series

Apocalypse
Haven
Anarchy
Minutemen
Civil War

The Yellowstone Series

Hellfire
Inferno
Fallout
Survival

The Lone Star Series

Axis of Evil
Beyond Borders
Lines in the Sand
Texas Strong
Fifth Column
Suicide Six

The Pandemic Series
Beginnings
The Innocents
Level 6
Quietus

The Blackout Series
36 Hours
Zero Hour
Turning Point
Shiloh Ranch
Hornet's Nest
Devil's Homecoming

The Boston Brahmin Series
The Loyal Nine
Cyber Attack

Martial Law

False Flag

The Mechanics

Choose Freedom

Patriot's Farewell (standalone novel)

Black Friday (standalone novel)

Seeds of Liberty (Companion Guide)

The Prepping for Tomorrow Series (non-fiction)

Cyber Warfare

EMP: Electromagnetic Pulse

Economic Collapse